EARTH ROAR

BOOK 7 IN THE EARTH SONG SERIES

NICK COOK

VOICE FROM THE CLOUDS

ABOUT THE AUTHOR

Somewhere back in the mists of time, Nick was born in the great sprawling metropolis of London. He grew up in a family where art was always a huge influence. Tapping into this, Nick finished college with a Fine Art degree tucked into his back pocket. Faced with the prospect of actually trying to make a living from his talents, he plunged into the emerging video game industry back in the eighties. It was the start of a long career and he produced graphics for many of the top-selling games on the early home computers, including *Aliens* and *Enduro Racer*. Those pioneering games may look crude now, but back then they were considered to be cutting edge. As the industry exploded into the one we know today, Nick's career went supernova. He worked on titles such as *X-Com*, and set up two studios, which produced

Warzone 2100 and the *Conflict: Desert Storm* series. He has around forty published titles to his name.

As great as the video game industry is, a little voice kept nagging inside Nick's head, and at the end of 2006 he was finally ready to pursue his other passion as a full-time career: writing. Many years later, he completed his first trilogy, *Cloud Riders*. And the rest, as they say, is history.

Nick has many interests, from space exploration and astronomy to travelling the world. He has flown light aircraft and microlights, an experience he used as research for *Cloud Riders*. He's always loved to cook, but then you'd expect it with his surname. His writing in many ways reflects his own curiosity about the world around him. He loves to let his imagination run riot to pose the question: *What if?*

.

For you, dear reader, who has accompanied Lauren and her team on their extraordinary Earth Song journey.

CHAPTER ONE

MY MIND SCRABBLED TO WAKE, cobwebs of sleep fogging my thoughts as the warbling sound rose and fell, raising the hairs on my neck. My eyes snapped open into the building glow of sunrise through the curtains and a shockingly loud call of the air raid siren reverberating throughout the cavern where Alice's log cabin was situated.

I sat up and my thoughts snapped into sharp focus as adrenaline began to flood my system. In an instant, I was grabbing my flight suit from the back of the chair and getting dressed.

The bedroom door rattled as someone knocked hard on the other side.

'Another damned air raid, we need to move it, Lauren!' Ruby shouted through the door.

'Oh don't you worry, I well and truly heard it. I'm on my way.'

'See you in the hangar,' she called back. That was followed by the sound of footsteps thundering away down the corridor.

I pulled on my boots, zipped up my flight suit, and rushed to the door.

This would make the eighth Kimprak raid in the last month alone, that had targeted Eden that our enemy had somehow been able to locate.

I sped out into the corridor and raced to the stairs, bounding down them three at a time.

The kitchen was deserted as I hurtled through it and out of the house.

The ducks were calling to each other in the simulated early morning as I sprinted along the path. A fine mist was also rising from the grass as the simulated environment heated up the cavern just like a real rising sun would have done.

I reached the rotating blast door that Ruby had left open to save me some precious seconds, and entered Alice's lab to find it packed with people.

As I wove my way through the crowd I spotted Alice, the president of the Sky Dreamer Corp, sitting in front of a bank of video feeds from the cameras on the surface. Jodie, the chief technical scientist, was sitting next to her, her face pensive. Next to her was Niki, our head of security, who looked most tense of all. And it was easy to see why. On the screens I could see blasts of shockwave vapour rippling out into the air from Eden's railgun point defence system, firing shots straight up into the sky.

I didn't even break my stride to get an update from them. That could wait until I was safely onboard *Ariel*, our anti-grav powered X103, the craft that had become my personal flagship. Somehow along the way, I'd been thrust into taking on the role of commander for the Earth fleet, and defending the base from this latest attack was very much part of my responsibility.

Instead of any words, Alice, Jodie and I just exchanged tense nods as I raced past them out of the lab and into the hangar. *Ariel* was already sitting on one of the launch pads, her ramp lowered, REV driving already quietly humming and waiting for me. As I ran up into our ship someone onboard was already raising the ramp behind me because in this situation every second counted. The ramp hissed closed just as I entered the flight cockpit where Erin our pilot was already in her seat. Ruby, our weapon's officer, in the adjacent seat was scanning the transparent CIC that curved around her.

Around us, the virtual three-hundred sixty degree curved walls that surrounded the flight deck were currently relaying a live view of the hangar outside.

'How are we doing, team?' I said as I dropped into my seat and pulled on my harness.

'Another day another dollar,' Ruby said as she shoved a fresh stick of gum into her mouth.

'The REV drive is still powering up and will be ready for liftoff in twenty seconds,' Erin said.

'All weapon systems are online and the prototype Hammer and Lightning torpedoes are already loaded,' Ruby added.

'Looks like the first field test for them won't be in a simulated attack but the real thing,' I replied.

Ruby nodded as I finished fastening my harness buckles. 'Delphi, turn on the Battle Command Centre please.'

'Initiating the Battle Command Centre,' our ship's AI echoed.

The view of the hangar shrank to a central screen, flanked left by a 3D map view and on the right the tactical options that were currently blank. On the zoomed out map view, three meteoroids ringed with red circles were heading straight down towards Eden. Fired shots from our defence grid marked in green were blazing up to meet the enemy asteroids. I could also see that a dozen of our X-craft that had been patrolling up in orbit were already chasing them down. Thanks to learning from previous experience those X-craft were keeping their distance as they harried the enemy as per their standing orders. The alien mechanised race had already proved themselves to be a formidable enemy and we weren't taking any chances now.

As I settled into my seat I felt a subtle shift in the gravity field.

'Fusion plant is running hot, REV drive is at speed, and hangar bay doors are open,' Erin said.

'Okay, then get us into this fight,' I said, casting a longing glance at the empty cup holder on my seat's arm and wishing I'd taken a few extra seconds to grab some coffee on my way here.

'Already on it, Lauren,' Erin said as she pushed the throttle forward.

The view of the hangar began to slide past—something that would never get old for me—and we began to rise into the air.

'Okay, Ruby, you better coordinate our ascent with Eden's defence grid,' I said. 'It would be better for all of us if we didn't stray into the path of a railgun round and manage to get ourselves shot down by our own side.'

Ruby practically eye-rolled me. 'Give me some credit, Commander, that's already been factored into our flight path.'

I nodded. The three of us had become quite the flight team, especially Erin and Ruby who could anticipate my orders before I'd even had a chance to issue them.

We exited the launch shaft into the jungle and there was a brief glimpse of tree trunks and thick foliage before we sped up past them. Then, in less time than I could blink, the jungle canopy was falling away beneath us.

Streaks of hypersonic rounds blurred up from the surrounding area with distant booms as the railgun grid continued to fire its salvos upwards. Each of those shots left a white track on the tactical map display a bit like the ancient arcade game, *Missile Command*.

But my attention was already focused on the three pulsing

red circles that were heading towards our world and that were surrounded by twelve of our X-craft from Earth fleet.

'Ruby, please turn on the fleet-wide channel,' I said.

She nodded and a moment later whoops and clapping were coming over our speakers as one of the red dots blinked out of existence on the 3D map.

'Take that, you bastards,' someone with a Mexican-Spanish accent said.

I cleared my throat with a cough. 'This is Commander Stelleck. Let's hold off on the celebrations for the moment. I'm still reading two Kimprak meteoroids left and we all know that all it takes is just one of them to crash with their bot-payload for all hell to break loose.'

'Roger that, Commander,' the Mexican guy replied, his tone meek.

I made a cutting sign across my throat. Ruby nodded and the comm light on my chair's arm blinked off.

'Wow, talk about busting their balls, Commander,' Ruby said shaking her head at me.

'I just want them all to keep focused until the last of those meteoroids have been taken down. Hopefully, there will be plenty of time later to celebrate down in the Rock Garden and I, for one, will be slapping their backs with the best of them. But right now we have a job to do.'

Ruby nodded.

She really got me now and so did Erin. But the thing I was most relieved about was that I no longer seemed to suffer from impostor syndrome from being the commander tasked with the huge responsibility of being in charge of the Earth X-fleet. The battle over Antarctica had seen to that. There, I'd seen front-line action with our ships, and although we'd had our noses badly bloodied, with help from, of all people, the USSF with their TR-3B fleet we'd manage to win that day. The fruits of that victory, namely an Angelus starship bequeathed to the human race, was now sitting hidden with a holographic camouflage field back in Antarctica. But for me, on a personal level, it had marked the turning point where I no longer cringed when I heard people refer to me as commander and could even refer to myself using that title. Yes, I come quite some way in my acceptance of a role that had been thrust upon me. If Tom had still been here, I was certain he would have approved and probably have said, *see, I told you so.*

On the tactical map a dotted white line had appeared in front of *Ariel* and was heading up into space depicting the flightpath that Ruby had already negotiated with the Eden Defence Control team.

As we followed it, *Ariel* began to rapidly gain altitude and my comm light blinked on again.

'Niki's on the line for you,' Ruby said.

I toggled a switch on my chair's arm. 'Hey, Niki, how are things looking from your side of Eden?'

'We're narrowing down our field of fire with the defence grid to one of the two remaining meteoroids. With the coordinated, concentrated burst that we're about to fire we should be able to atomise it before it gets anywhere near entering Earth's atmosphere. The only problem is that those Kimprak meteoroids keep dodging our fire with their damned manoeuvring jets. Anyway, heads up, because we're firing a barrage in three, two, one...'

From far beneath us on the jungle floor, there was a massive ripple of expanding shockwaves in the air that spread out like rain hitting a lake's surface. Then at least fifty projectiles, speeding almost too fast for the human eye to track, streaked past *Ariel* into the sky. The Battle Command system that I was using to control and monitor the battle tracked every single round on the tactical map.

Another thirty seconds ticked past and then one of the two remaining meteoroids blinked out of existence.

'We have confirmation from the fleet engaging the meteoroids that one of them has just detonated,' Ruby said. 'But as usual, there's still a cloud of Kimprak bots still heading down towards Eden.'

'Nice shooting, Niki,' I said. 'Sounds like the time has come for us to try out our new prototype torpedoes to mop up the rest.'

'Then we'll keep up the barrage. Good hunting, Lauren,' Niki replied.

'You too. Out,' I said as I toggled the comm channel off.

As stars filled the view ahead of us, two tactical options appeared that had been processed by the Battle Command system, *Alpha* and *Beta*. Both involved pulling our other X-craft that were already engaging the meteoroids back and then us firing a Hammer torpedo for the Alpha option and a Lightning torpedo for the Beta option.

'Okay, looks like the time has come to put the Forge team's hard work to the test,' I said. 'Delphi, initiate option Alpha.'

'Initiating Alpha,' Delphi replied.

At once, the green markers for our fleet about two hundred klicks ahead of us began to separate leaving a clear firing zone for us.

'Ruby, over to you,' I said.

'Yes, Commander,' she said with the wide grin of someone getting to play with a new toy.

Her hands flew over the CIC screen lighting up icons. Then she took a breath as she pulled the trigger on one of the weapon control joysticks.

A slight shudder passed through the ship as a lone torpedo was launched from one of the hatches and appeared on the virtual cockpit above us. A split-second later its rocket engine ignited with a flash of red and the large bulky Hammer torpedo with shark's teeth painted onto its nose—something the Forge team insisted was absolutely necessary for maximum performance—sped away from us.

Ruby sat back in her seat with her hands locked behind her head as she chewed her gum. 'I'm so looking forward to seeing what a Hammer torpedo can do to those bastards. Its warhead is packed with two thousand kilos of shrapnel, each piece of which is the size of a cannonball. Basically, it's the equivalent of firing a supersized shotgun round at the Kimprak.'

'If the demo proving flights against that boulder field are anything to go by, they should be pretty devastating,' Erin replied.

'We're about to find out now for sure,' I said, as we all watched Hammer torpedo speed towards the final meteoroid, the live view being relayed from its nose camera.

Already, puffs of jets were coming from the meteoroid's sides as it tried to dodge the torpedo with its name on it.

Then, with a pulse of light, the video blinked off as the torpedo detonated into shards on the 3D tactical map. Each fragment began spreading outwards in an expanding ball creating a huge debris field as the meteoroid flew towards it.

Erin was drumming her foot on the floor like she always did when she got stressed. Strangely that was never in the middle of intense combat, just moments like this when all she could do was wait with the rest of us. Ruby, meanwhile, was watching her readouts with slightly narrowed eyes like a cat watching its prey as the meteoroid entered the expanding shrapnel cloud of what were effectively cannonballs still travelling with the momentum that they'd inherited from the torpedo.

The effect was instant as the meteor ploughed into them. It was torn apart in multiple fragments that spun away and fragmented again and again as they struck more of the shrapnel cloud.

Ruby whistled. 'Impressive. I'll take three dozen to go because we've just achieved with just one Hammer torpedo strike what a whole barrage of railgun rounds managed to do.'

'Yes, but as good of a start as this is, we still need to land the knockout punch,' I replied. 'Hidden in the remains of that meteoroid will be a whole swarm of those Kimprak self-replicating bots that we still need to take out before they make it to the ground.'

'A Lightning torpedo is ready to do exactly that,' Ruby replied, itching to try it. 'Whenever you're ready.'

I nodded. 'Then you better go ahead.'

She grinned at me as her fingers flew over the console and then pulled the trigger.

Once again *Ariel* shuddered. This time, an elongated black torpedo with a blue nose cone and an appropriate lightning graphic painted down its side, launched from our ship. Moments later, it was streaking away towards the cloud of incoming rock fragments and the Kimprak killing machines hidden among them.

As the Lightning rushed towards its target, its nose cone camera began picking out small silver steel spheres among the fragments of rock. These were the Kimprak bots rolled up in their armoured ball-bearing configuration that was almost indestructible from anything but a direct hit.

'EMP pulse in three, two, one...' Ruby said.

A huge flare lit the atmosphere high above us on the central viewing screen as the torpedo video feed blinked out, then less than a second later a crackle of static passed through our displays. On the tactical map, a blue sphere was rushing out from the origin of the Lightning's detonation designating the electromagnetic pulse that was beginning to fade as it grew wider.

'Successful EM pulse detonation has been confirmed by our sensors,' Ruby said. 'Instruments confirm no harm to our systems thanks to them being battle-hardened and being sufficiently far away from the blast. Having said that, our ship would have only been taken offline temporarily if we'd been closer.'

I nodded as I stared at the rapidly approaching swarm of debris on the video screen.

'The question is, did it work on the Kimprak?' Erin asked.

'We should find that out any moment because we're receiving a video feed from one of our X103s in close pursuit,' Ruby said. 'Putting their camera feeds on our screen now.'

A zoomed-in view of the debris field appeared with at least thirty Kimprak in view. Every single one of them had uncurled into their trilobite form, but crucially their glowing red eyes had gone dark.

Ruby punched the air. 'Boo-yah! Take that, bitches.'

Erin was nodding. 'It certainly looks like that EMP burst knocked them out.'

A sense of relief surged through me. 'This will make all the difference when...' My words trailed away as one by one the eyes of the Kimprak started to flicker. 'Bloody hell, they're powering up again.' I was already scanning down the tactical options that had just appeared. 'Delphi, initiate Charlie option.'

'Charlie option initiated,' Delphi replied.

On the 3D tactical map, a stream of mini-gunfire opened up from our X-craft fleet, bullets streaming towards the Kimprak. On the zoomed-in video view we saw several of the Kimprak being sliced apart by the armour-piercing rounds as their eyes flared back to full brightness.

Our mini-guns opened up as Ruby got on the case and we raced towards the Kimprak too.

There had to be at least a thousand of the Kimprak remaining and I was painfully conscious that our window of opportunity to stop them was closing rapidly.

'Erin, how long till they reach the upper atmosphere?' I called out.

'Sixty seconds,' she replied as she looped us to the side of the swarm and then formed up with the rest of our fleet chasing after them, their mini-guns scything through the Kimprak's ranks.

My blood ran cold as the Kimprak began to curl back in on themselves. From our first encounter with them, we knew that in their armoured ball configuration they could survive the atmosphere. But the experience of launching that last torpedo was also conjuring up a possible solution in my mind.

'Ruby, launch another Lightning,' I said.

'But we already know the EMP pulse only lasts long enough to knock them out for sixty seconds tops,' Ruby said.

'Trust me, if I've got this right, then that's all we'll need,' I replied.

With a sharp nod, Ruby pressed the trigger and another Lightning torpedo leapt from one of our launch tubes and sped towards the Kimprak swarm.

Our X-craft fleet hurtled towards us even as they tracked the enemy. With a deft spin of the controls and one of the incredible right-angle manoeuvres *Ariel* was capable of, Erin switched our direction.

Now, in formation with the rest of the X103s, we were close enough to eyeball the silver balls reflecting light from the Earth beneath us as they raced towards it. And more specifically, towards Eden base, located in the Yucatán Peninsula in Mexico.

The need for secrecy had long passed since we'd started flying so many sorties above it and we had quickly worked out where the Sky Dreamer Corp's underground base was situated. Also, the need for ongoing security since the run-ins with the Overseers had stopped so that had also reset the requirement for absolute secrecy in that regard.

As our squadron of ships continued to pour fire into the

swarms of Kimprak, our torpedo detonated among their ranks with a flash of blue light visible overhead.

This time our virtual cockpit completely blinked off and suddenly our bridge was only lit by the glow of buttons around us.

Erin was already toggling switches on her console. 'We were a bit too close to the pulse that time, but our systems are already coming back online.'

With a soft hum, the virtual cockpit flickered back into existence to show that the Kimprak swarm was racing past us towards Earth. But the crucial difference was that their eyes were all dark again, and more importantly for my plan to work, they had uncurled into their trilobite forms as they raced by.

'Why are you just sitting there, Erin? Get after them,' Ruby said.

'We can't yet, our REV drive is still powering up.'

I glanced at the virtual cockpit to see that the rest of the wing were drifting too, the EM pulse had obviously had the same effect on them.

'Okay, Ruby, raise Eden and let them know that if my plan doesn't work it will be down to their point defence grid to take out those remaining Kimprak.'

'You mean your plan is still in play?' Erin asked as Ruby began toggling icons on her CIC screen that had just powered back up.

'Yes, and hopefully any moment now...'

Then, just as I hoped they would, the swarm started to glow first red, then orange, and finally white-hot as they left a trail of molten metal behind.

'They're burning up!' Erin said.

I let out a relieved sigh. 'Exactly as I'd hoped, Earth's atmosphere is doing the job for us. The Kimprak in their trilobite form are much more exposed to the intense heat of reentry.'

'You mean you planned to literally melt their asses?' Ruby said looking across at me.

I gesture towards the 3D tactual maps as every single one of the Kimprak robots blinked out of existence. 'Well it worked, didn't it?'

She snorted. 'You're so the boss. Well played, Commander, well played. Shall I cancel that order to Eden defence grid then?'

'Yes, and instead let the rest of the squadron know that I expect to see all of them in the Rock Garden later tonight to celebrate.'

'Yes, Commander,' Ruby said snapping me an almost polite salute.

Erin shook her head grinning at us. Then, with the REV drive back online, she curved us round back towards Eden as the wing of X-craft formed up behind us and we got ready to head home.

CHAPTER TWO

With the Kimprak raid, this had been a trickier Monday than most. That was the downside, but the one thing that always elevated this day of the week was that it was also curry night at the Rock Garden with an interesting Sri Lankan twist, thanks to Chef Pete Duminda. He normally worked at one of the main Eden restaurants, but come Mondays he always offered up his services to serve up a taste of his home country in the Rock Garden. Pete always referred to his dishes as simply curry and rice, but it was so much more than that humble title would suggest.

His menus included everything from cuttlefish curry to a sticky aubergine, one that I could never get enough of. Then there was also a rather mind-blowing barbecued chilli crab that Jack had once declared his undying love for. He certainly would have adored being here tonight, and I'd already made a mental note that when I headed back to *Tempest* I would ask Pete to make Jack some so I could take it to him. I knew the way to my man's heart.

It was in the Rock Garden that I now sat with Alice, Niki, and Jodie. Erin was sitting with Ruby at the next table who was holding centre court with her buddies from the security team. She also had a plate piled high enough with several curry combos to feed a small army.

Niki raised a glass of frozen chilled Icelandic vodka that he'd insisted we all try and clinked it against our glasses. 'Here's to a very successful demonstration of your new torpedoes, Jodie.'

Even though she clinked her glass against his, Jodie still frowned. 'Hmmm, a partial success. Those Kimprak are far harder to knock out than I expected. I'm going to need to do a lot more tweaking.'

I reached across the table and squeezed her arm. 'As far as I'm concerned, they worked spectacularly well and made a huge difference in our mission, especially the Hammer Torpedoes. They literally did the job of a hundred railgun rounds in a fraction of the time.'

That managed to elicit a small smile from Jodie. 'Yes, the kinetic closing speed of the area effect shrapnel blasts should make a real difference intercepting those meteoroids.'

'There certainly seems to be a lot more attacks than there used to be,' Niki said shaking his head.

'My guess is that they're using some sort of mass launcher, which is basically a scaled-up version of one of our railguns, and they're firing more as they close in on our solar system,' Jodie replied.

Alice frowned. 'They've certainly stretched both Earth and Psyche 16's fleets to the maximum trying to intercept them, especially as our printers work flat out to replace the ships lost in battle over Antarctica.'

'We shouldn't forget Area 51's TR-3B fleet either, that the Kimprak were somehow able to locate,' Niki added. 'According to our intelligence sources, they've come under bombardment almost as frequently as we have. But so far, like us, they've been able to keep them at bay.'

'Which is great news, but I just wish that we'd been able to keep the lines of communication open with the USSF,' I said. 'As we proved we can do at Antarctica, both sides should still be working together, combining our forces, rather than pursuing our own separate agendas.'

Alice sighed. 'I know, but I think in fairness, that the USSF losing so many ships has made them even warier of working with us.'

'If it helps to build some bridges, then I'm more than happy to share the schematics of our space torpedoes with them,' Jodie said.

'That is certainly something we could look at,' Alice said.

Jodie gazed down at her plate of aubergine curry with a side of spiced garlic okra. 'Yes, but maybe let me try to do something to at least increase the yield of the Lightnings first. Otherwise, they'll accuse us of trying to sell them a dud.'

Before I could respond, Niki held up a hand. 'I think we've talked enough shop for the evening, and besides, we have the meeting tomorrow to discuss all of that and the general state of preparations for the Kimprak mothership's arrival. For now I say we kick back, enjoy some great food and drink, and make the most of each other's company.'

'Absolutely,' I replied. Then I raised my glass to Jodie. 'Here's to you, Jodie. You never cease to amaze.'

A warm smile filled her face. 'And to you too, Lauren, for the exact same reason. Now let's fill our faces with this delicious food before it goes cold.'

'Amen to that,' Alice said, smiling too.

The barbecued crab was every bit as good as I remembered it

and I was making a mental note that maybe I should get two portions of crab for Jack when a very uncharacteristic squeal came from the next table. Ruby was up on her feet and rushing across the floor towards a red-haired woman.

It took me a moment to realise that it was Julie, who we hadn't seen for months as she'd been working out at Tranquillity base on Psyche 16, a massive metallic asteroid the size of a moon that we'd been mining to produce more ships. Julie had been helping to set up the automated factory production there. She looked every bit as lit up at seeing Ruby as both women threw their arms round each other.

Alice smiled at them as we all watched. 'Julie just got back from her tour of duty for some R&R time.'

'Oh, that's why Ruby was so keen we stayed an extra day before heading back to *Tempest*,' I replied.

'You mean she didn't tell you that she wanted to take a brief holiday with Julie, even if it was just a day?' Jodie said.

'No, but then that woman keeps her personal life close to her chest and I'm not one to pry. Anyway, she can certainly have her day because there's plenty that I can do here.'

'I hope you're ready for visitors soon,' Niki said. 'I'm looking forward to seeing how it's all been going onboard *Tempest*.'

'You're not the only one, it's high time I made a site visit to *Tempest* too,' Alice said. 'Videos and photos are all well and good, but there's no substitute for seeing it with my own eyes.'

'We'd be delighted to have you, and I'm sure you wouldn't overlook the chance to fly an X103 to get yourself there, Alice.'

Considering Alice was president of Sky Dreamer Corp that made all of this possible, including *Ariel*, and a former stunt pilot, the prospect of that made her eyes light up.

'Now, there's a wonderful idea,' Alice said beaming at me as we all returned our attention to our food.

It was at moments like this that I realised how all these people had become part of my extended family over the years. But at the centre of that family for me was Jack, and as always I found it hard to be parted from him even for a few days, like we were now. Not that we were joined at the hip, just life always seemed brighter when we were together.

But I knew Jack was having the time of his archaeologist life as he pored over the contents of *Tempest*, cataloguing everything he found. One of the setbacks that we'd suffered from the loss of seven of the micro minds—the AIs that helped rebuild and run *Tempest*—was the loss of the systems and databases that detailed all aspects of the starship. Even now, there were vast sections of the starship that still hadn't been explored.

Mike was having a similarly great time onboard *Tempest* too, up to his neck in tech and science as he worked alongside Lucy.

Yes, both the main guys in my life were in their happy place right now. As for me, even though I'd surprised myself in the way I'd stepped up to the role of commander, deep down I'd always be a woman who loved looking up at the stars and getting lost in the wonder of it all.

I pushed my plate away and helped myself to another measure of the rather great Icelandic vodka that Niki was sharing with us and then I stood.

I raised my voice so everyone in the Rock Garden could hear me. 'Hey, I would just like to raise a glass here to everyone in Eden, onboard *Tempest,* out at Tranquillity Base, and all the crews out there currently patrolling space. Whatever else we all are, we're one hell of a team working together to protect humanity. May we never lose our mojo.'

'Hell yes,' Ruby said, squeezing Julie's hand.

Everyone in the room was nodding, especially Alice who was smiling at me.

'Well said, Lauren,' she said as she raised her glass. 'May we never lose our mojo!' she called out.

'May we never lose our mojo!' everyone echoed as they raise their glasses and took a sip of their drinks. That was followed by raucous applause, led most of all by me.

CHAPTER THREE

We all sat in the briefing room around the large oval table in Eden. This was one of the regular monthly updates where everyone was kept up to speed with how preparations were going for the Kimprak invasion. It wasn't lost on me that the defence of Earth had become an ever more complex machine with many moving parts, and one of the biggest parts of that equation was now *Tempest* and the difference she could make. Everyone back in Antarctica was working flat out to make sure it could play a major role in the coming battle.

Around the table sat Alice, Jodie, Niki, and myself, me with a large pot of Lapsang Souchong tea and one of the many excellent bagels that Alice always brought to these meetings for us to share. Of course, normally I was at the other end of a video feed for these updates onboard the bridge of *Tempest,* otherwise known as the Citadel, so being here made for a novel change.

On the wall was a countdown timer to the Kimprak mothership arrival in our solar system and that currently stood at five months and twenty-two days and they were everywhere across Eden. It was Alice's not-so-subtle attempt to keep everyone focused on the task at hand, that we all needed to do everything we could to defend our world. It absolutely worked too, stopping meetings from running on too long. The unspoken priority was that we all needed to get on and actually do the things that we discussed in meetings like this one.

Alice, who'd been studying a tablet of notes and chatting to Niki, turned towards Jodie and me. 'Are you ready to start?'

We both nodded.

'Then let's get this meeting underway,' Alice said. 'Delphi, please initiate a conference call with *Tempest* and also with Tranquillity Base.'

'Initiating conference call,' Sky Dreamer Corp's omnipotent AI replied.

The large screen that filled the entire wall at the end of the meeting room switched from a view of rolling waves and was replaced with a mosaic of webcam feeds.

I immediately sought out Jack, because even a few days away from him felt like a lifetime. I spotted his video windows in the top left-hand corner where he and Poseidon, one of the Angelus AIs android avatars, appeared to be standing in a museum with statues and display cases that they'd recently unearthed in one of the unused habitation zones.

Jack looked a lot more tired than the last time I'd seen him thirty-six hours ago, when I'd departed *Tempest*. He looked a lot less lit up too. Probably just overdoing things, like usual, with his research work.

But at least the others on the conference call looked happy. Mike was in one of *Tempest's* engineering sections with Lucy, standing in front of a large room lined with a number of large spheres with pointy spikes sticking out of them, a bit like a silver sea urchin.

Below his video window was Troy, the commander of the Sol fleet. He appeared to be sitting in the control room of the Psyche

16 base. He had a mug of coffee in his hand and was nodding to us as his stream came online.

'Good to see you all again,' he said.

'You too,' Alice replied. 'So how are things going out at Tranquillity Base on Psyche 16?'

'Good, but first and foremost, I'm really sorry about the meteoroids that managed to get past our Sol fleet that you had to deal with. We just didn't spot them.'

'You can't expect to stop every one of them, Troy, some are bound to slip past,' I said. 'Remind me, how many have you managed to intercept over the last month?'

'A hundred and thirty-three so far, but I can't help feel personally responsible for every single one that gets past our ships.'

I knew exactly where he was coming from because it was the same way that I felt whenever anything went wrong here, like it was some sort of shortcoming in me as the Earth fleet commander. But of course, that sort of guilt trip was also all part of the role, which was just as it should be because it meant that we cared deeply about our people.

Niki nodded towards Troy. 'Look, I understand your feelings, but some are bound to slip through, especially as we now know they are using gravitational slingshots around the outer planets to vary their approach paths. That's why we have the Earth fleet under Lauren's command to mop up any that get through.'

'Absolutely, and Troy, to be honest, you're all making us feel a bit lazy here because you're leaving us hardly anything to do,' I said giving him a small smile.

He snorted. 'Lazy is the last thing that you guys are, Lauren.'

'Okay, maybe not,' I said with a broader smile. 'Anyway, all this should be thing of the past, thanks to Jodie and the Forge team's incredible work with the space torpedoes. I'm certain they're going to be an absolute game-changer.'

Troy nodded as he turned his attention towards Jodie. 'So you've conjured up another tech miracle for us, then?'

'I really can't take any of the credit because this was very much down to the work of the Forge team.'

But Mike was already shaking his head over the video link at his girlfriend. 'Way too modest as usual. You've been burning the candle at both ends. When you've not been helping me here, you've been poring over all the schematics for those torpedoes and making revisions right up until the last moment.'

Jodie pulled a face. 'I'm just trying to make myself useful.'

Alice fixed her with a direct look. 'Which you always over-achieve in abundance, as you well know, so for once just accept a compliment.'

'If you say so,' Jodie replied.

'She does, and so do I,' I said. Then I nodded towards Lucy standing next to Mike. 'Is there any news from any of those Guardian drones that you managed to launch from *Tempest* and send out into space, Lucy?'

'Yes, they are all on target to reach their designated coordinates ringing the solar system in interstellar space in about another week. Once there, we should have the early warning capability not only of the Kimprak meteoroids that are being thrown our way, but also of the asteroid mothership when it finally arrives.'

'That's going to make a huge difference,' Troy replied. 'With that knowledge, we'll be able to work out their projected trajectories and arrange a suitable reception committee. Anyway, what I really want to hear, is how things are going aboard *Tempest*, Lauren?'

'That goes for all of us,' Alice said.

I took a sip of my Lapsang tea and nodded. 'As you all are well aware by now, bringing *Tempest's* fusion drives back online has been our main priority and is in the final stages. But Lucy will be able to give you a better idea about that than me.'

She nodded towards the camera. 'Yes, it's one of the more fiddly parts of the internal structural builds that has yet to be completed. What hasn't helped was that a secondary critical system was badly out of calibration and was damaged during a test power-up last week. That, unfortunately, put us back a bit, but we're still on track for *Tempest* to have her fusion drive up and running in another two months.'

'Since when has *Tempest* been a she?' Mike asked, which made me smile.

'To start with, dearest, all craft in any human navy have traditionally been referred to as she, but more importantly, with *Tempest,* it's even more appropriate,' Lucy said.

'In what way?' Mike replied.

Lucy tilted her head to one side. 'If you'd ever been at the sharp end of a woman's scorn you *so* wouldn't need to ask that.'

Everyone laughed, apart from Jack who I noticed continued to look like someone enjoying a wet weekend at a seaside resort in England and who had just discovered all the fish and chip shops were closed.

'So, Mike and Lucy, I have to ask where you're both standing because it's more than a little bit intriguing?' Alice asked, seemingly oblivious to Jack's dour mood.

'We're actually in one of *Tempest's* four factory E8 molecular printer rooms,' Mike replied.

'Yes, to say you're like a kid with a new toy would be a serious understatement,' Lucy said raising her eyebrows at him.

'Can you blame me? I mean, think of Eden's 3D industrial printers, but something that's a hundred times more efficient. Each printer contains discreet pockets of the E8 that can model everything down to the sub atomic level when building something up to a hundred metres across.'

Lucy was nodding. 'The molecular E8 printing rooms can literally create everything you need and all in one go. But it's probably better if we show you what we just created in the last hour.' She took hold of the camera that had been filming the two of them and swung it round.

Everyone gasped, as there before us was a fully finished Pangolin.

'You're seriously saying that you finished that in only an hour?' Niki asked.

'You better believe it, and every single aspect of the Pangolin too, from the computer systems down to the padding in the flight seats,' Mike replied. 'Unlike moving things into our reality from the E8 zone within *Tempest,* which is restricted to relatively small objects, these molecular printers can cope with far larger ones. The only downside is that they do need to draw significant power from the main E8 sphere and can't be used when the weapons systems are powered up, so no printing more torpedoes during a battle for example. But with enough raw material in the storage holds, we can build as many ships as we like, which is yet another reason we should get *Tempest* over to Psyche 16 sooner rather than later, so she fills her boots directly from the surface of the asteroid.'

'As fantastic as this news is, there is a logistical problem here that I can see,' Alice said. 'We've barely got enough pilots as it is.'

'Ah, that's why we're not proposing printing just X-craft with these.'

My eyes widened. 'Why, what did you have in mind?'

'To print something that Jodie has been discussing with me, but until now we didn't have the capacity to produce. Here, let me show you.' Mike reached forward to take the camera from Lucy and then the view swung round towards a rectangular boxy craft, shaped a bit like a ten-metre-long coffin. A metre long metallic tube extended from its nose.

Jodie stared at it. 'You produced a prototype of the Wolfpack battle drone, Mike?'

'It seemed as good a test subject as any and I know how stretched you and the Forge team have been there at Eden.'

Lucy was nodding. 'We thought we could help out by creating one of them for you from one of your schematics for us to be able to play with.'

Jodie was beaming at them. 'Oh that's just fantastic news, but does it actually turn on?'

In answer, Mike grinned at her. 'Delphi, please initiate a ten-metre hop with Wolfpack drone prototype one.'

'Initiating ten-metre hop,' Delphi replied, her voice echoing round the space where they were standing.

In absolute silence, the craft rose ten metres from the floor, glided forward, and then lowered itself onto the ground.

'As you can see, it uses a full micro REV antigravity drive, and the really crazy thing is that only took an hour to print. Using all three printers we can produce around seventy-five drones a day.'

Alice was already nodding enthusiastically. 'This could be a real game-changer and could directly help with our lack of flight crews.'

Jodie was now nodding. 'Yes, I came up with the idea of the Wolfpack to address exactly that. It was actually an idea I got from Boeing's Loyal Wingman drone program that's designed to augment a fighter plane's capabilities in combat by slaving the control of the drones to the pilot. But rather than carrying missiles, ours will be armed with a high-powered laser based on Angelus tech.'

'So you're saying these are sort of a scaled-up, anti-grav powered version of a WASP?' I asked.

'In many ways, but their lasers should be more than enough to take out individual Kimprak,' Jodie said.

'Now you're talking my language,' Niki said. 'Along with the new space torpedoes, this transforms what we can bring into a battle with the Kimprak. And of course, we mustn't overlook what difference *Tempest* can make too.'

'Absolutely,' I replied. 'And talking of military strategy, I was thinking of a way that we could build some bridges with USSF for a joint strategy to battle the Kimprak together. As you know, after the Antarctica battle, we rescued USSF pilot Don Jacobs who'd been shot down. Last week, his new artificial heart was completed, so he's nearly ready to be discharged from *Tempest's* medical facility.'

Alice shook her head. 'The medical wonders onboard that starship are extraordinary, especially the Angelus' use of nanobots. If we weren't preparing for all-out war, I would be diverting huge funds to take that technology to the rest of our world.'

'Hopefully, that can happen one day after we've dealt with the Kimprak,' I said. 'Anyway, Don is more than up for helping us persuade the USSF.'

'Good. Let's make that a priority,' Alice said 'That also neatly brings us onto our other favourite topic, namely the Overseers.'

Niki scowled. 'Once again there's not been a single scrap of intelligence about them over the last few months. It's as though they dropped off the face of the planet. The only notable exception is in the UK. It seems they may have had a major role in Prime Minister Alexander Langton seizing the top job and who appears to be very much under their influence.'

'Bloody hell, I always knew that guy was bad news. Is there anything we can do about it?' I asked.

'Not for now, but let's just say we're putting together a dossier on him that can be released to the press when the time is right,' Alice replied. 'But apart from that, the trail goes cold regarding the Overseers, and there hasn't been a single sighting of Colonel Alvarez anywhere either.'

'Which makes me feel even more uncomfortable,' I said.

'You're not the only one,' Alice replied with a thin smile. 'However, the main point still stands that the Overseers appear to no longer be a major thorn in our sides. So for now, as far as I'm concerned, that's something I'm more than happy to accept with open arms.'

I might have nodded with the others, but deep down it all had me more than a little bit worried. Could this really be a sudden capitulation by the Overseers? Even if the secret organisation did feel there was nothing more they could do to stop our efforts, it wasn't like Alvarez to withdraw from a fight. And the one thing that still bothered me was that he had once boasted to me that they had well-advanced plans to deal with the Kimprak. I'd always assumed he was talking about the TR-3B fleet they had built out of Area 51. But what if it was something else?

Alice's gaze landed on Jack's video window. 'So how are things going with your exploration of *Tempest*, Jack?'

Now everyone's attention focused on him and I was struck again by just how mute he'd been so far in the meeting.

His weary eyes looked out at us, his expression pinched. 'Really well, if not a little exhausting.'

'You sound like you're pushing yourself way too hard,' I said.

Jack managed a faint smile. 'You know me when it comes to anything archaeology, even if this is an alien one. Anyway, I'm happy to report that Poseidon and I have been making steady progress. Although we still have a way to go yet, with the whole stern section of *Tempest* still to be explored. Anyway, I've included details of what we've found in the report I've attached to the meeting notes that you're free to read when you have a moment.'

'I'm looking forward to it,' Lucy replied.

'There are a few bits in there that fill in some of the jigsaw puzzle about *Tempest*,' Jack said.

'You can run me through them in person when we head back tomorrow,' I said.

'Yes, that would be good,' Jack replied as his gaze slid away from mine and immediately I had a sense that something was wrong, especially when he was normally so enthusiastic about sharing his latest discoveries with everyone.

'Okay, is there anything else that anyone wants to cover before we wrap up?' Alice asked, obviously not picking up on the same vibe that I was.

'Just that, now I've finished with torpedo prototype work with the Forge team, I'd like to hitch a lift back onboard *Ariel* if that's okay, Lauren?' Jodie asked.

'Fine with me.'

'And me,' Alice said. 'It's certainly about time you worked alongside Mike again.'

'You can say that again,' Mike said. 'So much to show you and there's quite a few systems I could really do with your help on.'

'Then you shall have it,' Jodie said beaming at Mike.

'Then, if there is nothing else, let's draw things to a close there,' Alice said.

With a series of nods and then goodbyes, the video feeds closed down. But as I headed for the door, Jack's behaviour had me more than a little concerned. The first thing I intended to do when I got back to *Tempest* was check in with him to make sure everything was really okay.

CHAPTER FOUR

Ruby was barely speaking to me as we began our journey towards Antarctica onboard *Ariel*. But that was hardly surprising as I'd refused her request to extend her R&R with Julie. I'd nearly relented and called in a surrogate pilot, but Niki had a quiet word in my ear about how a flight crew was a tightly knit unit and how even on what was effectively a shuttle flight, she should be with us, just in case anything happened.

In the heightened state of alert that we were all living in currently, a Kimprak bombardment landing on our heads at any moment was definitely a very real possibility, at least until we had the new torpedoes built and deployed. So for now, I would just have to suffer Ruby's mood until she eventually came out the other side of it. Not that I had much headspace left for it.

But of course, I also had a personal reason for wanting to stick to our schedule. Jack's whole withdrawn attitude had really unsettled me. The one thing that I knew for sure was that the sooner I saw him, the sooner I'd be able to reassure myself that everything was okay with him—or maybe not.

Below us on the virtual cockpit, the ocean sped past, gentle waves sparkling under a bright blue sky as we headed towards the southern pole of our planet.

Erin was as focused as usual on her flying, and Jodie was lost in looking at technical schematics on her tablet. They were every bit as quiet as Ruby, who was absolutely giving me the silent treatment. So everyone was leaving me to the churn of my own thoughts about Jack, when the comm light blinked on Ruby's CIC screen.

'We have Niki on the line for you, Commander,' Ruby said without even looking at me.

I nodded and toggled the comm switch on my chair's arm.

'Hi, Lauren,' Niki said. 'There's been a development, and I'm afraid I'm going to need you to deviate from your flight path to check it out. You're the nearest X-craft we have to deal with it.'

I had to suppress a surge of frustration because any deviation would mean a delay in talking to Jack. 'What is it, Niki?' I asked.

'We've had reports about a possible meteorite coming down in an area of Eastern Australia in Dalrymple Heights, Queensland. Delphi picked up reports of it crash-landing near a remote farm up in the hills.'

'But that could just be an ordinary impact,' I replied.

'It would have been, if we hadn't lost contact with the person who called it in. Not only that, but nothing has been heard from a local police officer who was also dispatched to the area to investigate.'

'You're saying this could be a Kimprak meteoroid that slipped past our defences?'

'Maybe not a whole one, but possibly a fragment we didn't spot that slipped through. And even if it was carrying just a single Kimprak, at the rate those damned things replicate it could be enough to cause a major situation if we don't nip it in the bud. I'm already dispatching a task force to investigate, but you could be there a good thirty minutes ahead of them if only to give us a situation report.'

'Actually, we're well equipped for the mission, even if it is a Kimprak meteorite,' Jodie said. 'We still have some Hammer and Lightning torpedoes loaded onboard.'

Ruby nodded. 'Yeah, if there are any Kimprak there we're in a good position to deal with them. Also, it's my home country that might be coming under attack here, so I'm all in. Especially as we also have a Tin Head in our hold and a whole WASP swarm all loaded up with armour-piercing rounds. But like always this is our commander's call.'

From the expression on her face, I could see that any attitude from Ruby towards me had vanished, and as always, she was the very definition of professionalism when it came to an active mission. When it came down to it, we all knew any Kimprak making it down to the surface made any personal issues, even my own, secondary to dealing with a potential live invasion threat.

I met Ruby's expectant gaze as they all waited to hear my answer. 'Of course, we're going to investigate. Let's just hope it's a false alarm. Erin, could you please take us to the impact site.'

'Already all over it, Lauren,' Erin replied as she deftly adjusted *Ariel's* thrusters and we started heading sideways to our original heading at Mach eight.

I'd always been a fan of the original '50s movie version of *War of the Worlds*, and as we descended towards the impact site, it almost felt like we were about to live through a real-life version of it.

In the darkness below, an impact crater was glowing with a deep red light. A short way off, a police Toyota Land Cruiser had been parked, its blue lights still flashing. According to the metadata tag overlaid over the virtual cockpit, there wasn't a light to be seen at the farmhouse sitting on the hill, from where the original sighting had been reported.

'This is all looking a bit too quiet for my liking,' Jodie said.

'I agree,' I replied. 'Ruby, we need to scout out the area to see what's happened before we risk touching down.'

'Okay, let's launch our WASP swarm to see what we're dealing with, especially around that impact crater,' she replied.

'Good. How long till backup gets here?' I asked.

Ruby glanced at one of her sub-displays on her CIC screen. 'About twenty-five minutes now.'

'Then let's start gathering intel.'

Our weapon's officer nodded and toggled a few buttons. A moment later a window appeared split into a four-by-three grid, a different video feed in each of them from the WASP drones currently in our hold. In the background hung our lone Tin Head robot who Ruby had nicknamed Slick, which had been scrawled on the side of his squat, neckless head in red paint. A XM556 mini-gun—a scaled-down version of one of the weapon systems that *Ariel* used—had also been fitted as an extension to his right arm. The attachment basically made Slick look like an extra straight out of *Terminator*. But at least this mechanical beast was on our side, rather than trying to wipe out humanity like his Kimprak brethren.

With a whir just audible through our hull, the twelve WASP drones dropped away from our fully stealthed ship. Also, as we'd approached the site, Erin had made sure our active camo system was engaged so that anyone who might be on the ground wouldn't spot the giant flying saucer sitting in the air just a thousand feet over their heads. That would only create some tricky questions that Eden's security team would then be forced to try and suppress.

Our WASP swarm separated into a pre-programmed search

pattern. A number of them headed outwards, but the bulk of them concentrated their attention on the smouldering crater below us. Ruby increased the size of their video windows on the virtual cockpit until we were encircled by them.

We all paid most attention to drone six, otherwise known as Dopey according to its metadata tag and so named by Ruby as she did with all our robotic craft, as he headed straight down towards the crater.

As Dopey neared the target the red light became so intense it was impossible to see anything that might be sitting in the crater.

'Switching Dopey to thermal imaging mode,' Ruby said.

A false colour image appeared in his video feed, but once again it was hard to make anything out because of the intensity of the heat at the bottom of the crater.

Ruby sighed. 'Well, that made diddly squat difference to clearing up what's at the bottom of that bloody crater. I'm going to have to let Dopey get closer.'

I nodded, but my attention was now on drone three, otherwise known as Grumpy, who had just reached the police car and was now slowly circling it to reveal that there was no one in it.

'Okay, I realise there could be an innocent explanation for where that policeman has gone, but does anyone else have a really bad feeling about this?' Jodie asked.

Erin, Jodie, and I all nodded as we watched Grumpy track in for a closer look. It was as he was swinging around that I noticed something glittering on the ground.

'Hey, Ruby, can you back Grumpy up and point his camera towards that patch of ground,' I said gesturing towards it on the screen.

'Sure...' She pressed a few icons and hovering, Grumpy swivelled his camera downwards.

Picked out by the spotlight attached to the side of his camera, were five bullet casings lying on the ground next to the police car.

Then Jodie gasped as a trail of blood appeared just in front of it and lead away back towards the crater, complete with significant drag marks.

'Oh shit, I don't think you need to be Sherlock Holmes to crack this case,' Jodie said.

'Exactly,' I replied. 'Okay, Ruby, let's try and get Dopey as close as possible to the crater to see exactly what we're dealing with. Meanwhile, have a Lightning torpedo ready to fire straight down at it if anything so much as twitches down there.'

'Whoa there, even with *Ariel's* shielding that's too close to be on the safe side,' Jodie said. 'Better to withdraw to a few miles up and launch from there.'

'"Nuke them from orbit," in other words,' Ruby said giving me a wry smile.

'Seriously, a quote from *Aliens*?' I replied.

'It's the only decent sci-fi movie that's ever been made, in my not so humble opinion.'

'That will be because it's got marines and lots of guns in it, right?' Erin said raising her eyebrows at her friend.

'Yeah, that's the one,' Ruby replied grinning back at her.

I shook my head at her, but smiled. 'Okay, withdraw us to a safe distance, Erin.'

Our pilot nodded and *Ariel* rose quickly into the sky. Ruby had already returned Dopey's video feed to normal vision mode, as the thermal image wasn't helping identify anything, apart from a lot of heat radiating off the crater.

As the WASP drone neared its target, my heart clenched as I spotted more blood leading up over the lip of the crater and down into it. If there were Kimprak down there, and there was every reason to think that there could be, just how many more of them were there by now? Of course, there was one even worse scenario. They might have already fled the nest and were scurrying across the countryside. If that had happened, we might already be looking at a nightmare scenario, where the Kimprak bots carried on replicating like an out of control bunch of cockroaches in a dodgy takeaway kitchen.

Dopey had almost drawn level with the lip of the surrounding crater when there was a brief flicker of movement within it. Then we had a brief glimpse of an image straight out of a horror movie.

The body of the police officer lay crumpled at the bottom of the crater and he was covered in a swarm of the Kimprak trilobites that were burrowing into his flesh. Already half his face had been eaten away and newly hatched trilobites were burrowing out of his chest cavity.

Before Ruby could react, one of the metallic bugs leapt straight up at Dopey and his video feed blinked off.

'Launch that damned torpedo now!' I shouted, any sense of detachment shattered by the grisly spectacle that we'd all just witnessed.

'Lightning torpedo is away,' Ruby said as she pulled the trigger on her joystick.

A shudder passed through *Ariel* as the torpedo sped out of the weapon port, straight down towards the target.

The views from the other WASPs showed them all firing towards the crater as Kimprak trilobites began to scuttle out.

A split-second later, a huge pulse of light lit up the landscape as the EMP torpedo detonated. On the virtual cockpit, there was an overlay of an expanding circle of blue marking the electromagnetic pulse's progress across the landscape far below us. As it reached the visible lights of the scattered houses in a small town a good ten klicks out from the impact site, they blinked out as the pulse fried anything electronic. A snowstorm of static briefly flickered across our cockpit view before clearing again.

'Get us down there now, mini-guns hot and throw in a Hammer torpedo for good measure,' I said.

Erin and Ruby both nodded and then *Ariel* shuddered again as a Hammer torpedo streaked away from us leading the charge.

Less than two seconds later, the crater lit up with a fireball, propelling cannonball shrapnel out that blasted the entire area, a few stray ones slamming into the Toyota Land Cruiser and rolling it onto its side. Erin adjusted the REV drive, and hot on the missile's trail, we hurtled straight down.

Ruby flicked off the safety and spooled up our mini-guns, firing a stream straight down into and around the crater.

With a brief surge of negative-Gs, Erin brought us into a hover just a couple of hundred feet from the bottom, blazing through the metal trilobites that had frozen up as they'd scuttled away, their pinprick, glowing, red demon eyes now all dark, thanks to the EM pulse.

'Okay, another sixty seconds tops and they'll recover,' Jodie said looking at the clock she'd pulled up on her screen.

'Deploy our Tin Head,' I called out. 'The more guns we can deploy the better.'

Ruby nodded. 'Slick is away!'

On the virtual cockpit, our robot hurtled straight down and landed hard into a crouch position, his hydraulic legs absorbing the impact. Moments later he was standing tall, his XM556 mini-gun tracer-fire blazing out and picking off the Kimprak.

'Twenty seconds before those damned things reboot,' Jodie called out, looking at her display.

Ruby placed a counter on the virtual screen of the number of Kimprak *Ariel's* and Slick's sensors were picking up. Fifteen seconds raced past and the count was still at two hundred.

'Come on!' Ruby said as she blazed fire down into the crater and Slick continued to mop up any that had attempted to flee.

At ten seconds, the number was down to a hundred.

I could already tell that this was going to be tight, but then a blindingly obvious idea struck me. 'Erin, quickly reorientate

Ariel so Ruby can use the topside mini-gun as well,' I called over.

Erin nodded and spun the ship around, the gyro-stabilised deck keeping the flight deck level throughout the manoeuvre.

Ruby shot me a grateful look as she opened up with the second mini-gun as well. Twin streams of armour-piercing death rained down into the crater and immediately the number of Kimprak kills started to double.

As three seconds raced by, twenty-three Kimprak remained.

My hands were clawing into my chair as the final moments ticked down, and it was literally down to the last two-hundred milliseconds when the Kimprak numbers finally dwindled to zero.

Ruby thumped the air. 'Boo-yah!' Then she cast me a broad grin. 'So yeah, okay, maybe you had a point, after all, dragging me away from Julie.'

I snorted and shook my head at her. 'Okay, but before we really start celebrating we better land and do a ground sweep to check that none of those bloody things escaped.'

Erin nodded and righted *Ariel*.

'Let's do this,' Ruby said.

Jodie dug around in her pack and pulled out a metal box fastened with sturdy clamps and some sort of control unit attached to it.

'What are you planning to do with that?' I asked.

'Something I've been desperate to do since this started. If there is a live Kimprak out there, I want to capture it.'

Ruby gawped at her. 'You have to shitting us?'

'Relax, it generates a closed EM field within the container that will keep the Kimprak offline. The opportunity to examine a live specimen is too good an opportunity to miss. Especially since I need one to experiment on so I can increase the effective yield of our Lightning torpedoes.'

I glared at her. 'You are *not* bringing one of those things onboard *Ariel*.'

'Yes, I agree that would be reckless. That's why we'll put it in the hold. If there's even a hint of a problem, you can literally drop it like a bomb. Then I was thinking Ruby could slice it to pieces before it even hit the ground.'

'That shouldn't be a problem,' Ruby said.

'Okay, not entirely thrilled with this idea,' I said. 'Let's just hope there isn't an escaped Kimprak to capture anyway.'

I unstrapped my flight harness and headed to the weapon's locker, as Erin began to lower *Ariel* towards a patch of scrubland just beyond the abandoned police Land Cruiser.

CHAPTER FIVE

'Oh, bloody hell,' I said as we stood next to the remains of the crater. Ruby had just pointed out the marks in the ground from multiple tiny metallic feet. They led away from the crater and headed up towards the distant farm on the hill.

'Looks like we have a bear hunt on,' Jodie said. The only thing stopping her from rubbing her hands together with glee was the EMP case she carried.

'Can you please not look quite so pleased about it,' I said as we all looked at the farmhouse. 'Of course, you do realise it could be anywhere by now and multiplying like crazy?'

'Actually, I think it's a very safe bet that it will have made its way to the farm,' Jodie replied. 'The fastest way for a Kimprak to replicate is to consume metal and seeing as it wasn't able to snack on that police vehicle because it was under fire, assuming a certain level of intelligence, I would imagine it would head for the next source of concentrated material that it can munch its way through.'

'In other words, that farm, which probably has plenty of metal in a thing like a tractor,' I replied.

'Yep, and almost certainly a ute, if I know my Aussie farmers, which translates as truck to the rest of you,' Ruby replied as she stood from where she'd been examining the tracks.

She checked the magazine on her Heckler & Koch MP7 as she eyed the treeline ahead of us. Just to make completely sure she was suitably armed for this mission, she also had an M32 grenade launcher slung over her shoulder. Ruby was never one to take chances.

I'd opted for a Benelli M3 tactical shotgun loaded with flechette cartridges that Ruby had assured me would be enough to shred even a Kimprak in its armoured ball configuration. I also had my trusty LRS pistol on my belt, its magazine loaded with armour-piercing rounds.

Jodie was only armed for this mission with wide-eyed enthusiasm and a broad grin, like this was some sort of Enid Blyton adventure. Then again, I suppose that's always going to be the attitude of a scientist who doesn't get out of the lab much, and who probably also doesn't fully appreciate just how dangerous the situation really is. I had, of course, tried insisting that she stay aboard *Ariel* with Erin, but she'd crossed her arms and refused point-blank. So here we were, nursemaiding a scientist on what could be an extremely dangerous mission, just so she could hopefully bag a Kimprak that she could have some fun studying.

But the irony of that line of thought wasn't lost on me either. I'd once been a scientist too, albeit specialising in the area of radio astronomy. That old life had disappeared overnight when we'd captured the Sentinel broadcast back at Jodrell Bank, and events since had moulded me over the last five years into the battle-hardened soldier and commander that I was today. But then again, that was the sort of crazy curveball that life throws at you when you think you have everything all nicely worked out.

Ruby and I were both suited and booted for the mission with full combat gear on, including our helmets with their built-in

HUD system. In contrast, Jodie was just wearing body armour that we'd both insisted she had to wear if she was determined to accompany us on the mission. That little interaction also showed me just how far I'd come in Ruby's estimation because she would have wanted to put me in the same box once, but now she seemed to see me as a fellow soldier. More importantly, Ruby also knew she could rely on me in the thick of the action, which was an entirely mutual feeling.

We'd already checked on our WASP drones that, it turned out, had simply dropped out of the sky when the EMP pulse had happened. Unlike *Ariel,* and due to the issue of weight, they weren't battle-hardened. Jodie had declared them a write-off when she'd checked over the one that had nose-dived into an embankment. But in contrast, Slick was fighting fit and towered over us, his single blue-lit eye staring out into the darkness as he stood guard like some sort of robotic Goliath.

Ruby had already reloaded the hefty magazine for his mini-gun after it had been almost fully depleted after his help in exterminating the Kimprak around the impact crater.

'Okay, Slick, you stay right behind us,' she said turning to our Tin Head. 'I don't want you trampling over any tracks that the Kimprak left.

'Affirmative,' Slick replied with a suitably impressive deep male voice.

Ruby nodded and we set off, with her acting as our tracker, stopping every so often to study the foot scrapes on the ground.

'I thought the Kimprak could devour anything, Jodie, so why not just start burrowing into the ground?' I asked as we continued along the track between the trees and started to ascend the hill to the farmhouse.

'Substances like rock take far more processing and time on their part to create another replicant. Refined metals are a far more speedy way for them to multiply. That's probably a priority for our lone Kimprak right now.'

'I don't much fancy the chances of anyone who lives there,' Ruby said.

'Let's try not to be pessimistic here,' I said. 'Working on the basis they might have somehow survived, let's see what we can dig up about them. Delphi, who lives in the farmhouse?'

'A George Robinson, age forty-two, and his daughter, Ellie Robinson, seven-years-old,' Delphi replied through the speakers built into my combat helmet. 'George is a widower, his wife Helen Robinson died during childbirth. His tax return for the last year was—'

'Yes, we get the general idea, Delphi,' I replied shutting her off.

'Oh damn, there's a kid in there,' Ruby said shaking her head.

A brief image of a young girl being attacked by a Kimprak flooded my imagination in unnecessary, gruesome detail. But that's what comes from watching too many sci-fi horror movies.

'Erin, are you seeing anything on *Ariel's* sensors yet?' I asked into my helmet's mic.

'Nothing so far,' she replied over the comm. 'On the plus side, that means I haven't spotted any bodies outside it either.'

'Yet,' Jodie said and then grimaced. 'Sorry, just me thinking out loud.'

'Don't worry, we're all thinking it,' I said. 'So keep everything crossed that they're both still alive and let's do everything we can to keep it that way.'

Jodie and Ruby both nodded and we increased our pace. Slick followed a short distance behind us with the soft whir of his caterpillar tracks moving over the terrain.

At last, we crested the hill to see the farmhouse sitting just over a hundred metres away, a closed wooden and metal barn to one side. I pulled up a live video feed in my helmet's HUD from *Ariel*. Our ship was barely visible against the canopy of stars, apart from a slight disc-shaped distortion in the air over the farmhouse.

I couldn't see anything suspicious on the video feed, just hopefully a sleeping household who knew nothing other than having seen the meteorite fall at the foot of their hill. But as much as I would have loved that to be the case, the Kimprak's trail that was heading straight towards their home told another story.

'Okay, let's head in, Ruby, but leave Slick here with Jodie just in case everything is okay,' I said. 'Probably better not to show up on their doorstep with an eight-foot robot in tow.'

'Hey, I'm not staying here,' Jodie said.

'Yes, you bloody are,' I replied. 'This is potentially a serious combat situation and to be perfectly honest, you'll be more of a liability. Keeping you alive will distract us from a very dangerous enemy.'

Jodie squared up to me, her face hard, but the barest head-shake from Ruby seemed to defuse her. She sighed.

'Okay, okay, I understand, although I'm so not happy.'

'I can more than cope with your disappointment if that means you're alive,' I replied.

Jodie made a harrumphing sound but didn't quite manage to suppress a small smile.

'Okay, Ruby,' I said. 'Let's head in.'

She nodded and flicked off the safety on her MP7.

Keeping low, the two of us crept forward, following the trail towards a gravel-covered yard in front of the single-story farmhouse.

It was deathly silent as we neared. Then Ruby cursed softly under her breath.

'What is it?' I asked.

'There will be no tracking anything anywhere over that stuff.'

She gestured towards the gravel. 'Damn, what I wouldn't give to have some WASPs left.'

I nodded. 'Erin, how long until those reinforcements get here?'

'They're twelve minutes out,' she replied over the comm.

'Twelve minutes is too long,' I replied. 'Okay, we're going to have to do this the old fashioned way and do a sweep of the area. I'll try the house whilst you have a look in that barn.'

'Understood, Commander.' Ruby dipped her chin towards me before she crept off for a door on the side of the barn and I made my way to the front porch of the house.

I kept my Benelli shotgun ready for anything scuttling out of the shadows towards me. But despite my revving heart rate, I reached the porch without incident.

The screen door was closed and everything was dark beyond it. I was far too aware that if the occupants hadn't heard anything then an armed soldier turning up on their doorstep would likely scare the shit out of them. Dropping my shotgun's muzzle towards the floor, I took a breath and knocked on the doorframe.

'Hi, is anyone in?' I called out.

I strained my ears to hear a response. I was about to knock again, when I heard the faintest sound of a board creaking. Maybe it was all that time in the field, but my instinct kicked in and I threw myself sideways. A split second later twin shotgun blasts ripped through the screen door.

'Hold your bloody fire!' I shouted as I cocked the Benelli.

'Leave us alone,' a man's voice called back. 'I'm armed and I'll do whatever's necessary to defend my daughter.'

The guy sounded beyond scared, and apart from anything else, I needed to find out why.

'Are you okay, Lauren?' Ruby's voice asked over the comm.

'I'm fine. Just a bit of misunderstanding with the owner. Leave it to me.'

'Roger that,' she replied.

This time I took a bigger breath. 'George, isn't it?'

'How do you know my name?' he asked, his voice coming from somewhere deep inside the house.

'Because we're here to help you and your daughter, Ellie.'

'You're here for that thing?' he said, the panic in his tone ratcheting down a fraction.

'Thing?' I asked.

'A metallic cockroach that killed my daughter's dog and then scuttled off before I could stop it.

I heard the sound of a child trying to suppress a sob.

My mind raced to come up with a plausible excuse to explain it and us. 'Yes, it escaped from a lab. It's a new form of military combat robot that's gone rogue and we're Special Forces come to deal with it.'

'Don't believe you. Prove it.'

'Just lower your weapon and I'll show you,' I replied.

'I'm not lowering anything.'

The guy sounded beyond freaked out and no wonder, if he'd already had a run-in with the Kimprak. But I needed to gain his trust and quickly.

I'm held my Benelli at arm's length in front of what was left of the screen door and then placed it on the ground. 'Okay, I'm unarmed so please don't shoot.' I took a deep breath, raised my visor and stepped in front of the doorway again, my hands up this time.

The first thing I spotted was a guy with a beard pointing a double-barrelled shotgun at me.

'Well, we're off to a good start,' I said. 'At least you haven't shot me yet.'

'Oh, there's still plenty of time for that, especially if you're responsible for that dammed metallic critter that killed our dog, Meg.'

'No, we are in no way responsible, but like I said, I'm part of the Special Forces team sent to deal with it.'

A young girl with long blonde hair appeared next to the man and stared at me with saucer-shaped eyes.

George immediately dropped to her level, placing his shotgun on the floor and taking her by the shoulders. 'I told you to stay in the back room, Ellie.'

'I heard you talking, Dad. Who's this lady?'

He cast me a narrow-eyed look, before returning his attention to her. 'A friend who's come to help us get rid of that silver bug who killed Meg.'

Tears filled Ellie's eyes and George hugged her to him.

My heart squeezed at the sudden transformation from the tough Aussie farmer, to simply a man trying to protect his daughter.

'Ellie, my name's Lauren,' I said squatting before her so I could look her in the eye. 'Don't worry, we're going to squish that bug flat for you.'

She gave me a searching look over her dad's shoulder and then nodded.

'George, where exactly did this robot bug kill your dog?' I asked.

Before he could answer, there was a staccato burst of submachine gun fire coming from the barn.

'Don't worry, I think that just answered my question,' I said.

George grabbed his shotgun. 'Let's go and finish off that bloody metal thing that's taken residence in my shed.'

But I was already shaking my head. 'No, you take Ellie to the back and stay there until this is over. Leave the extermination to us.'

He nodded as I stood. I grabbed my Benelli and started sprinting towards the barn just as another burst of submachine gun fire echoed from inside it.

'Ruby, talk to me, are you okay in there?'

'Just about holding my own, but barely, Commander.'

'I'll be with you in ten seconds,' I said.

I reached the side door that had been left open and rushed inside. But as I took in what was going on, I skidded to a stop.

A pickup truck and the tractor next to it had been half eaten away by hundreds of Kimprak. Dozens of them were surging towards Ruby who was doing her best to pick them off with her MP7.

I immediately started firing my Benelli into their flank, the flechettes slicing them apart a dozen at a time. But then a whole load more of them leapt from the vehicles and came scurrying towards me.

'Get Slick in here!' I said over the comm.

'He's already on his way,' Ruby said as she ejected a spent magazine and clipped in a fresh one.

With an explosion of wood, our Tin Head didn't bother with the door and instead charged straight through the wall, his mini-gun barrels already spinning. With a barking roar of fire, he poured bullets from his XM556 into the hoards as they leapt forward to attack the new combatant. The barn was quickly filling with the smell of cordite, the walls peppered with holes as the three of us blazed away with everything we had.

Within moments, destroyed Kimprak were littering the floor. But as fast as they fell, they were being consumed by their comrades who, in a matter of seconds, were depositing more ball-bearing-eggs that were already unfurling into fresh bots.

'Shit, this isn't going to hold them off for long,' I said over the comm. 'We need to fall back.'

'Form up behind Slick so he can give us some cover as we get the hell out of Dodge,' Ruby replied.

With another blast of the Benelli, I cleared a path and rushed to her as Slick stepped in front of us, his mini-gun blazing as he took out wave after wave of the Kimprak.

'Stick with us, Slick,' Ruby called out.

'Affirmative,' the Tin Head replied.

As a group, we started back towards the hole that Slick had created in his crashing entrance into the barn. As we all continued to lay down a wall of fire as we backed out of the hole, I spotted something growing in the seething mass of Kimprak that had been devouring the tractor. But then we lost sight of it as we cleared the exit.

My brain was already whirring as to how we could contain this situation that was quickly sliding south. 'Erin, get Delphi to use *Ariel's* mini-gun fire to destroy anything that so much as shows its face out of that barn.'

'On it, Lauren.'

As we backed away from the barn, still pouring rounds into it, we spotted a gleaming mass of silver bots rolling towards the door like a metal sea. They scuttled out through the hole in the wall and raced towards us. But then the ground erupted around them as a withering stream of armour-piercing rounds fired straight down from our stealthed ship, ripping into the wave of death scuttling towards us. The hailstorm of rounds vaporised them instantly into metal shards and halting the tide that had been surging towards us.

My relief was short-lived, as we spotted a larger robot-version of the Kimprak, its limbs made from hundreds of the smaller robots that had linked together. A deep resonating roar, raw and brutal, intended to instil absolute fear in its prey instantly made my heart beat faster.

The Kimprak that had started to fall back, began to surge forward again.

'Shit, that has to be some sort of command unit and I'm

guessing that's the Kimprak equivalent of a rallying battle cry,' Ruby said as she slid a fresh magazine into her MP7.

'Then we need to concentrate all our fire on it and drive it back. I want it contained in the barn for a moment longer,' I shouted as I aimed the Benelli at the thing and blasted one of its multiple legs away that was quickly replaced by the smaller Kimprak that rushed to reform it with their bodies.

'Any suggestions, before we have our arses handed to us, Commander?' Ruby asked as she blazed a fresh round of bullets at our nightmare attackers.

'I have, actually. Erin, fire every single AIM missile you have onboard *Ariel* into that barn.'

'But you're too close, you'll be caught in the blast wave.'

'Don't worry about us, we're about to fall back. Ruby, time to get busy with that grenade launcher of yours and lay down suppressing fire as we make a hasty retreat back to the farmhouse.'

'Oh, it will be an absolute pleasure,' she replied.

Ruby unslung the M32 just as Slick's mini-gun spun to silence as he finally ran out of ammo. She aimed the grenade launcher towards the door, and with a series of popping sounds, fired three shots at what I was already thinking of as the robot queen.

As the grenades thudded into her, they exploded with bright flashes, ripping her apart.

'Retreat!' I shouted to Ruby.

We both turned and sprinted back towards the farmhouse. We reached the porch together, throwing ourselves through the door onto the floor inside.

'Fire those AIM missiles now, Erin!' I shouted into my helmet's mic.

'Roger that,' she replied.

I glanced over my shoulder to see a rippling fire of AIM

missiles seem to appear out of mid-air as they burst from *Ariel's* invisible weapon ports and raced towards the barn. A split second later, a series of explosions roared through the building and it disappeared in a massive fireball, totally engulfing the Kimprak swarm. As the shock wave slammed into the house I pressed my head into the floor, hearing the sound of splintering wood and shattering glass all around us. Then the roar of the explosion was blotted out as my ears were numbed to silence.

Bile tanged at the back of my mouth as the world finally stopped shaking. Then, gradually, sound began to return to my numbed ears. The roar of flames was coming from where the barn had been standing only a few moments before, but was now nothing more than a splintered, burning wreck of wood and twisted corrugated roof panels.

Ruby and I slowly got back to our feet as we both looked out at the mess. Kimprak limbs and abdomen sections were scattered everywhere across the yard, but crucially nothing was left moving.

A gasp came from behind us as George stepped past, staring out at the devastation that had just been rained down onto his quiet life. Then I became aware of a child sobbing and looked round to see that Ruby had scooped Ellie to her as they both looked out at the devastation.

Then, maybe for the first time in this war, it really struck me what exactly we were fighting for here—the ordinary lives of people like George and Ellie who would be affected if the Kimprak made it past our fleet. And it was then that I vowed that would never happen, even if it ultimately cost me my life.

CHAPTER SIX

My HEAD still ached from the explosion as I dosed up on paracetamol from the medical locker onboard *Ariel* as we continued our journey onwards to Antarctica.

We'd handed over dealing with the aftermath of the encounter with the Kimprak, to the reinforcements that had turned up literally a minute after we'd wiped out the bots with the final intense missile bombardment.

'Those poor people,' Jodie said shaking her head across at us from her flight seat.

'Yeah, I know, but the important thing is that they're alive,' Ruby replied.

'Absolutely, and barns can be rebuilt,' I said. 'I've already been on the line to Alice and she's confirmed that she'll make sure they're fully compensated for what happened. Of course, money is just part of the equation, and she's already arranged for some of Eden's trauma medical therapists to go and give the family whatever emotional support they need to get through this.'

'I feel most sorry for the daughter,' Erin said. 'That was the sort of nightmare that could scar you for the rest of your life.'

But Ruby was shaking her head. 'Actually, I think Ellie's a tough kid and will make it through fine. She sort of reminds me of myself at that age, and the main thing for her is that the good guys, AKA us, turned up and got rid of the scary monsters that killed her dog. Trust me, that will count for a lot.'

'But what about the dad? Will he keep quiet?' Erin asked.

'Let's just say Alice put a couple of extra zeros on that compensation cheque,' I said. 'Mind you, having spoken to him, he's not keen to talk to anyone because he realises just how crazy it will sound.'

'And what about that local policeman who wasn't so lucky?'

'His next of kin can't know the truth, so it will be made to look like a bad traffic accident where next to nothing was left of his body. Then, unexpectedly, his relatives will discover that he had a massive life insurance policy, so that will at least help in a practical way. We might not have been able to stop him from losing his life, but we can at least make the future better for his family.'

'I'm not sure I'm entirely happy with all this subterfuge,' Jodie said. 'Surely his family deserves to know what really happened to him?'

'And I hope they do one day when we've managed to defeat the Kimprak once and for all. But to avoid the inevitable mass panic that would naturally spread if word got out, we all have to continue to keep a lid on all of this for now.'

Jodie sighed. 'We all know that far too well.' She glanced at her monitor that had a live view of our hold where Slick had once more taken up residence. But of more significance, was the metal EMP crate held suspended in a pair of pincers directly over the cargo bay doors.

Erin followed her gaze and shook her head. 'I still can't believe you risked bringing one of those things aboard.'

'Honestly, there's nothing to worry about,' Jodie replied. 'Not only was the Kimprak bot inside that box totally deactivated by that missile strike, even if it did somehow manage to reboot itself, that EMP field inside that crate will keep it inert. And like I said before, any sign that something's gone wrong and we'll drop it like a hot potato out of the hold and you and Ruby can take care of it with our mini-guns.'

'Oh, you can count on it,' Ruby said.

'So, what about that command unit we encountered at the end of the fight, any thoughts on that?' I asked.

'It's certainly an interesting development, especially since, up until now, we thought Kimprak used a hive consciousness. But that unit suggests they can create higher intelligences when they need to.'

'Yes, it certainly acted like the equivalent of an officer ordering its soldiers around,' Ruby said.

Jodie nodded. 'Which is very intriguing in itself and I'm hoping that's something we could use to our advantage in future battles.'

'How so?' I asked.

'Not sure yet, and I need to talk this through with Lucy, but I have a few ideas bubbling.'

'Well, you won't have long to wait,' Erin said. 'ETA for the Antarctica site is just five minutes.'

As intense as the battle had been, a fresh sense of foreboding took its place in my gut. I wouldn't have much longer to wait to find out what was really going on with Jack.

Below us, Antarctica's snowy plain stretched away with not a thing out of the ordinary to be seen anywhere—just as intended. The reality was, thanks to Photonic Mass Projector that *Tempest* utilised, the starship was hidden by a holographic shield that was currently programmed to look exactly like the surrounding snowy tundra.

Ariel descended towards the snow-covered surface following a pre-programmed flight path that had been loaded into our navigational computer. A series of blue, wireframed rectangles expanded below us on the cockpit floor as Erin took us in to land.

As the ground grew ever closer, it still didn't betray the illusion. My brain screamed at me that we were going to crash into the surface. Then, like always, my stomach rose in anticipation of what was about to happen, where instinct overrode experience. But then, just like always, a round section of snow shimmered and vanished directly beneath us. Revealed in the snowy surface was a large round tunnel made from krine, the Angelus super material that had tensile strength twenty times greater than any metal or alloy.

Erin dropped *Ariel* down into the shaft manually, even though the starship's docking system could have easily taken over. She'd frequently told me she preferred to perform the landing manually because, as she liked to say, *practise makes perfect.*

She began to slow our ship as the tunnel opened out beneath us into a vast three-klick-wide hangar. The huge room was brightly lit thanks to glowing krine panels in the ceiling. Stretching away to either side of us, sitting on launch pads, were at least two hundred X103s just like *Ariel* and also X104s, the heavily armoured Pangolin variants of our burgeoning Earth and Sol fleets.

'They haven't wasted any time building those things,' Ruby said gesturing towards at least ten Thunder and Lightning torpedoes that were being transferred from a rack by a group of Tin Heads and were being loaded onto a Pangolin.

'Looks like Mike and Lucy have already been busy with the molecular printers,' Jodie said. 'That's ridiculously impressive. I only sent them the blueprints right before we left Eden.'

'If they crank them out at that rate, there's no reason why every X-craft can't be fitted with them,' I replied.

Jodie nodded. 'We can easily squeeze four into an X103 and at least eight into a Pangolin. If we build more, they can be flown as a fleet autonomously by a weapon's officer.'

'Oh, just let me at them,' Ruby said.

'Patience,' I replied smiling.

Erin manoeuvred us sideways and *Ariel* began sliding over the others ships, many of which had engineers swarming over them, towards *Ariel's* designated landing pad and where a landing cross pattern of green lights were now pulsing inwards. As we began to descend, I spotted the door open in one of Eden's transport pods that had just landed, and Lucy and Mike step out onto the deck. There was no sign of Jack and the ominous feeling that I'd been carrying inside only grew more intense.

It had only been a week since we'd last seen each other, but even being apart for that short amount of time felt like too long. And unless I was totally deluding myself, I was certain Jack felt the same way, so him not being there to meet and greet me was a very big deal indeed.

Then I spotted the phalanx of armed Tin Heads surrounding the landing pad, with the same number again of security guards.

'It looks like Niki got the memo about your little science project and contacted *Tempest* ahead of our arrival, Jodie,' I said.

'And as I keep telling everyone, that's totally unnecessary because the Kimprak can't do anything whilst it's inside that box,' Jodie replied.

'Better safe than sorry,' Erin said as she brought *Ariel* into a perfect, gentle landing. A short while later the hatch was open and I was descending it with Jodie, Erin, and Ruby.

Mike already had his arms stretched out towards Jodie. She headed up to him and wrapped her guy up in a tight hug. That only served to underline Jack's absence more starkly. Even Lucy's enthusiastic hug did little to help.

Lucy pulled away from me and gazed into my eyes. Then her expression pinched. 'Are you okay, Lauren?'

I quickly nodded. The last thing I wanted to do was air what could be little more than paranoia on my part.

'Yes, all good, just a bit wiped out,' I said.

'I'm not surprised. It sounds like you had quite the adventure on your way back.'

'You can say that again,' Jodie said. 'But Lauren, Ruby, and Erin had the situation totally under control.'

I raised my eyebrows at her. 'I'm not so sure about *totally,* but we managed to do what needed to be done. Anyway, we need to brief you all about a new sort of Kimprak that we encountered.'

Jodie nodded enthusiastically as she took Mike's hand in hers and steered him towards *Ariel's* hold. 'It was some sort of command unit that seemed to be operating at a higher level of intelligence.'

'Now, that sounds interesting,' Mike said. 'Did you manage to get any specific data about it?'

'Not directly,' I replied. 'Although, there's our helmet cam footage you can study.'

'Maybe we can learn something about it from the Kimprak you were able to retrieve,' Lucy said. 'Speaking of which, where is it?'

Jodie beamed at her and raised her smartwatch to her mouth. 'Delphi, please lower the Kimprak specimen from the hold.

The hold doors opened beneath *Ariel* and a moment later the silver box with its constellation of blue lights was lowered by a robotic arm.

Jodie grinned at Lucy. 'Don't say I never bring you any presents.'

The security guards and the Tin Heads already had their weapons trained on it.

'A bit of overreaction guys,' Jodie said shaking her head.

'Maybe, but just to be on the safe side, we'll transfer it to a secure lab where you can analyse it to your heart's content,' Lucy replied.

Jodie nodded. 'Sounds great. This should help our research significantly. There may even be some traces of code left that we can analyse for the command unit.'

Lucy gave the silver box a thoughtful look. 'Hopefully, we can analyse it to see if there's any way we can hack into the base code.'

'You mean, as in be able to control them?' I asked.

'We won't know until we try, but possibly eventually, yes,' Lucy replied.

Despite the sense of worry hanging over me about Jack, that lifted my mood a fraction. 'Well, if you can find the kill switch for those bloody things, then I'm all in for it.'

'Let's see what we can do,' Lucy replied.

My gaze alighted on one of the transport pods that had been parked next to the landing pad. 'First things first. Have you seen Jack anywhere, Lucy?'

'According to his tracking data, he's in the E8 hall where he's been for most of this week. I can take you to him, if you like?'

'That would be great, thank you.'

'Then follow me.'

A short while later, I was sitting in the transport pod with Lucy as it took off and was moving away quickly towards a small tunnel in the far end of the enormous hangar.

Beneath us, several of the torpedoes were carefully being loaded onto another Pangolin and a group of Tin Heads. In an attempt to distract myself from the churn of my thoughts, I gestured towards the torpedoes.

'Those E8 molecular printers are obviously already proving their value.'

'Like you wouldn't believe,' Lucy replied. 'We also have a second printer that is almost ready to go online and we're going to start producing more of the Wolfpack battle drones as well.'

'You sound like you've made significant progress in the week that I've been away,' I said.

'Like you wouldn't believe,' Lucy said as we reached the tunnel and entered it. 'You're about to see another example of what we've been up to in the main habitation zone. One of the avatars introduced a member of the science team who's a keen paraglider, to the nanobots environment modelling computer and well...you'll see the result of that for yourself in a moment.' She gestured towards the exit of the tunnel that we were now heading towards.

Grateful for the distraction, I craned my neck as we exited into the wide-open cavern. I could see the familiar sight of the Angelus city's crystal towers rising in the distance over a park-land that included forests and lakes in the foreground. But it was what was at the opposite end of the chamber that we were travelling over that actually made me gasp.

Where what had been a series of sweeping fields that led up to the curving walls when I'd left just a week ago, was now a range of rolling green mountains. Above them, several paragliders with brightly coloured canopies were turning in lazy circles in the air.

I turned to stare at Lucy. 'They modelled a mountain range just so they could paraglide over them? Seriously?'

'Yes, and why not? And as you can see it's really taken off as a recreational activity, pun intended, and the guy who dreamed this all up is now teaching people how to do it. It's become quite the pastime for people to knock back with when they're not working.'

'As long as no one breaks their necks trying it out.'

'Absolutely no danger of that, my little sunflower. The automated systems in *Tempest* constantly monitor every aspect of the ship, including gravity settings. If someone were to lose control, even for a moment, they would be surrounded by an anti-grav bubble and lowered gently to the ground before they'd even realised they had a problem.'

I nodded. 'Do these landscape modelling nanobots mean that we can change any aspect of this environment we like?'

'Yes, absolutely. Mike's already thinking it would be great to have an artificial sea, complete with waves, in one of the other unused habitation zones.'

'So he could go surfing, in other words?'

Lucy grinned at me. 'Hey, everyone has to have their hobbies.'

That actually managed to get a chuckle out of me, which was something of a miracle considering my current mood.

'Oh, one other piece of great news. Don Horton is finally out of the infirmary and is desperate to talk to you about doing his part. He thinks the fact that we saved his life will go a long way to convincing key senior USSF officers that we're not the threat they think we are.'

'That sounds good, but I think I'll leave it until tomorrow to discuss it with him. Today has been quite the day, and all I have energy for right now is Jack.'

'Of course,' Lucy replied, her expression growing serious again.

I turned away to gaze out at the view, trying to ignore the growing ball of anxiety in my stomach as we travelled through the rest of the chamber in silence.

As we reached the city itself and began to travel between the krine towers, I spotted a group of our crew walking along one of the raised boulevards towards one of the towers that we were now using for accommodation. Then we were past them and had entered the tunnel that led to the next chamber.

As lights strobed slowly past us, I was as tense as I'd ever been on any mission. What flavour of bad news exactly was I heading into?

A moment later we'd emerged into the E8 chamber that was as breathtakingly spectacular as always. A giant shimmering ball of energy hung in the air, its surface occasionally rippling as giant electrodes arranged around it crackled with plasma that was arcing from it into them. The sheer scale of the glowing sphere was brought home by the size of the tiny, human-scale walkways that encircled it.

This energy sphere was actually a pocket of the higher reality E8 contained within our starship. The incredible energy available within it was drawn off with a range of vast electrodes and conduits that encircled the E8 sphere. These powered all of *Tempest's* systems with the exception of the fusion engines, which were currently being built and ran independently in case there was any hiccup in the E8 power supply.

We swept towards the energy sphere, and as our transport pod passed through its outer membrane that separated our reality from the higher one of E8 within, I felt the usual tickling sensation over my skin as the air grew briefly viscous. The view of the surrounding chamber began to dance with refraction patterns as though we'd just dived beneath the surface of the sea. Then the world grew rapidly darker around us, and suddenly we were through it into the star-filled endless space within the sphere of the higher reality.

Hanging in the void, a point of light in the distance started to grow larger and as we drew nearer it gradually resolved as a platform lit with bright lights. A moment later, our transport pod was slowing to a stop at a doorway leading off the platform.

Lucy started to stand, but I gently took hold of her arm and shook my head. 'Do you mind leaving me to it with Jack?'

Her eyes widened. 'Of course, you two need to *catch* up.' Then she grinned at me.

'Well, you know what they say, absence makes the heart grow fonder.'

'Apparently so. Well, don't let me cramp your style. You go and be with your gorgeous man.'

I managed a smile despite my growing anxiety as I turned towards the door and headed for whatever was waiting for me with Jack.

CHAPTER SEVEN

I STEPPED into the E8 circular hall with its tessellated ceiling that contained the tetrahedron micro minds set into it like glowing gemstones. Each of these large crystals contained the consciousness of Lucy and the other avatars that had been designed to run the starship and also gave it a sense of self-awareness.

Despite the dreadful sense of anticipation swirling around inside me, my heart lifted at seeing Jack standing at a lab bench filled with laptops, notebooks, half-eaten sandwiches, and cold mugs of coffee. But as I took in his appearance my worry notched up again. He looked far more tired than he had on the video call, like he was carrying the weight of the world on his shoulders.

A single avatar was standing with his eyes closed in one of the alcoves in the curved walls. I recognised him immediately as Poseidon. He was the micro mind consciousness that we had first met at the Richat Structure that had turned out to be the site for the real Atlantis. It was where Poseidon, as his name suggested, had been worshipped like a god. It had turned out, that he had a real thirst for ancient human history, a passion that almost matched Jack's own. So it was little surprise to anyone that Poseidon had become Jack's right-hand guy when it came to researching the history of the Angelus starship.

Of course, that wouldn't have been necessary at all if it hadn't been for the Overseers destroying one of the micro minds that had contained a lot of the critical information about the starship, and along with it, the history of the Angelus. All the avatars had once shared that knowledge, but now there was a huge gap in their collective memory. Thankfully, we'd quickly discovered that there was plenty of material onboard *Tempest* to learn from and unpick the clues.

I stepped towards Jack, my heart already racing in anticipation of whatever had driven him into his current state.

At hearing my footsteps he turned, and the lines that had been crinkling his forehead a moment ago smoothed out.

'Lauren, you are seriously a sight for sore eyes,' he said. As I reached him, he took hold of me and gently kissed me.

'You too,' I said as I held onto him. It took a considerable effort of will to let go of him again.

'So what's wrong, Jack?'

His gaze immediately tightened on me. 'Did Poseidon blab to Lucy, despite promising me that he wouldn't?'

'You've lost me. Lucy didn't say a thing.'

Jack's eyes narrowed. 'Right... Okay, that's good, because the fewer people who know about this the better.'

Immediately my worry spun up to maximum. 'So my instinct was right, something is wrong, then?'

Jack reached out and held my shoulders in his hands. 'On the surface, it certainly looks that way, but please know, I was going to tell you about this anyway. This secret is too big for me to just hang onto without it eating me up. Also, apart from everything else, I need your help to figure out just how seriously we need to take it. However, before we get to that, I better start at the beginning and how it started with the discovery in one of the sealed labs.'

'I didn't know there were any sealed labs.'

'It was a surprise to Poseidon too when we stumbled upon it, and it took him a lot of work to hack the protocols that had been used to keep it locked,' Jack said. 'But when we finally gained entry, we found a lot of esoteric equipment, including incredibly accurate strontium clocks and numerous historical archives from all the sites where micro minds had been placed. There's several lifetimes worth of material for me to research in there. Anyway, it was in that lab that I discovered what I need to show you...' Jack rummaged in a bag and withdrew a crystal orb. I recognised it as an Empyrean Key as he handed it to me.

The air caught in my throat as I took in just how beautiful the object was. In many ways it was like my stone Empyrean Key, that was, apart from the obvious difference. It was made from a pale turquoise crystal like I'd once seen in a blue ice cave in Iceland during a winter holiday. This carved orb also appeared to be lit from within by a white bead of light that was refracted through the fissures in the orb to illuminate them like frozen bursts of lightning.

'It's beautiful,' I said with a sense of awe as I turned it over in my hand.

'It is,' Jack replied. 'And it turns out, this particular Empyrean Key belonged to one of the Angelus scientists who lived their lives out aboard this very ship, some guy called Tuul.'

'And who was he, then?'

'In a nutshell, he was a rogue scientist that, despite being warned not to, was actively researching time travel.'

I stared at him. 'You have to be kidding me.'

'Not at all, and he was deadly serious about it too, according to the records in his lab that Poseidon was able to recover,' Jack said. 'Tuul persisted in his research despite being warned off, but when it spilled over into using this very E8 hall, the high council ordered his lab to be shut down and all his research materials to be confiscated.'

'So what happened to this Tuul guy?' I asked.

'That's the mystery of it,' Jack replied. 'According to the records in his lab, the guy simply vanished with one of the ship's science research avatars before he could be seized. Although, you can imagine the rumours that swirled around, that he used his own research to escape back into the past. According to Poseidon, the less sensual and much more accepted version is, that unable to face the humiliation, Tuul managed to shut down all the security monitoring systems thanks to a computer virus he let loose to cover his tracks. It was also that same computer virus that wiped out nearly all records of his work. Then Tuul left the ship in an escape pod to live out his days uninterrupted, presumably somewhere on Earth, to pursue his research. Wherever he went, despite many searches, he was apparently never heard of again.'

'So, you're seriously suggesting that this guy may have discovered a way to time travel?' I asked.

Jack scraped his hand through his unruly mop of blond hair that looked like it hadn't been washed in a week. Certainly going by the faint odour of stale sweat emanating off him, he'd been a stranger to showers for at least a couple of days, which was out of character for him.

'I'm not exactly sure what he discovered, so it's probably better if I just show you.'

My heart beat a little faster as he headed over to one of the closed doors in the E8 hall that we'd never been able to enter despite all our efforts. As Jack neared it he raised his hand and the door shimmered as a bowl-shaped recess materialised in the middle of the door.

'You're saying this is a like that key for that temple door back in Peru?' I asked.

'Pretty much, although what's on the other side of this door is wildly different to any ancient chamber.'

He raised the crystal Empyrean Key and placed it into the recess in the door which simply dissolved into thin air. As it did so, the crystal orb remained hanging there until he took hold of it with his hand and removed it again.

A short gantry led out into the middle of a spherical room beyond the doorway, and at the end of it was some sort of control column on which was what looked like a trackball control. There was also another recess next to that which looked precisely the right size to fit the Empyrean Key that Jack had in his hand.

But what immediately drew my attention lay beyond all of that. A large globe made from triangular screens sat in the middle of the room encircled by a walkway. Only one of the screens was currently lit up. It took my mind a moment to realise it was playing a video of a scene that I actually recognised. It was the temple at Atlantis that Jack and I had both witnessed for ourselves when Poseidon had transported us there in the sim that he had created of the ancient city over in E8.

Jack turned to me. 'Welcome to the Hall of Dreams.'

'The what?' I asked.

'Poseidon told me it's basically something straight out of myth and legend, even for Angelus AIs. Very few of these rooms ever existed and where they did, they remained completely hidden to all but a chosen few Angelus, and certainly no avatars were ever allowed to enter them. But as you can see for yourself, it's this Hall of Dreams that's allowing us to witness one of Poseidon's memories from Atlantis. I've discovered the same is true when any of the avatars are docked next door. I've literally been able to see their dreams as a three-dimensional hologram in the centre of the room. What's amazing is that I also quickly discovered that most of the avatars seem to recall moments from their lives where they were hidden in human settlements.'

'Hang on. You're saying that AIs actually dream?' I said.

'Apparently, yes. Poseidon informed me that Angelus AI's can enter a dream state where they can do the equivalent of defragging their micro minds, much like our biological brains flush out the toxins during a sleep cycle.'

I gestured towards the image of Atlantis playing on the sphere. 'So, reliving previous events from human history would fit into that?'

'Yes, and a whole wealth of memories are available to any of the micro minds and their dreams are often shared, which is something I've actually witnessed in here where multiple screens have lit up with the same memory. As you can probably imagine, it's an incredibly exciting discovery for me as an archaeologist. With this, we can have a direct glimpse of key moments during human history. But what I wasn't expecting was that they could also dream about the future.' His face grew drawn again.

'Sorry, what did you just say?' I asked.

'AI dreaming was an area of intense research for Angelus scientists who were studying what was known as the Procession Plan.'

'And what's that when it's at home?' I asked.

'Literally the study of the future apparently. It was the science that formed many of their strategies for protecting life across the cosmos. They used AIs as a way of gazing into the simulated future, not a certainty as such, because there were never any absolutes as it was just a sim. More of a likely outcome based on statistical and behavioural modelling, but apparently it was never an exact science.'

'Hang on, has any of this to do with whatever has upset you, Jack?' I asked as I lightly touched his arm.

'It has everything to do with it, but it's probably better if you just see it rather than listen to any more explanations. Follow me.'

With a growing sense of foreboding, I followed Jack into the room. I didn't need to be a psychologist to realise that whatever he'd seen had left him traumatised.

CHAPTER EIGHT

With a shimmer of light, the door rematerialised behind us, shutting out the view of the E8 hall as we stepped into the spherical room. Grim-faced, Jack headed out onto the walkway towards the pillar, and just as I guessed he would, placed his crystal Empyrean Key into the recess on top of it.

At once, each of what had been blank triangular screens on the sphere, filled with fragments of Atlantis that formed a larger view that used all the screens. But there was one key difference. Rather than a single triangular view, this image was spherical and one that I quickly realised I could walk around and examine from any angle. But as I did exactly that, the view on the other side shifted as though I was looking out at the actual Atlantis. It was as though the sphere was acting like some sort of magical portal that gave me a full three-sixty view of the surroundings.

'Bloody hell, Jack, if that's a dream it's the most three-dimensional one that I've ever seen,' I said.

'I promise you, it's far more than that.' He placed his hand on the orb and spun it forward like a trackball. As he did so, the view suddenly shifted towards the harbour.'

'Whoa, you can actually decide which part of the city you want to see?' I asked.

Jack nodded. 'I can literally go anywhere I want. Like I said, this really is an archaeologist's dream. And before you ask, yes, I can pull up the dreams of any of the avatars when they're docked into their alcoves next door. I hope she doesn't mind, but I actually used Lucy's memories when she was docked next door to explore Skara Brae and it was beyond my wildest dreams.'

'That sounds like an invasion of privacy. You probably should've asked her first. But that aside, why all the secrecy, Jack? I would have expected you to be shouting this from the rooftops.'

'Because I discovered that if you get at least seven of the avatars docked next door, it's not just the past you can look into.'

'You're talking about the Procession Plan being able to predict probable outcomes, aren't you?'

'Exactly. According to Poseidon, the Procession Plan apparently uses the combined consciousness of a number of micro minds in a form of AI lucid dreaming. Even the Angelus had little understanding about how it worked, but they used it to plan how best to protect emerging intelligent species that it showed might be in danger. Then they went around the galaxy putting things in place to avoid the usual mass extinction events that normally plague young civilisations.'

I nodded. 'That sounds like what we call the Great Filters, which is the theory that something usually leads to the destruction of civilisations before they can master intergalactic travel.'

'That's pretty much what Poseidon told me as well,' Jack said. 'And that's what led to the Angelus leaving us *Tempest* so that one day we could use it to defend ourselves against a threat like the Kimprak.'

I tilted my head to gaze at Jack. 'It almost sounds like was the equivalent of seers gazing into their scientific crystal balls in order to see the future. But seriously, how could you ever cover every eventuality to create a *happy ever after* scenario for every sentient species across the universe?'

'Basically, you can't,' Jack replied. 'Poseidon said it's like trying to juggle billions of balls and keep them all in the air at the same time. What happened at Alpha Centauri is evidence of exactly some sort of failure in the Procession Plan when the Kimprak were able to strip mine that system killing off all life there. I guess it's a case of having to decide which species are priorities. Luckily for us, the Angelus felt that Earth, and specifically the human race, was one where extra effort and energy was deemed worthwhile. But the most sobering thing that I learnt from Poseidon about all of this, is that the Procession Plan comes down to a numbers game, trying to make certain outcomes become a reality even though not all do. Having said that, the Angelus did everything they could to stack things in our favour.'

A chilling thought struck me. 'Is that it, Jack, have you seen that despite everything the Angelus did and everything that we're doing now, that we're still about to lose to the Kimprak?'

He held up his hands. 'No, I don't know the outcome of the coming battle with the Kimprak mothership. But there is a key moment from that battle that I did see, and that I need to share with you. Then we can decide together what to do with the information.'

'So, what is it, Jack?' I asked in a quiet voice, already deeply apprehensive about where this conversation was headed.

'I best start with explaining of how I stumbled across this particular vision, prediction, or whatever you want to call it. I'd been working non-stop in here, analysing the past experiences of the avatars through their dreams when I actually fell asleep myself. Not really surprising, when I'd worked for fifty-six hours straight without a break.'

'Jack!'

He held up his hands. 'I know, I know. I just got a bit carried away. But it was then that I had the most vivid of dreams, one that seemed so real it was like I was actually there. Also, crucially, it was one that, just like the avatar's dreams next door, the system was able to record. And that's why I brought you here, Lauren, because you specifically need to see this.'

The churning feeling in my stomach was back in full force. 'It's really bad, isn't it?'

'I'm afraid there's no way to soften this. Yes, it is,' Jack replied, his voice gentle.

I held his gaze. I needed to know. 'Okay, we better get this over with. Time to show me what you saw.'

Jack nodded and selected the trackball type control next to the Empyrean Key. As he rotated it, a series of images spun past on the sphere before us. I glimpsed Skara Brae no longer a ruin, but a thriving community filled with people, which I thought had to be one of Lucy's dreams. I even caught a brief view of a large gold-tipped pyramid covered in smooth white limestone before it was replaced by the next image. Then I gasped because there I was, Lauren Stelleck, onboard what could only be the flight deck of *Ariel*. Ruby, Erin, and Jack were there too.

As I walked around the sphere to get a better look at what was going on, I saw a view of what had to be the Kimprak asteroid mothership on *Ariel's* virtual cockpit. Countless glittering points of light that could only be individual Kimprak bots surrounded it like a dense field of stars. The wreckage of ships, both X-craft and TR-3Bs were floating everywhere.

In the distance behind us, loomed the vast bulk of *Tempest*, thousands of streams of laser fire shooting out from it and scything through another swarm of the Kimprak that were streaming from the constellation. But the asteroid mothership had been attacked by something huge and a vast hole had been blasted out of the side of it...a hole that *Ariel* was plummeting towards, as strange glittering tracer fire rose from the Kimprak ship.

On the virtual cockpit, there was also a view of *Ariel's* hold in which there appeared to be four warheads with some sort of countdown that had just ticked down past two minutes. This had all the hallmarks of one of my famous seat-of-the-pants plans and looking at the evidence, I would guess that we'd turned *Ariel* into some sort of flying bomb.

Jack stared at the scene before me, casting an occasional glance in my direction, obviously checking to see what my reaction to all this was.

From the other Lauren's tense expression on that flight deck, it was obvious that whatever was happening was very bad.

Ruby was blazing mini-gun rounds into the Kimprak swarm who were attempting to block our path to their mothership.

Then I spotted a massive rock hurtling up from the mothership straight towards *Ariel*. Flanked on all sides by tracer fire, Erin had no way to avoid the projectile. With a sickening impact that threw everyone in the cockpit around violently, the rock barrelled into *Ariel's* side, sending her spinning. The blaring of alarms wailed. Smoke billowed and rapidly filled the cockpit as respirators fell from the ceiling that everyone quickly strapped on.

'Hull breach, eject now, structural integrity has been critically compromised,' Delphi announced.

The other version of me had an even wilder look on her face. One that I recognised. One that meant she was about to do something really stupid.

'Okay, Erin, let Delphi take over flying, we need to abandon ship' the other Lauren called out.

'She's going to have a hard time doing that because the stabilisers are shot to hell,' Erin replied. 'I need to manually fly her in if we have a chance of doing this.'

Lauren unbuckled her harness and approached her. 'No, we're abandoning ship and that's an order. Everyone to the escape capsule now. Delphi, take over flight control towards the navigation marker.'

'I have control,' Delphi replied.

Then the future version of me was herding the crew as they all staggered across the tilting flight deck as the stabilising gyros began to fail.

This other Lauren was just behind Jack when she dropped back slightly for a moment. As soon as everyone had entered the escape pod she smashed her hand down on the button and the door slammed closed behind them. Jack whirled round to stare at her through the porthole.

'Don't do this!' his muffled voice shouted as Lauren turned away, her face pale.

A moment later, I watched on the virtual cockpit as the pod shot away from *Ariel*.

I knew exactly what the other Lauren was going to do before she did it because she was me and it was exactly what I would have done in that situation. First, I would make sure that everyone I loved was safe. Second, I would finish the job by myself.

And that was exactly what played out as I watched the other Lauren drag herself across the now violently tilting flight deck and strap herself into Erin's flight seat. Then the other me began to turn *Ariel* back towards the gaping hole and pushed the throttle to the max.

The countdown on the virtual cockpit had reached the last ten seconds as the stricken ship dove straight down into the dark abyss in the side of the asteroid. There was a brief glimpse of sheared conduits lining the broken rocky walls as *Ariel* sped past them.

As the timer ticked towards zero, my mind numbed as I witnessed what was happening.

Jack joined me, taking my hand in his, eyes glistening.

But it was already obvious to me he knew how this particular movie was going to end.

The other Lauren's face was calm. I was certain that she knew she was about to die and somewhere along the line had made peace with that fact as the countdown reached zero. There was a millisecond of intense white light building in the cockpit and then there was nothing at all as the window into the future faded to black.

I turned to Jack, the tears now freely streaming down his face.

'I'm so sorry, Lauren,' he whispered taking my hands in his.

I managed a vague nod as he pulled me into a fierce hug and held onto me. But that somehow only helped to fuel the deep sense of desolation that was already raging through me. I was going to die, and now I knew when and how it was going to happen.

CHAPTER NINE

THE FOLLOWING morning I opened my eyes to a mosaic of coloured light dancing across my face. I was in the penthouse of one of the taller city towers that Jack and I had claimed and now referred to as our loft apartment, albeit one with its own aerial sky pad for our transport pod.

The windows all glowed with light from outside thanks to the simulated night cycle that had given way to the golden simulated dawn, which Lucy had set up in the habitation to support our human night-time circadian rhythms.

Jack's arm was wrapped protectively over me. Without turning round I could tell just by listening to the gentle rhythm of his breathing that he was still fast asleep, and that was good because he needed to catch up on some rest. I just wished the same had been true for me because I'd woken up with a splitting, teeth-grinding headache. That wasn't surprising after the restless night I'd endured after what I'd witnessed had really begun to sink—I was going to die in the battle with the Kimprak.

That same thought had played endlessly through my mind into the small hours. There had been tears as I'd scrabbled to process it. Jack had done his best to be my rock, of course, but he wasn't in much better of a state. Even making love had only offered a brief respite. That same mood felt like it was draining the beautiful, multicoloured light from the windows and turning it monochrome. I knew that particular emotional filter was going to be hanging over me for some time. How anyone came to terms with their certain death I had no idea.

Worse still, was that I'd already agreed with Jack that we couldn't tell Lucy or anyone else about what we'd seen. The reason for this necessary subterfuge, and the reason why Jack hadn't mentioned it to anyone, had quickly become obvious as we'd talked it through. If we told anyone about what we'd seen they would almost certainly try and stop it from happening.

On the surface that sounded like a great plan, but what if it was the only way that we could win the battle with the Kimprak? Flying *Ariel* straight into the mothership loaded up with some sort of warheads certainly looked like a desperate final strike against the mothership to try and take it out. If that didn't happen as we'd foreseen it, there was a strong possibility that we might be throwing away our only chance to save Earth from the Kimprak invasion. And so our discussion had circled endlessly about what we should do. Damned if we did, damned if we didn't.

The one thing I knew might help shake off the shadows was exercise. I certainly needed to burn off the nervous energy already raging through me somehow if I was to be good to anyone today.

Carefully, I moved Jack's arm so as not to disturb him, because the poor guy had stayed up half the night with me before sleep had finally claimed him.

I slipped out of bed and padded as quietly as I could across the perfectly temperature-controlled crystal floor and headed to the arched chamber to one side of the main living area we'd set up as a dressing room.

A short while later, courtesy of our transport pod that had whisked me to another part of the city, I was running along one of the wide boulevard walkways. I'd already settled into a steady rhythm and almost felt like I was floating, my shoulders still, my pelvis and legs doing most of the work. I began to concentrate on the cycle of my breathing as a form of meditation, the exercise beginning to settle the churning of my mind.

Yes, this had been a good idea.

The alien city towers made from krine and crystal rose up all around me, their shapes flowing into each other like the trunks of some alien high-tech tree. High above, a lone transport pod was flying towards one of the tunnels that led to one of the rear engineering sections still in the process of being reconstructed, like many aspects of our starship.

Far below the raised boulevard that I was running along, the parkland extended into the city like a river of trees and grass between the buildings. There were ornamental flower beds down there with the most delicate white petals that would give the best of our Earth roses a run for their money.

Ahead of me, the pathway forked. One way headed off in a circuit that ringed the entire city and was about a twenty-kilometre run. The alternative route headed towards a building that sort of reminded me of a tall version of a football stadium, although this one had a domed crystal roof.

According to Lucy, the building before me was known as the Temple of Transmutation. The fact was that I'd fallen in love with it the first time that Jack had introduced me to it, not least because there was the most astonishing sculpture inside.

Instinctively I turned towards it as I reached the junction. Yes, that was probably the best place for me to get myself together.

I reached the steps and jogged up them to the round crystal entrance. As I neared it, the glass panels retracted into the walls like a camera iris opening. As I stepped inside, I heard the sound of distant running water, and a heady fragrance a bit like the smell of honeysuckle hit my nose. The source of that smell was ahead of me—blue-fronded flowers that curled back in dense bunches like grapes and hung from palm-like trees. When a botanist on the science team had discovered them here, she'd at once christened them Midnight Orchids based on the fact that they seemed to release their greatest scent in the small hours of the night cycle.

Despite everything that I'd been feeling, that scent reached into me and start lifting the tension I'd been carrying. The magical effect of this room was considerably magnified by the green walls that were covered with creepers and fine white flowers. They reached up to the mosaic crystal ceiling with its stylised Angelus, their hands outstretched and holding the hands of those next to them in a ring. That was all breathtaking, but none of it compared to what was in the middle of the room.

A water column fell from the centre of the roof, surrounded by a shaft of light that pierced the slight gloom of this place and made rainbows play across the spray breaking away from it in endless dancing patterns of light. The waterfall fell straight down in slow motion, which made it even more mesmerising. Poseidon had told me and Jack that the gravity field within this building had been adjusted to achieve the effect.

The waterfall was also falling through the middle of what this entire temple was named after, namely, the Day of Transmutation statue, which was an extraordinarily exquisite piece of artwork. The statue consisted of a series of naked Angelus figures that were being drawn up into the air, the tendrils of their plasma angel-like wings were spread wide like a group of swallows taking flight. They had been arranged around the waterfall to make it look like they were soaring towards the source of the light shaft above them. All of them had a look of serenity on their faces.

I headed towards one of the many benches that encircled the statues.

Then, without warning, as the peace of that place really took hold of me, the tears that I'd managed to keep suppressed since the revelation about my death, finally came. As I gave into everything that I'd been suppressing—the frustration, the fear, the thought that I couldn't do anything to stop my destiny—roared through me and I sobbed my heart out. I was no longer the commander of the Earth fleet, I was just a woman whose soul was shattering.

For once, I did nothing to try and fight my grief, letting it all go until gradually the tears began to slow. I don't know how long I cried, but eventually, I felt a sense of lightness take hold inside me.

It was in that moment that a sixth sense alerted me to the presence of someone behind me. I turned around to see Lucy watching me with worried eyes.

I smeared away the last of my tears. 'How long have you been there?'

Lucy headed over and sat down next to me, taking my hands in hers. 'Long enough, Lauren, but I didn't want to disturb you. I don't suppose there's any point in asking what's wrong?'

I actually managed a small smile for my friend. 'No, as much I want to, I'm afraid I can't discuss it. But anyway, I feel much better for a good sob.'

'Please just tell me that you and Jack are okay?'

'Yes, this is nothing like that, just the weight of responsibility starting to weigh me down.' It was hopefully enough of the truth for Lucy not to pursue it any further, because if she did I knew that everything would be in danger of just tumbling out.

Concern filled her eyes. 'You've been under so much constant pressure, but sometimes just letting go, like you just did, is what you have to do before you can start to come out the other side.'

'Since when did you get so wise, Lucy?'

'You forget I've been around the human race in one form or another for a very long time. And in so many ways you remind me of my creators, the Angelus.' She raised her chin towards the statues soaring towards the roof before us.

'What were they like?' I asked.

'Kind and considerate would be the main takeaway, and in so many ways not unlike humans, although when your species is at its best. Unfortunately, many humans do seem to have a tendency to concentrate on the wrong things, like the pursuit of possessions rather than things that really matter like each other and the natural world around them. I think that's one of the many reasons the Angelus created this temple, as a way of reminding themselves of those connections. But what I can tell you, is that I don't think that in all my considerable years of consciousness, that I've ever met a human being who has ever burned brighter in their life than you, Lauren Stelleck. You really are quite something.' She raised her hand to cup my face.

'You're not so bad yourself,' I replied smiling.

'Okay,' I said, gazing at the statue. 'As Ruby would say if she could see me now, time for me to suck it up and get on with the job.'

'That's the spirit,' Lucy replied with a small smile. 'Anyway, I tracked you down because I have news. I've been working my way through the US military databases for anything that could help us and I came across the design of a B83 nuclear warhead that has a yield of 1.2 megatons. Basically, it's the biggest nuke in the US military arsenal and could easily be adapted to be carried in one of our new torpedoes. Anyway, I've already discussed it with Jodie and the Forge team who are going to throw every resource into developing it into a working design.'

My mind was already processing this new bit of information. What if the warheads I'd seen in *Ariel* in the Hall of Dreams had been one of these? If so, it seemed certain aspects of that vision were already set to come true, but I needed to make sure my best poker face was on display.

'That sounds like a good move,' I said.

'It is. Oh, and Captain Don Horton has been asking to see you. He's just going through some last-minute checks for his artificial heart in the gym. If he passes the battery of tests that the medical team is putting him through, then he'll be formally discharged from the infirmary. Anyway, he apparently has some ideas about who he can best reach out to at the USSF.'

Once again, based on the vision where we'd seen plenty of destroyed TR-3Bs, that suggested that Don was going to be successful in setting everything in motion for our negotiation with the USSF.

It seemed that events were already conspiring to propel me into the future I'd seen. But then, I also needed to keep reminding myself about what Jack had told me, that if what we had a glimpse into was part of the Procession Plan it also wasn't written in stone. So maybe, just maybe, there was a way through this where we won and I got to spend the rest of my life with the man I loved.

I met Lucy's gaze. She wasn't so much looking at me, but rather *into* me.

'I have a good feeling about him, so let's go and see him now,' I said. 'But first, I need to check in with Jack because I don't want him waking up in an empty bed and panicking. The last time he saw me I was a real mess.'

Lucy peered at me. 'And you're not now?'

'No, I'm in a much better place, no doubt partly thanks to my present company but also to this beautiful building.'

Lucy gazed around us and nodded. 'Yes, it really is something, isn't it?'

'It really is,' I said as I stood and breathed in the rich heady scent of the flowers. Then together, and strangely for me, with a fresh sense of hope, that maybe everything might not be lost after all, we headed for the doors.

———

As we entered the gym it was obvious that Alice had thrown a lot of money at it, installing the very best equipment from running, rowing, and stepping machines to lots of weightlifting gear and benches. The irony was, now with the E8 molecular printers online we probably could have just made them ourselves rather than transporting them in.

I spotted Don straight away because he was the guy sprinting at top speed on the treadmill, surrounded by a small scrum of doctors. They were staring at him with slack-jawed amazement as they looked at the readouts on a display measuring his statistics.

Lucy and I headed over towards Mary, one of our chief medics who'd been monitoring Don throughout his recovery.

'How's Don doing, Mary?' I asked as I reached her.

'Like you wouldn't believe, Lauren. You see this sprint he's doing?'

'Yes, and it's very impressive, especially for someone who has had major heart surgery.'

'Then you'll be even more impressed that he's been able to keep this up for over thirty minutes so far without a break and his heart rate is barely above normal levels.'

'Bloody hell, that's incredible. So this new heart isn't so much a replacement, as more of an upgrade?'

Lucy nodded. 'Yes, it's using the same engineering that was used to create my android body using biomechanical engineering.

That new heart will probably outlast every other organ in his body by a factor of five.'

'So basically, we've turned him into the Six Million Dollar man,' I said.

Mary gave me a blank look, but Lucy was already nodding.

'You're talking about that old classic sci-fi series where they replaced the damaged parts of a former astronaut with mechanical replacements that gave him superhuman strength,' she said.

'Glad to see you've been swotting up on our old sci-fi, but basically, yes. So the key question now is, are you happy to finally discharge him because we need to chat with him?'

'Goodness, yes,' Mary replied. 'He's passed every test we could think to give him with flying colours and is good to go.' She waved her hand at Don. 'Okay, I think we can call this a wrap. Lauren's here to talk to you.'

'But I was just getting into my stride,' he said without so much as sounding even faintly breathless.

'You can knock yourself out later if you like, but for now, we're done and you are fit to resume duty, Captain Jacobs.' Mary snapped him a salute which made him smile.

A moment later the treadmill was whining to a stop, and Don was heading towards us towelling down the barest hint of perspiration on his face. 'So what are my stats looking like, doc?' he asked.

'Exceptional, as you well know. If you ever want to give up being a pilot, I think you have a real shot at entering the Olympics.'

He grinned wider. 'Running the sixteen hundred at a flat-out sprint would certainly raise a few eyebrows.'

Mary laughed and did that whole playing with her hair thing that instantly told me there was a bit of a spark between the two.

'Anyway, I have other patients to attend to, talking of which if you see Mike, Lauren, do tell him that we can replace his prosthetic leg with an Angelus engineered one which will be better than his original one.'

'Wow, that's incredible,' I replied. 'I'm sure he'll be thrilled to hear it.'

'I'm sure he will.' She turned towards Don. 'See you later, maybe?'

'Oh, you can count on it,' he said giving her a wink that made her grin.

Lucy and I raised eyebrows at each other as we headed over to the water cooler with Don.

'We need to discuss how I can return the favour for saving my life and set things up for a meeting with the USSF, Lauren,' he said as he helped himself to a cup of water.

'Which I'd be more than happy to discuss. But I also have to tell you that as much as I would love for you to return to the USSF and your old life, unfortunately, we have no way of knowing just how far into the USSF the Overseers reach still extends in their ranks.'

'So in other words you don't want me to reveal anything about this incredible ship that you've snagged yourselves, right?' Don asked.

'That's the one, but only because it would entirely be in the Overseer's playbook to try and steal it for themselves,' I replied. 'They would literally throw whatever it took at us to make that a reality. But that's something you already know all about.'

'Yes, I do. It cost the life of my best buddy, Zack, and that's something I'm never going to be able to forgive them for. So let's cut to the chase, I'm happy to stay here for now and be your bridge builder to make sure that both the USSF and your forces are fighting on the same side of this coming battle. But there is one condition.'

'Which is?' I asked.

'That you allow me to join your fleet, Lauren, and take command of one of your ships.'

'Are you sure you want to do that after what happened? I mean, are you really ready to get involved in combat missions again?'

'Absolutely, I've never been more certain of anything in my life. I am and always will be a flyboy. I was born for this fight. So don't have me sitting it out on the bench when I should be leading by example to the other USSF officers. Allow me to fight by your side.'

'Then you shall have your own command, Don, and that's a promise,' I said.

He beamed at me. 'You, ma'am, have just made my day.'

I grimaced. 'Yes, but please don't call me ma'am because that always makes me feel like a hundred and three.'

Don snapped me a salute, grinning. 'Understood, Commander.'

Lucy's eyes widened as she tilted her head to the side with a look of concentration. 'Oh bloody hell, not that.'

'Is something wrong?' I asked.

She looked at me, her face pale. 'Everything's wrong, Lauren. I just heard over the avatar-to-avatar internal comm system that one of our Guardian probes that we sent out to the edge of the solar system has just relayed a message. The Kimprak mothership has arrived three months early and is about to enter our solar system.'

Don and I both stared at her, my blood turning to ice. All our carefully considered plans to prepare for the Kimprak invasion had just well and truly been blown out of the water.

CHAPTER TEN

I HAD GATHERED ALL the key people, and had invited Don along too, for the urgent meeting in the Citadel, otherwise known as the command bridge of *Tempest*. It had been absolutely transformed since I'd last been there a week ago thanks to the tireless work of the nanobots and had gone through a major refit.

Now, all the critical flight systems and the weapons and science stations had been moved into a semi-open amphitheatre-style arrangement with tiers stepping down to the large central hologram projector in the middle. My captain's chair was situated towards the back of the amphitheatre on one of the higher tiers, which had been my idea so I was able to see everyone else on the bridge at a glance. In a battle situation, even something as trivial as direct eye contact could make a real difference in a life or death situation. A glass wall separated us from the rest of the flight deck where avatars and humans could be seen working side by side on *Tempest's* secondary systems.

Lucy had just powered up the main display and Troy was gazing out at us from a video window that was now hanging in mid-air in the main hologram. But far more impressive was a fully rendered 3D image of Alice that could actually walk around if she wanted to and who was sitting in her wheelchair before us. That was thanks to Jodie and the Forge team, who had started to make full use of the starship's sophisticated holographic photonic mass projection system and had installed a sister system to the one here in the situation room back at Eden.

Alice was currently holding up her hands to try and regain some order. 'Okay, we're not going to get anywhere if everyone tries to speak at once, so let's start with you, Lucy. Have you got any additional intel about the Kimprak mothership that you could share with us?'

'Actually, I have,' Lucy replied. 'I now have a Guardian drone tracking it half a light-year out and slowly reeling it in. It's also stealthed, so hopefully the Kimprak won't pick up on its presence. Unfortunately, the Guardian's still too far away to make out any real detail as the return signal from the radar is presenting a very scattered profile that doesn't make much sense. We're currently analysing it to try and work out why.'

'That aside, I think the burning question that we'd all like the answer to is, how come the Kimprak are due to arrive three months ahead of schedule?' Mike said.

'That's a good question, and one I've also been analysing with the other avatars,' Lucy replied. 'Our best guess is that maybe the Kimprak managed to increase the power of the laser beam that they used to propel their solar sail. That's the problem with predictions, they don't always come true.'

I tried to ignore the pointed look that Jack gave me.

Ruby crossed her arms. 'Look, people, we could talk about that all day long, but let's get to the part where we discuss what the hell we're going to do about it? Because unless I'm the only one thinking it, it's hard not to think that we're totally screwed by this latest development.'

Niki grimaced. 'No, it's not just you, Ruby. We've definitely been caught on the back foot here, especially with *Tempest* still not being flight ready yet.'

I nodded. 'So that brings us to the first most pressing question, how long before that mothership reaches Earth?'

'Not as soon as you might think, despite the fact they're still travelling a third of the speed of light,' Lucy said. 'Thanks to that, they will actually slow things down a lot before reaching here, otherwise, they'll just zip straight through our solar system. So metaphorically speaking, they need to apply the brakes. They'll do that by using the gravity well of one of the bigger planets to slow them down before slingshotting themselves on towards Earth at a far slower speed. Based on its current trajectory it looks like the mothership is heading straight towards Jupiter to do exactly that.

'We've already run a few calculations and to answer your question, I would say we have about three months before they reach Earth, rather than the six months we'd predicted before this new development. Having discussed the implications with the ship's avatars, our advice would be to take on the Kimprak out at Jupiter so there is plenty of time for a rearguard action if we lose the initial battle. That would mean we would need to intercept them in seven weeks max.'

'But there's no way the main fusion drive will be online by then,' Jodie said grim-faced.

Jack traded a knowing look with me. Of course, unlike the rest of them, we'd already seen a potential glimpse into the future where *Tempest* was very much in evidence, battling with the mothership in what had to be the final battle over Jupiter. I gave him the barest nod.

'There has to be a way to get *Tempest* into this fight, even if we have to tow the damned thing,' I said.

Mike's eyes widened a fraction. 'Lauren, you're a bloody genius.'

'I'm more than happy to be called that, but how so, exactly?'

'Think about it. *Tempest's* anti-grav systems are already fully operational and they are way more efficient than our REV drive design. Thanks to that, despite *Tempest* weighing in at over two billion metric tons—and yes, you did hear me correctly—the anti-grav systems can reduce its effective mass to just an astonishing three thousand metric tons.'

Alice narrowed her gaze on him from the hologram. 'Which is incredible, but I'm not sure where you're going with this, Mike.'

'I am,' Jodie said. 'You're thinking that we could actually airlift *Tempest* out of Earth's gravity well and tow her into space, aren't you?'

Mike grinned at her. 'You nailed it in one, and all based on Lauren's throwaway idea.'

'Oh, now *that* I like the sound of,' I said. 'Plus, despite the holographic field that *Tempest* is generating, I would feel far more comfortable getting her into space and away from any potential prying eyes.'

'Hang on, even if we get *Tempest* into orbit, are you seriously suggesting we tow her all the way to Jupiter?' Alice asked.

But Jodie was already holding up her hand to stop her. 'Actually, there is still a way to make that happen. We could prioritise bringing *Tempest's* backup ion drive system online. Although, it has nothing like the speed capabilities of the fusion drive, the ion drive is huge and would certainly be capable of propelling *Tempest* to Jupiter in the time that we have left.'

'That sounds more promising,' Alice said visibly relaxing.

'So what about the fact we're still going to be short of a lot of ships and crews to take on the Kimprak?' Troy asked from his video window.

'I think, because time is now a much rarer commodity, we need to switch our priority from building more X-craft to the Wolfpack battle drones. As we've already discussed, each ship can have a number slaved to their systems. Maybe we could increase that number, Jodie?'

She nodded. 'I can't see why not and that would effectively greatly increase their firepower.'

'It sounds like we all need to brainstorm this further, but this has been a promising start,' Alice said. 'The universe has thrown us a curveball and we're just going to have to do whatever it takes to knock it out of the park.'

Don who'd been following the conversation in silence, coughed. 'Actually, you are all overlooking something obvious, and that is prioritising those negotiations with the USSF for our forces to fight alongside one another. They may have suffered significant losses at the Antarctica Battle, but you can guarantee they will have been working flat-out on building more ships since then, just like you have. The one thing for certain is that we need to win the USSF's trust and quickly, so I'm going to suggest something that I don't think any of you are going to like. But if you want to make this a sure-fire bet, then I think this is your best option.'

'Tell us what's on your mind, Don,' Alice said.

'Why not let the USSF know about *Tempest* and offer to give their TR-3Bs a ride out to the battlefield at Jupiter too. TR-3Bs ships aren't equipped for long-duration missions like your Pangolins and what the USSF needs right now is the equivalent of an aircraft carrier, which apart from anything else, is exactly what *Tempest* offers them at this crucial time. In my humble opinion, it's time to start being open with your former enemy if you all do want to give Earth the best shot at surviving.'

We all stared in shocked silence at Don, because he was suggesting trading the biggest secret that we had, and one that had cost many lives to secure. But before I could begin to object, Alice was already nodding.

'You're saying if we really want to build an alliance that we need to make a major gesture,' she said.

'I am, and if you want something to swing their vote, then I tell you now, telling them about *Tempest* is the answer,' Don replied.

Ruby stared at Alice with a marble-hard stare. 'Hang on, then we might as well hand the keys of *Tempest* over to the Overseers and be done with it.'

'Actually, there could be a way to cover even that, a sort of *you can see but don't touch* arrangement,' Jodie said. 'We have several hangars that we're not using, so why don't we just give the USSF one of those and seal off its access to the rest of the ship.'

'You mean, keep them in a form of quarantine without access to any systems that could give us problems?' Mike asked.

'Exactly, but the only problem is that we are inviting onboard a potential enemy combatant.'

'Oh, please,' Lucy said. 'Without wanting to sound a bit big-headed, *Tempest's* point defence system could cut those ships to shreds if they tried anything like that. Also, it would be easy peasy lemon squeezy to adjust the gravity field within their hangar and crush their ships to the size of a sugar cube if they do decide to get a bit frisky.'

'If we are seriously suggesting that this as an option, then I insist on fully vetting every USSF officer for any possible Overseer agents among them,' Niki said. 'Having said that, I'd be more than happy to share whatever intelligence we have about the Overseers with the USSF so they can start weeding them out of their ranks beforehand.'

'Now, that is something that I think certain high ranking officers would find very interesting,' Don said. 'There has been a suspicion for some time that the USSF has been infiltrated and until now they've had no way of identifying who those people were.'

'I hear you, buddy, but if it's any comfort it's not just the USSF but every major military in the world,' Jack replied.

'Not to mention worming their way into governments, including my own,' I said.

'I think I can muster up a lot of support to deal with this dry rot,' Don replied. 'And apart from helping to identify compromised military personnel, may I also suggest that we share the footage of the Kimprak mothership from the Guardian with them? Apart from *Tempest* herself, if anything is going to get their attention, it's going be that.'

Alice's hologram gazed at all of us. 'If anyone has any objections then now is the time to air them.'

I turned the thought over. The shortened time frame really did change everything, and besides, my little glimpse into the future had also shown TR-3Bs fighting alongside our ships.

I nodded slowly. 'You'll get no objection from me. I honestly don't think we have any other choice when the future of our whole world is on the line.'

Everyone's gazes settled on Niki who looked like he had just sucked on a lemon.

He held up his hands. 'Okay, okay, I might not like it, but I can still see the sense in it. But I'm also going to assign a triple guard detail to any hangar that they're using, even if Lucy can crush them to the size of a sugar cube.'

'Then it sounds like we're in agreement,' Alice said. 'Don, please go ahead and reach out to your contacts as soon as possible.'

He nodded. 'Leave it with me. I'll see what I can do, ma'am.'

'Okay everyone,' I said. 'It sounds like we all have a lot of work to do now that the deadline has been brought forward, so we all better get to it.'

A moment later we were forming into little huddles, locked

into intense conversations about what would happen next because one thing was for certain, there was suddenly an awful lot to discuss.

CHAPTER ELEVEN

THE CITADEL'S flight control deck looked more like mission control, thanks to all the control stations that were lit up and currently crewed. Sitting in the captain's chair, the haptic holographic screens displayed a bewildering display of charts and readouts and control interfaces around me that were being operated by the majority of the avatars. The avatars were being shadowed by some of our people as we slowly started to collectively get our heads around how to operate this starship that had been bequeathed to us.

Jack, Lucy, Mike, and Jodie were here too for this crucial moment in our plan. I was already sick with anticipation at the attempt to lift *Tempest* into orbit. There was so much that could go wrong, most of the crew had been temporarily evacuated to the E8 sphere where the avatars had created a temporary parkland for them to take shelter in.

I leant forward in my seat as I examined the relayed video views that were filling the central holographic display as a series of floating panels. We'd raised the Citadel into its above-hull position ready for this operation. Around us, the Antarctica illusion conjured up by the photonics mass projector shield stretched away. The key detail which gave away that things weren't quite what they first appeared to be were the hundreds of silver cables rising into the sky from the seemingly featureless ice-encrusted surface.

Mike shook his head. 'If anyone is out there and sees this, it will be the most bizarre sight ever, thanks to all the X-craft being camouflaged. To them, it would probably look like a forest of silver vines rising into the sky.'

'Then it's just as well that *Tempest's* sensors show no sign of anyone out there for at least a six-hundred-klick radius,' Lucy said as she peered at some sort of 3D radar sensor display that was before her. 'Mind you, it's confusing the bejeebers out of the penguins and the seals out there though.'

'Just please tell me that you remembered to hack any satellites overhead to render those cables out of the scene?' I asked.

'Already done, my little sunflower,' Lucy said. 'Apart from us and the local fauna, no one will have any idea of what we are trying to do here.'

I turned towards the others. 'Talking of which, are you sure there's absolutely no way that I can persuade the rest of you to watch this onboard the relative safety of an E8 with everyone else?'

'If you think I'm going to leave your side, you have another thing coming,' Jack replied.

Mike and Jodie nodded.

'Besides, we need to be here to monitor all the systems during this attempt,' Mike said.

Lucy glanced back over her shoulder and raised her eyebrows at him. 'I think the other avatars and I have that part covered, but I learnt a long time ago to stop trying to persuade you humans against anything that you have set your hearts on doing.'

'A very wise strategy,' Jodie replied, who appeared to be

viewing a whole bank of energy displays in a window floating in front of her chair.

'Okay, if anything does go wrong, is everyone clear on what they have to do?' I said.

'Yes, we all make our way over to E8 to join the others where we can ride out anything that happens here,' Mike said in the tone of someone repeating the instructions of a teacher. 'Which obviously, isn't going to happen as this will be a silky-smooth ride up into space.'

'I hope I don't end up ironically quoting you on that,' I said as I returned my attention to the video feed from the hangar that we stored our X-craft fleet in.

On it, the last of the ships had departed through the launch tubes leaving only a handful of craft left in the hangars that were in various stages of maintenance, the rest already out on patrols. Mike and Jodie had run the calculations several times over with Lucy and assured me that theoretically, four hundred plus X-craft that we'd been able to muster for this operation would have more than enough redundancy built into the airlift operation, even if a third of them had to pull out for any reason.

I raised my hand to the holographic screen being projected in front of my seat and with a flick of my fingers, I felt the haptic feedback of a solid surface beneath them as I swiped the view on my console to the side. The view of Hangar one that had been on my screen, was replaced with a live feed from *Ariel's* cameras. Ruby and Erin were currently aboard *Ariel* and they'd already taken up a position high in the sky over *Tempest*. With another flick of my fingers, I transferred that view to the main hologram display in the middle of the Citadel's flight deck.

I stood up and headed, not just towards the hologram, but into it. The light flickered over my skin as the projectors adapted to my presence disrupting it. Then I was standing in the middle of the projected 3D image of *Ariel's* flight deck with Ruby and

Erin on either side of me. It was so real that it was like I was actually there looking out at *Ariel's* virtual cockpit display around me. The only thing that broke the illusion was the fact that I was standing partly within a chair like some sort of video game surface collision bug.

From Erin and Ruby's vantage point a bright blue sky extended over the glistening Antarctic snow-filled plain below them. Despite being invisible, the other X-craft were being rendered by the virtual cockpit system.

Jack came over to join me in the middle of the hologram. 'Our X-craft all look like UFO-shaped balloons with strings trailing down from them.'

That raised a small smile from me. 'Don't they just. I still can't get my head around the idea that despite it being pretty much most of our whole Earth fleet, that it will be enough to get us into space.'

'Yes, it's a bit like watching a bunch of ants trying to tow Mount Everest to a new location, so I take your point,' he said returning my smile.

'Great analogy.' I chuckled. 'You seem a bit brighter than you did a few days ago, Jack. Any particular reason why?'

Jack turned to look at me and dropped his voice to a whisper. 'Well, as I see it, there's two ways I can deal with that vision. I can either mope around just waiting for it to happen. Or I can do everything in my power to avoid it ever happening by working my ass off.'

'And I'm guessing you've decided on the latter based on your change in attitude?'

'Absolutely. I'm in the process of putting together a new expedition with Poseidon to explore *Tempest's* stern that we still haven't managed to survey yet. I'm hoping that we might find something that will help us in that final battle and specifically change the outcome of what we both saw in that prediction.'

'That sounds like a much healthier approach to me,' I replied, squeezing his shoulder.

But despite Jack's enthusiasm, and what was obviously a fresh sense of purpose, deep down I couldn't help but wonder whether the Procession Plan prediction algorithms had already factored in anything we might be able to do, even with all of *Tempest's* resources thrown at it. But there was absolutely no way I was going to rain on his parade, especially when part of me had already accepted that if we were really going to win this battle that it might cost me my life.

Lucy joined us in the middle of the hologram. 'So far, everything is looking good for this lift attempt, guys. Windspeed is a very modest two-miles-per-hour and not a cloud to be seen. This is the very definition of the best weather that Antarctica has to offer. *Tempest's* anti-grav drive is spinning up to full power and our starship's effective mass is heading south rapidly. We should be good to go for a lift attempt in five minutes when the last of the Earth fleet get to their designated lifting positions.

'And you're absolutely sure nothing can go wrong?' I asked.

'As much as is possible,' Lucy replied. 'There's always the wildcard that something fails, but that's highly unlikely.'

I nodded. 'Good to hear.'

'I always like to be the bearer of good news,' she said as she headed back to her console.

Jack leant into me and dropped his voice to a whisper again. 'Look, whatever else was in that prediction we did see *Tempest* there for the final battle. That tells me that this is going to be a walk in the park.'

'That's what I keep telling myself,' I replied, deliberately not addressing the elephant in the room, that in that same prediction was where I had died.

On *Ariel's* virtual cockpit in the hologram, we watched the last dozen dots of the final X-craft rising from the opening of one of *Tempest's* hangar bays. Our starship, far below the X103 and despite also being invisible thanks to a photonic holographic shield, was beautifully rendered on *Ariel's* bird's-eye view.

At this distance, the starship's design was as breathtaking as she was huge. The Citadel, where we were sitting, was a tiny teardrop-shaped dome at the pointy end of the starship. The rest of the craft stretched back behind it in a sort of sweeping triangular deltoid shape. An elliptical wing section encircled the rear part of the ship where two large fusion drive nacelles extended from the port and starboard sides. At the rear, was a sort of scooped out section where a massive single rocket bell engine was housed. If everything goes to plan, the backup ion drive would be utilising that once it was brought online after we reached orbit.

The only thing missing externally, according to Lucy, was the jump drive itself that distorted the space-time field around this behemoth of a ship. If we'd had that, we could have travelled instantly between two points anywhere in the universe. Unfortunately, that incredible ability had been lost because the plans to rebuild and operate it had been buried within one of the micro minds that the Overseers had managed to take out. Even though our starship was partly crippled by Angelus standards, the hope was that it would be more than enough as-is to tip the coming fight in our favour.

Jack, Lucy, and I watched the last X-craft slowly rise into position, each trailing its tether behind them until finally, Jodie gave us a thumbs-up.

'Okay, the fleet is in position,' she said.

'*Tempest's* anti-grav drive is approaching maximum output,' Mike said. 'In three, two, one...' He glanced across to me. 'Okay, *Tempest's* effective mass has been reduced by ninety-nine percent. We are good to attempt the lift operation.'

Lucy nodded. 'Okay, then everyone best get back to their

seats, which have their own emergency gravity field if anything goes wrong,'

A moment later, I was sitting in the captain's chair again. 'Delphi, please open a channel to everyone in Earth fleet.'

'Affirmative, ship-wide channel is now open,' Delphi replied.

I took a moment to centre myself as the others on the command deck looked at me.

'Hi, everyone, this is Commander Lauren Stelleck speaking. We're ready to begin lift operations. Delphi will take control of each of your ships so that this manoeuvre can be coordinated across our entire fleet for what will be a very finely balanced operation. Good luck to us all and we will hopefully see you all soon in space for a celebratory drink. Out.'

With a wave of her fingers, Lucy overlaid the main holographic display over a zoomed-out view of all the Earth fleet with *Tempest* below them, all marked with metadata tabs.

My gaze automatically sought out and found *Ariel* near the zenith, alongside *Thor*. I knew Niki was aboard *Thor*, having decided to join them for this critical operation.

'Delphi, begin operation *Rolling Stone*,' I said.

'Operation *Rolling Stone* has begun,' the AI replied.

On the main hologram, we watched as each craft in the fleet began to rise slowly, drawing the cables taut beneath them.

I felt a hand take my mine and looked to see Jack beaming at me.

'Here we go,' he said as we both looked through the surrounding windows at the view.

There was a slight shudder that grew stronger and was followed by a cracking sound that echoed throughout the Citadel.

Lucy already had her hands up as we all cast her worried looks. 'You can all relax, that's just ice breaking free that has built up round *Tempest's* hull.'

'Now you tell us. I nearly spat my coffee out,' Mike replied shaking his head at her as he placed his mug back in the chair's cupholder that had been one of the other upgrades I'd asked for.

Another longer groan from the breaking ice was followed by softer rumbles as indicators lit up showing the increase in the amount of lift being generated.

'Delphi is increasing fleet's REV drives to maximum, whilst also throttling up their multimode rockets,' Lucy said.

I pulled up the live feed from *Ariel* on my hologram console in front of my seat. I could immediately see that the cable dropping away from her had become piano-wire-taught.

A series of explosive booms came from all around us as the snow and ice around the starship seemed to dislodge all at once. Then, suddenly, *Tempest* was moving, pulling free and rising. Avatars and humans alike clapped and cheered.

I reached over and squeezed Jack's hand as Mike and Jodie did the same.

'You see, anything is possible when we all put our minds to it,' Jack said.

'It is, isn't it?' I replied with a fresh sense of hope.

Together we both looked out at the Antarctica landscape stretching around us. Snow was tumbling away from *Tempest* as she cleared the ground and my heart soared with her as she began to quickly rise away from it.

One of the views from the cameras mounted in the belly of the ship displayed a large crater that was being left behind by our departure.

'It's going to leave some Antarctica scientists very puzzled when they come across that hole in the landscape for the first time,' Jack said.

'Isn't it just,' I replied smiling at him.

Tempest began to accelerate, the ride silky smooth now that we'd lifted off. Above us, the constellation of ships were working in perfect harmony just like Jodie and Lucy had been planned.

Small alterations were being made to each of the ship's controls as our army of X-craft worker ants continued to haul our starship into the sky.

The landscape was opening out into a vast expanse of snowy plateaus and ice-covered mountains. It was then that it struck me that in our distant past, *Tempest* must have made this trip in reverse when its Angelus crew had brought her in to land. What must the Angelus crew have thought as they'd approached our planet for the first time?

As we passed a hundred thousand feet and the sky began to darken, and the tension I'd been carrying was just starting to lighten, there was a sudden lurch. Multiple alarms seemed to warble out at once as the deck began to lurch to starboard. At the same moment, dozens of thrust indicators started to turn red on some of the fleet as Delphi commanded them to max out their engines.

'What the hell is happening, Lucy?' I called over to her as she and the other avatars' hands flew frantically over the controls.

'We've had a partial power failure in one of *Tempest's* anti-grav generators that's dropped back to sixty-percent efficiency,' she replied with a tight expression. 'We're trying everything we can to bring it back online, but it's going to take us five minutes.'

'But that's five minutes we don't have,' Mike replied, his face pale.

Jodie was nodding. 'There's absolutely no way that the Earth fleet will be able to maintain this altitude, let alone lift us.'

'Then, can we begin a controlled descent?' Jack asked.

'Again, not enough time,' Mike said staring at his displays. 'We'll have crashed long before then, bringing down most of our fleet with us if they don't cut the tethers.'

'Bloody hell, but there has to be something we can do,' I said, frantically looking around the flight deck for an answer to magically materialise.

And then as *Tempest* started to tilt even more I saw it on one of the monitor views of the hangar bay—a large number of Wolf-pack drones that had already been built.

'Lucy, launch all available Wolfpack drones now!' I called out.

She stared at me and then quickly nodded as comprehension filled her eyes.

Jack was staring at me. 'You're going to use them to help our fleet?'

'That's the general idea. But as there obviously isn't time to connect them by cables, we'll just have to position them beneath us to provide lift. Although they haven't got the lift-power of one our X-craft, there are enough of them to make up for it.'

'Your *seat-of-your-pants* plans are genius sometimes,' Jodie said.

'It's amazing how a bit of primordial fear sharpens my thinking like that,' I said as the localised gravity field built into each of the flight deck chairs activated with a slight shudder.

I felt an immediate shift of localised gravity as my bum was now pinned to the seat even as the flight deck tipped past thirty degrees.

Like a swarm of dark seeds, three hundred Wolfpack drones shot out of the landing bay doors and gathered beneath the enormous spaceship.

Lucy and the other avatars had opened up hundreds of control windows, their reactions working ten times faster than any human could have as they controlled the swarm. One by one we watched them latch onto the bottom of the hull like some sort of mechanical leeches. The similarities to the way the Kimprak attacked their victims wasn't lost on me. But the difference here, was that the drones were very much on our side, and more importantly, directly under our control.

Another judder went through the Citadel as *Tempest* was

slowly righted. The metadata tags were practically all flashing red as the Wolfpack and the X-craft fleet resumed *Tempest's* ascent into space.

I hardly dared breathe over the next five minutes in case I jinxed it, but slowly the Earth began to curve away beneath us. Then, one by one, the red warning tags started to go out on all of our ships as our planet's gravity well began to lose its grip on the giant alien starship.

As we rose free of Earth's atmosphere a deep black darkness engulfed us, followed by pinprick-sharp stars that started appearing one by one. Then, the alarms finally fell silent. Lucy and the other avatars shared a relieved look.

'Full power has been restored to the anti-grav system,' Lucy said. 'We're in the clear people,.'

This time there wasn't any applause, but everyone seemed to breathe a sigh of relief.

As the localised anti-grav field in my seat was switched off it only heightened the sensation of me sagging into myself as the tension flowed away.

'So it seems a bunch of ants can shift a mountain after all,' Jack said grinning as he reached out to squeeze my hand again.

I nodded and shakily got to my feet. 'I don't know about anyone else, but I really need that stiff drink now.'

'Heck yes,' Jodie said.

I nodded. 'Lucy, please relay my thanks to the entire fleet and tell them that the drinks will be on me when they get back onboard.'

'Absolutely,' Lucy said smiling.

'Just as well you don't have to pay for the bar bill,' Mike said.

'Under the circumstances, I don't think Alice would mind,' I replied.

'Hey, no cost involved as you all can have any drink you desire, courtesy of the molecular printers,' Lucy replied.

'Oh my god, we really have fallen into the world of *Forbidden Planet* somewhere along this journey,' Jack said, which made me burst out laughing as I hugged him.

I stood hanging on to him for a moment, just looking out at the stars and the fleet of ships manoeuvring towards us. I might not have a lot of time left, but I vowed, then and there, to make the most of every moment and that started tonight, celebrating what was, without a doubt, a very real reason to do exactly that.

CHAPTER TWELVE

I WAS PRETTY sure that every member of the flight crew had made it down to the parkland for the impromptu celebration after word had gotten out, especially when they heard there was free *whatever you fancy* booze on offer.

With Jack next to me, I sprawled out on a lounger that the nanobots had conjured for us and watched Ruby and Erin wildly dancing to the techno music that was playing on a massive speaker system that one of the technicians had quietly printed.

The avatars were mixing it up with the best of us and throwing themselves into the party vibe with both android feet. Poseidon, much to everyone's amusement, had even mastered body-popping moves thanks to a quick crash course from Mike.

Lucy was heading towards us with Slick, who was sporting a bowtie that had been looped round her neck, just behind her. He was carrying a silver tray in his pincer hands and on which two drinks were balanced. Much to my approval, I spotted that one was a margarita for me, and going by the beads of moisture on the outside of the glass, a very cold beer for Jack. With the absolute precision of advanced robotics Slick presented us with our two beverages of choice.

'Seriously, you've reduced our state of the art Tin Head to a waiter?' Jack asked as he helped himself to the beer.

'Hey, I didn't want the big guy to miss out on the celebrations. He would have sulked,' Lucy said. 'You should listen to how much the Tin Heads bitch about you lot when they're left out of the fun.'

I stared at her. 'They do?'

'Gotcha,' Lucy said grinning at me. 'You humans are so gullible sometimes.'

Smiling, I shook my head at her. I was feeling like a different woman compared to the one who'd been paralysed not long ago by the thought of her own death. Strangely, as I'd gradually come to terms with the idea, it actually felt liberating. It's not often in life that you get to know your own sell-by date. Besides, as Jack kept reminding me, it wasn't a given.

I took a margarita from the tray with a *thank you* thrown in Slick's direction just in case he did actually have some rudimentary feelings buried deep within his metal skin. Then my eyes widened at the first sip.

'Wow, Slick makes a pretty excellent margarita,' I said.

'And also serves a damned find cold beer,' Jack added, wiping the foam from his lips. 'You should let Kilroy know. I'm sure he could do with some extra help down at the Rock Garden back in Eden.'

Lucy draped a protective arm around what would normally be the shoulders, but in Slick's case, because of the height difference, ended up being around his waist. 'You ignore them, big guy. You're always going to be with me.'

'Hang on, let me get this straight,' I said. 'You're an AI in an android body with a robot sidekick now?'

'Hey, it's the way I roll. Anyway, I wanted to see your faces for the big reveal to the crew.'

'What big reveal?' I asked giving Lucy a suspicious look. The last time she'd attempted to surprise us was with the breakfast culinary creation of pickled herring, combined with maple syrup pancakes. It still made my stomach heave just thinking about it.

'Now that we're in orbit, I thought it might be rather nice for the crew to see a view of Earth over the parkland, if only because it will help remind everyone what a beautiful planet you have that we're all fighting to keep exactly that way.'

'Great idea, so what are you going to do?' Jack asked. 'Project a live view onto the ceiling, a bit like Alice does with the virtual skydome back in her cavern in Eden?'

'Oh, we can do way better than that,' Lucy replied. 'I told you before that the krine metal alloy that *Tempest* is built from has many properties, including exceptional strength. Well, another useful feature is that passing a mild electrical current through it alters its transparency, so if I do this...' She clicked her fingers and the entire ceiling became a vast girder-panelled window. Now, above us, framed by the Milky Way behind her, was Earth in all her glory.

A collective gasp went up from the assembled crowd as all eyes turned towards the view.

Mike, Ruby, Erin, and Jodie who, until a short moment ago, had been dancing together, all headed over.

'Did you do this, Lauren?' Jodie asked. 'Because it's utterly breathtaking.'

I gestured towards Lucy. 'I can't take any of the credit for this. This is all Lucy.'

Mike gave her an impressed look. 'Very cool, Lucy. And I'm guessing that whatever you've just done to the roof panels to make them transparent doesn't also reduce their structural strength?'

'Nope, just as strong, and that's without taking into account the extensive gravity shielding beyond it.'

The music had fallen silent as the people around us looked up, all mesmerised by the spectacular view of our world. If the Angelus had seen this view, no wonder they'd been so determined to protect our fragile planet.

Of course, I'd had plenty of time to witness the beauty of Earth like this aboard *Ariel*, but for many of our crew, this was probably the most sustained view of our world that they'd ever experienced.

I don't know who started the clapping, but in a ripple effect it spread outwards and within moments everyone was joining in, hands raised towards our mother world. It was a deeply touching moment and I had tears in my eyes when Jack glanced across at me.

'This is the *why*,' he said.

'Yes. Yes, it really is,' I replied as I looped my arm through his and squeezed. 'And even if saving this extraordinary planet of ours costs us everything, then it will still be worth it.'

Jack's gaze fell away from mine. 'Maybe...'

It sounded to me like the two of us weren't quite on the same page about me throwing myself under the bus if that was what it took.

But as the applause continued I also got a sense that I wasn't the only one feeling that protecting our precious planet was worth everything. It was obvious that I was surrounded by like-minded people, who would put their lives on the line to defend it too.

As the clapping began to fade, someone made a deafening two-fingered whistle.

'Let's get back to partying people, whilst we still can,' Ruby called out over the PA as she cranked the sound back up and the throbbing dance music filled the park.

Whooping, people began to dance. Swinging her hips with

the best of them, Ruby headed towards us beckoning with both hands.

'Shall we?' Jack asked.

'I think it would be rude not to,' I replied as I kicked my shoes off and began dancing with him under the light of our homeworld shining down on us.

My head was slightly throbbing the following morning after one too many margaritas made their lingering presence known. As my mind surfaced from a dreamless sleep, otherwise known as passing out, I also felt a dull throb in the back of one of my calves. It was then that the memory of the giant conga line came back to me. Ruby had been behind me and had slightly misjudged one of her dance kicks and it had landed squarely on my calf. When I'd glanced down later I had an impressive bruise to show for it.

Now, I needed some painkillers.

Feeling a bit too sorry for myself, I stretched my foot across to wake Jack so he could sympathise with my fragile state. But rather than feel either of his legs, all I felt was empty space where they should have been.

I cranked my eyes open a slit which was definitely a mistake, because even the soft light from the stained glass window felt like someone was shining a thousand-watt searchlight into my face.

'Jack?' I called out.

When there was no reply, I struggled into a sitting position, my bleary eyes gradually focusing on the room around me. There wasn't any sign of Jack, but next to my bed were croissants and a glass of fresh orange juice propping up a handwritten note.

'*Off to hopefully change the future. Love, Jack xxx*'

I was immediately wide awake, my hangover forgotten. Of course, today was the day that Jack was heading off with Poseidon to explore the far reaches of the ship. Having already discussed it with him, I realised it was a journey that was easily going to take a considerable amount of time. He'd probably be away weeks while they covered all the areas of *Tempest* that hadn't yet been surveyed.

I glanced at the clock and it had just past 10 a.m. ship time. If I hurried, I might just be able to catch him. I leapt out of bed and quickly got dressed.

Thanks to Jack's location beacon being broadcast by his smartwatch that all crew members wore, I tracked him down to one of the massive storage lockers in one of the industrial areas of the ship. Over the last few months, they had been a hive of logistic activity and we'd gradually filled them with equipment transferred from Eden to augment things that had already been created with the molecular printers. Everything we might possibly need was already in there for the voyage to Jupiter and our rendezvous with the Sol fleet. Troy agreed that combining our fleets there, was our preferred joint strategy to take on the Kimprak.

My transport pod landed next to another one already parked up. Through its large transparent blister-like dome, I could see that it had already been loaded with a huge amount of equipment from the storage facility. Crammed inside, there seemed to be everything from what looked like ground radar equipment to shovels and trowels, which as I well knew, were two pieces of essential equipment for any self-respecting archaeologist.

That had to be a force of habit for Jack, as I couldn't imagine there would be a whole lot of dirt around for him to actually dig into, unless he was going to explore the hydroponic farms onboard that augmented *Tempest's* ability to print food.

According to Lucy, that was because some of the Angelus had always sworn they could taste the difference between printed food and real food. It seemed our own modern-day organic movement had a long and prestigious alien lineage.

Jack and Poseidon appeared in the doorway of the storage locker, pulling a pallet piled high with provisions behind them.

As I left my transport pod, I headed over. 'Remind me again just how long you're planning on being gone, guys?' I said.

'As long as it takes, but obviously, I can be back here in a heartbeat if you need me,' Jack replied.

'But why not just return each night?'

'Who says I'm going to be getting much sleep? This is way too important for that.'

Poseidon sighed. 'You should try talking to him, Lauren. I've tried to persuade him that he should pace himself on this expedition. It will be alright for me, as I can simply plug myself in when I need a charge, but human batteries tend to run down a lot more quickly than android ones.'

'You heard the man, Jack. Come back every night to a comfy bed and more importantly to me in it.'

'You have no idea how hard it is to resist that thought, but I'm going to need to take rain raincheck on that, Lauren. But when I'm back by your side again, I'm not going anywhere, and that's a promise.'

'I'm going to keep you to that. I just hope all this effort will be worth it.'

'We really think it will be,' Poseidon replied. 'I was researching a truncated database file and it references a major production facility near the stern of the ship that's currently in the process of being reconstructed.'

'But we have plenty of E8 molecular printers already, and although, admittedly, another one would be useful," I said, 'what's the big deal with this one?'

'The scale of it is ten times larger than anything we have now, suggesting it was used to build things that were really huge,' Jack said.

'Such as?'

'We're not absolutely sure, but whatever it is, is very heavily armoured,' Poseidon replied. 'Suggesting that it was a very important facility.'

'Okay." I sighed. 'I can see why you think it must be significant, but just promise me you'll be in touch the moment you have any idea what it is.'

'You have my word,' Jack said. 'But I've got a good feeling about this.'

'You better bloody have if it's going to drag you away from me for so long.' I took hold of his shirt and pulled him in for a kiss before letting him go again. 'And just remember, I expect regular updates.'

'Then virtual postcards with "wish you were here" written on them it will be. Anyway, shouldn't you get spruced up? Isn't Alice due here for that big meeting with the USSF delegation today that Troy has been busy negotiating with?'

'Oh, bloody hell. I thought that was tomorrow.'

'No, Alice is en route and should be arriving in about fifteen minutes,' Poseidon replied. 'The Earth delegates will be here about an hour later. Niki Linden has been busy organising the security for the meeting and has been trying to get hold of you.'

'Damn it, once again I've left my smartwatch on the bedside cabinet. Okay, I better dash and get ready. Anyway, the best of luck guys.'

They both nodded and Jack blew me a kiss that I returned as I leapt back into my transport pod. A few moments later, I was speeding back towards the tunnel that would take me back to the city for a meeting that could change everything.

CHAPTER THIRTEEN

ABOVE US IN landing bay one, *Thor* exited the shaft and flew towards us as we stood waiting for its arrival.

Lucy turned to me. 'About the USSF visit later today, I feel like we should be rolling out the red carpet for them.'

'I know what you mean. This is a symbolic moment, at least if it goes well,' I replied. 'But I was also talking to Don about it and he said that since we'll be talking to senior military brass rather than a politician that they wouldn't be expecting that sort of treatment.'

'In that case, we'll give it a miss then,' Lucy replied.

'So, when is the USSF delegation due to arrive anyway?'

'Around 4ST,'

'ST?'

'Sorry that's an abbreviation for ship time,' Lucy replied. 'Anyway, I was thinking there's still plenty of time to give Alice a tour of the latest developments. Especially, of the progress that Jodie and Mike have already made helping our avatars bring the ion drive online.'

'I'm actually looking forward to seeing their progress for myself,' I replied. 'It feels like I've barely seen them in days.'

'I know, busy busy bees, bless them,' Lucy replied.

Thor began its descent, and with the softest of hums, the X104 settled onto its landing pad a moment later.

I took in the newly painted hammer logo on its side. Niki had been threatening to paint one of those onto his ship for ages, so he'd obviously persuaded someone on the maintenance team to actually do it for him. The man was really into his Norse mythology.

The ramp lowered and a few moments later Alice wheeled her chair down the ramp with Niki just behind her.

Alice's eyes were already hungrily taking in the vast hangar around us. 'Oh my goodness, the photos, videos and even the holograms really don't do this justice. The sheer size alone is breathtaking.'

'If you think this hangar is impressive, just wait until you see the rest of the ship,' I replied.

'Which I'm looking forward to and I will, later. But first, let's go and see this incredible engine room that I've heard so much about from Jodie. It sounds like quite the feat of engineering.'

'I haven't seen it myself,' I replied. 'I'm looking forward to seeing it too.'

'I promise neither of you will be disappointed,' Lucy said with a smile.

———

Niki excused himself to check in with the security arrangements for the USSF delegation, and Alice, Lucy, and I exited the hangar.

The first thing that struck me as the doors to the engine room swooshed open was the tingle of static that brushed over my skin, bringing with it a mild tingling sensation. A loud humming echoed through the open doorway to the dimly lit room beyond. That noise was occasionally punctuated by a strange whooshing and the crackle of what had to be some sort of energy discharge.

'It sounds very productive in there,' Alice said.

'It was as silent as the grave the last time I was here and was basically a featureless chamber,' I said.

'Oh, there's been a lot of change since then,' Lucy said with a broad smile.

Even though I'd seen the reports about the progress being made here, nothing quite prepared me for what we saw as we followed Lucy through the doorway and out onto a walkway.

What had been an empty tubular-shaped chamber about five klicks long and two wide had been completely transformed. Once again, the scale of the Angelus engineering in here, like so many aspects of this huge starship, was breathtaking.

A vast shimmering wall of energy spanned the far section, through which it was just possible to see streams of glowing particles flowing through the air to form vast conduits and giant ringed capacitor coils.

At the top of the engine chamber stood a large metal teardrop jet engine-like structure. A large pipe travelled from the end of it and disappeared into the shimmering wall.

Far more impressive was a giant round mirror-chromed sphere in the middle of the chamber. It had to be easily three hundred metres wide and had a complex constellation of power conduits linking it to the walls like a giant spiderweb.

Positioned around it were six, large cylinder-shaped structures orbiting it like elongated satellites and connected to it by more metal pipes.

The sphere's smooth surface didn't appear to have a single panel weld, apart from several hatches built into it, one of which stood open at the end of the walkway we were standing on.

Working next to it we could see the tiny ant-like figures of people walking in and out of it which immediately gave a sense of scale to the huge structure. The other remarkable feature in the otherwise flawless sphere were a number of hexagonal windows. There was also a second large tube leading away from it with a series of large torus rings wrapped round it, like the other large pipe, it disappeared into the shimmering wall as well.

'Oh my,' Alice said as she took everything in. She pointed towards the area beyond the rippling energy wall. 'Is the area beyond that still being created?'

'Yes, they're still being unpacked from the quasicrystal that this ship was stored in,' Lucy said. 'There are a number of areas that are still being reconstructed, but this area has been prioritised for obvious reasons.'

'And how long until they bring this all online?' Alice asked.

'Let's go ask Jodie and Mike,' I replied. 'They've been working flat out on all of this.'

As we made our way to where Lucy thought they might be, the sphere hummed quietly, and now that I was closer, I could see that the hexagonal windows had a faint blue light emanating from them. There was also a heavy thunderstorm smell of ozone which gave the air a sharp, fresh taste to it that was growing stronger the closer we got.

Alice was looking increasingly impressed. 'Even if you hadn't told me that this was the engine room, I could still tell it was because there's already a tangible sense of power emanating from this chamber.'

'Yes,' Lucy replied. 'And just imagine what it will be like when all the systems in here are up and running.'

It was a good five minutes before we finally reached the sphere where the science team was working alongside the ship's avatars. As we neared, I spotted Jodie and Mike among them, both scrutinising a holographic schematic floating in the air and that appeared to be displaying a cross-section of the sphere that they were standing in front of.

Mike was the first one to spot us and opened his arms with a beaming smile. 'Welcome to our kingdom,' he said.

'And what a kingdom it is,' Alice replied.

'Yes.' Jodie nodded. 'Even without *Tempest's* jump drive, the ion and fusion drives are still the stuff of engineering dreams.'

'We can see that,' I said. 'Maybe you could talk us through what this impressive equipment actually does.'

'Okay,' Mike said. 'Let's start with the ion drive running along the top of the chamber, which is the barrel-shaped device. By Angelus standards of engineering, it's actually very low tech.'

Jodie nodded. 'It's basically an electric propulsion system that uses xenon ionised gas accelerated towards an anode and creates a low level of thrust. The advantage of this drive design is that it can be sustained pretty much forever, allowing *Tempest* to gradually increase speed. It also draws very little in the way of power, so is effectively a backup drive system if the main fusion drive is offline for any reason, like it is currently.'

'So the billion-dollar question is, how long before the ion drive is ready?' Alice asked.

Jodie grinned at her. 'The headline is that it should be online within the next twenty-four hours.'

Alice and I stared at her.

'And when exactly were you going to tell me this incredible news?' I asked.

'Now, because we wanted to see the look on your face when we told you,' Mike replied. 'Anyway, thanks to that, *Tempest* should be able to head out tomorrow for the rendezvous with the Sol fleet.'

Mike placed his hand on the surface of the large metal sphere that we were standing next to and tapped it. 'It's just such a shame we can't bring the fusion online sooner.'

'How fast can the fusion drive propel *Tempest*?' I asked.

'Easily ninety-five percent the speed of light, far faster than the ion-drive can manage even after years of acceleration,' Mike replied. 'The problem is that it needs an awful lot more power than the ion drive. When the *Tempest* has finished all its internal building processes then we'll eventually be able to finish reconstructing it. But if we had it now, we could travel out to Jupiter in a matter of days. Unlike the ion drive, it can produce rapid acceleration. Unfortunately, with all the other work that's currently drawing power, we won't have it ready in time for the Kimprak's arrival at Jupiter.'

'Well, the good news is that at least the ion drive will be online and that will mean that, at the very least, *Tempest* can fulfil her role as a giant aircraft carrier,' Alice said.

Lucy closed her eyes for a moment and then opened them again. 'Talking of which, our sensors have just detected a TR-3B squadron of six ships approaching the designated rendezvous point. Don is talking to them now and has confirmed that Commander Hamilton who will be leading the USSF negotiations is aboard.'

'Then let's hope we can persuade him to see sense and combine our forces before it's too late,' I replied.

CHAPTER FOURTEEN

ALICE, Niki, Don, Lucy, and I were waiting in the empty hanger bay watching the three TR-3Bs coming into land on the pads.

Niki scowled at Alice and me. 'I would be so much happier if both of you were wearing full combat armour. I wouldn't trust these people further than I could spit right now.'

'And as we both keep telling you,' I replied, 'what sort of message would that send to the delegation?'

'That we're not going to allow them to piss us around,' Niki replied.

'Look, I allowed you to bring a whole security detail to stand guard over us.' Alice gestured to the security team positioned around the pads, interspersed with Tin Heads armed with their mini-guns. 'I think that's a reasonable compromise, don't you?'

Niki did his impression of a bear in a bad mood, complete with growling, which made Don bite back a smile.

Of course, our head of security wouldn't have been happy unless we'd been behind a blast-proof krine crystal wall, and only then if we were wearing body armour as well.

Obviously still exasperated with us for being so unreasonable,

Niki switched his attention to Lucy. 'You're absolutely sure that they haven't got a nuke stowed on any of those TR-3Bs?'

'We've already had *Tempest* run multiple sensor sweeps and she's not picked up so much as a firecracker onboard those ships,' Lucy replied. 'And before you ask, I've already hacked into their ship's systems, including their internal cameras, and there is absolutely nothing to raise any suspicion.'

Niki pulled a sceptical face. 'Ever heard of a Trojan Horse?'

I scowled at him. 'Look, I know you're paid to be paranoid, but I think you need to notch it down a fraction.'

'There's absolutely no chance of that until our *guests* have departed,' he replied.

Don met Niki's gaze and shook his head. 'I think you're going to be pleasantly surprised by Commander Hamilton. The guy is strictly old school. He's very much a man of his word and his handshake is a binding contract. Just as importantly, he holds considerable influence with both the flight crews and senior staff right across the USSF. If we're able to win him over today, I tell you now, he's the right man in the right place to do business with.'

Niki's sceptical expression was ramped up to eleven. 'We'll see about that.'

Looking at the others I shrugged. 'None of us can't say we didn't try.'

'That we most certainly did,' Alice replied giving me an amused smile.

With a much louder hum than our own X-craft, the TR-3Bs followed an animated series of lights set into the floor that was leading them to their designated pads.

'So, those TR-3Bs crews haven't actually seen *Tempest* yet in all her glory, is that right, Lucy?' Alice asked.

'Correct. The Photonic Mass Projector's holographic field would have presented nothing but an empty patch of space in which the entrance to a hangar appeared to be hovering. Based on the conversations in their cockpits right now, they think they're just entering some sort of stealthed space dock rather than anything that might be part of a much larger starship.'

'Good, it might be useful to keep a few cards up our sleeves about *Tempest* for now,' she replied.

'Aha! So I'm not the only one who's feeling a bit paranoid then,' Niki said.

'Paranoid, no. However, not showing our full hand in a negotiation until it suits us, then very much yes,' Alice said.

'I hate to sound a bit like Niki here, but shouldn't you be considering wearing a disguise or something, Alice?' I said. 'You do realise that when they see you they will be able to link all of our operations to Sky Dreamer Corp?'

'I do. However, I think the time to hide our light behind a bushel is far past. When the Earth's fate is hanging in the balance the time has come for the Sky Dreamer Corp to come out and make a stand, not just against the Kimprak invasion, but also against the Overseers and everything that they stand for.'

I exchanged looks with the others and then we all nodded.

'Well said, Alice,' I said. 'And I think I speak for everyone here that we're all behind you in this decision.'

'Yes, that even goes for your resident grouch,' Niki said.

Alice laughed. 'That's always good to know, dear friend.'

A hissing sound came from the hatches of all three TR-3Bs and a moment later marines began to emerge, quickly taking up defensive positions around the steps of their craft, their rifles drawn and eyeballing our security team, and particularly our Tin Heads, with considerable wariness. The human contingent of our security team were returning their gazes just as suspiciously, their own weapons aimed back at the soldiers.

But Niki, despite his bluster, was already turning towards his people. 'Weapons down everyone. Let's start as we mean to go on.'

'Well said,' a bald man with a Louisiana accent said. His penetrating blue eyes swept over the soldiers as he emerged from the TR-3B. 'And you heard our hosts, stow your weapons too, Marines.'

His people frowned at each other, but did as they'd been ordered and lowered their carbines as our team did the same.

'That's much better,' the man said. 'I never did like a Mexican standoff.'

Don leant a fraction in towards us. 'That's Commander John Hamilton,' he said quietly.

'I think we all worked that part out for ourselves,' I whispered back.

Hamilton headed towards us, flanked by two of his marines who were still watching the security team with eagle eyes. Then the commander's gaze locked onto Don and a wide smile filled his face.

'Good to see you again, Captain.'

Don snapped his commanding officer a salute. 'You too, sir.'

But then Hamilton's face fell a fraction as he looked at Don. 'I was really saddened to hear about the loss of Zack. An excellent officer and a good man.'

'And a good friend too, sir. But like so many of our own and many of Commander Lauren Stelleck's crew, they all died heroes defending our world.'

Hamilton nodded as his gaze turned towards the rest of us and sought me out specifically. 'Ah yes, and if I'm not mistaken, the very same lady who managed to steal one of our TR-3Bs from under our noses at Area 51.'

'The very same, but that happened several lifetimes ago,' I replied holding out a hand.

Hamilton nodded and then a smile curled the corners of his mouth as he took my hand and shook it. 'Which, if nothing else, shows a certain amount of impressive resourcefulness.'

'Lauren is far too modest to admit it, but she has that in spades, which is why she's now commander of our Earth fleet,' Alice said.

Before I could jump in and introduce her, Hamilton's gaze widened. 'Alice Jefferson, is that really you?'

'You, sir, have me at disadvantage, do you know me?'

'Of course, I do. You just need to picture me with a full head of curly hair, several pounds lighter. Although you probably knew me by my flight handle, Snow Goose, thanks to my former golden locks.'

Now it was Alice's turn for her eyes to widen. 'Snow Goose, that hotshot pilot that always gave me a run for my money at all those stunt flying competitions?'

Hamilton grinned. 'The very same, ma'am.'

And just like that, I felt the mood of the people gathered round us shift. There was history between these two and that could make all the difference for the coming negotiations.

'So how on Earth did you manage to get yourself into this situation?' Hamilton asked.

'It's a very long story and there's a lot to tell,' Alice replied. 'So why don't I be a good host and extend some real southern-style hospitality like you used to give me and we go and break some bread together whilst I catch you up on everything that's happened. Then we can get down to the real business of thrashing out a treaty to take on two common enemies.'

'Two?' Hamilton replied.

'Oh yes, obviously the Kimprak, but also the Overseers that have held a pernicious hold over the US and other major governments of the world for far too long.'

'Ah yes, you're referring to the security dossier that Don supplied us with?'

'I am, indeed.'

'And if you haven't already taken action you have to straight away,' I said. 'You have no idea how bad it—'

But Hamilton was holding up his hand. 'Commander Stelleck, I'll need to stop you right there. I wouldn't be here if I hadn't taken your intelligence briefing seriously. I can assure you that wheels are already in motion and arrests are in progress. And not just in the US either. We have shared intelligence with other governments right around the world. Most have been responsive, although there have been some surprising abstentions from countries we have always considered to be major allies.' He gave me a slightly pointed look.

'As in my own country, you mean?' I asked.

'Let's just say your intelligence agencies, MI5 and MI6, have been less than helpful.'

'I wonder if that has anything to do with the new PM, Alexander Langton,' Lucy said.

'Possibly, but that doesn't sound good,' I replied. 'Anyway, that's a conversation for another time. The main thing, is that you've begun to move on the Overseers?'

'We have, but we can discuss that shortly. So, Alice, let's get to that hospitality that you were offering and then we can get the real negotiations underway.'

'Let's,' Alice replied. She nodded to Niki. 'You are to stand your security team down.'

He gave her a sharp look. 'But with all due respect—'

Her intense look made Niki's protest die in his throat.

Hamilton was also nodding to his soldiers. 'You heard the woman, you are to stow your weapons and remain here with our ships.'

His people exchanged looks with each other with the same lack of enthusiasm that was currently engraved in Niki and his security team's faces. But one by one they did as they were ordered, as our security team did the same, both sides still warily looking at each other.

'There's an obvious amount of mistrust on both sides among our people,' Alice said. 'So let's lead by example and start building those bridges. If you'd like to join me in my ready room I'll get you fully up to speed with what we're doing to prepare for the Kimprak invasion and how, if your side is willing, we could work together to defend our planet. I also happen to have a very fine twenty-year-old bourbon that I've been looking for an excuse to open and I can't think of a better occasion than now.'

'Now that, I like the sound of,' Hamilton replied.

As Alice turned away with the commander, at once one of the soldiers started to follow him. Immediately Niki stepped forward and was in his face.

'I don't remember hearing that you were invited to that particular party,' Niki said.

The other guy's eyes became slits as he stared back at our head of security. 'Fortunately, buddy, I don't take my orders from you and I intend to do everything in my power to protect my commanding officer.'

'There's no need for all this attitude,' I said stepping between them. 'Will you please both calm down?'

They glowered at each other past me, but then Niki stepped back and shrugged.

Hamilton's gaze sharpened on the marine as he turned back towards him. 'Stand down, Edwards. Unless you're hard of hearing, you must have heard what was a direct order. You are to remain here with the rest of the team.'

'But, sir—'

A swipe of Hamilton's hand cut off the soldier's protest. 'You heard me, Marine. As Alice said, this is all about building bridges and that starts with me trusting our host who happens to be an old friend.'

'Of course, sir.' Edwards snapped Hamilton a salute.

Alice turned her wheelchair towards Lucy, Don, and me. 'If you'd like to join us, I think we'll begin by giving Commander Hamilton a tour of *Tempest* before we get down to business.'

'You're going to do what now?' Niki asked staring at her.

'You heard me. I can't think of a better way of building trust between our two sides then by showing the considerable asset that we have at our disposal.'

I found myself sympathising with Niki's obvious discomfort about the situation.

'I have to say, Alice,' I said. 'Now I've had time to think about it, I have some reservations about this too.'

'I thought you might, but without getting into it again just please trust my judgement in this matter.'

I gave her the longest look. Like Niki, my job was partly to be paranoid and to see potential threats in every situation. But I also knew Alice was an excellent judge of character and sometimes her instincts were far better honed than mine.

I slowly nodded. 'Of course, Alice. Then let's get this tour underway.'

She smiled at me even as Niki scowled at me. But it was the little nod of approval that Lucy, who'd remained quiet for most of the meet-and-greet, gave me that meant most of all. She was far more astute than she let on sometimes, and if Lucy approved of Alice's approach, then that was another major tick in the box that I should trust her judgement on this too.

Putting my reservations aside, I followed the others towards the transport pod that awaited us.

'Holy crap!' Commander Hamilton said as he stared out from the top of the Crucible at the vast expanse of the starship around him.

'That's pretty much the same reaction everyone has when they see *Tempest* in her entirety for the first time,' I replied.

He turned to us, his eyes wide. 'And you say that this vast starship was tucked away at the heart of our planet since the dawn of human history?'

'That's right. At least the blueprints for *Tempest* were, it was then reconstructed by the merged micro minds using some very exotic E8 physics,' I replied.

Lucy nodded. 'This ship is the Angelus' legacy to your species. A legacy I might add, that the Overseers were blindly intent on destroying, Commander Hamilton.'

'Please, you can all call me John. And I have to say, I find myself in agreement that I can't believe that the US military was involved in trying to destroy this in what amounts to an act of mindless vandalism.'

'If it's any comfort, it wasn't just the US military that was suckered by the Overseers,' Alice said. 'That organisation's modus operandi is all about maintaining their shadowy control of our world, and that includes destroying anything that they can't directly control.'

'All I can say is, if I ever get my hands on this Alvarez character, he's going to regret the day he was damned-well born,' John said.

'Speaking of which, have you had any more information on his whereabouts?' I asked.

John shook his head. 'It's like the guy has disappeared off the face of the planet. According to our intelligence services, he and his people cleared their desks and disappeared from Area 51 about four months ago and haven't been seen since.'

'I find that almost as unnerving,' Alice said. 'I find myself worrying about what they're are up to now.'

'Nothing good, you can be sure of that,' I said.

Alice nodded and then gestured towards a door in a curved area to the rear of the Citadel that had been set up as a meeting room. 'Anyway, let's start talking turkey about how we can work together to kick the Kimprak's butts and make them wish that they'd never tried taking on the human race.'

'You really are someone I can do business with,' John said.

'Oh, you better believe it,' Alice said with a wide smile.

CHAPTER FIFTEEN

THE NEGOTIATIONS HAD ENDED up going far better than any of us had any right to expect. John and his squadron of Astra TR-3Bs departing to head back to Earth had of course been a reality check. To absolutely no one's surprise, trying to make the new alliance work had been anything but smooth.

Despite what Alice and John hoped for, there had still been a lot of suspicion on both sides as former enemies tried to mentally and practically pivot towards working together. Niki had certainly been less than impressed and had been on something of a personal security crusade to double up on security protocols.

That was why I was currently standing outside hangar bay two with Niki and Don peering through the window of a closed krine blast door. Also, just to make sure there was absolutely no chance of anyone getting out of that hangar, it was guarded by four Tin Heads and six of Niki's security officers ready for the arrival of the TR-3B fleet of eight hundred plus ships.

I scowled, gesturing towards one of Tin Heads sporting a mini-gun. 'Is this all strictly necessary, Niki?'

'As far as I'm concerned, yes, it damned well is. Despite all of

Alice's cosy negotiations and guarantees that Hamilton has given us, I wouldn't trust the USSF any further than I absolutely have to, especially with their people now boarding *Tempest* in significant numbers.'

'Has anyone told you that you're something of a cynic when it comes to human nature?' I said.

Niki scowled, but before he could reply, Don jumped in.

'This might surprise you, Lauren, but I'm actually with Niki on this. I can tell you for a fact that no one arriving now will even raise an eyebrow that there are armed guards on the doors. I can also guarantee that if the situation was reversed, the USSF would do exactly the same. Trust is a tricky thing to build and has to be earned by both sides.'

I sighed as my initial indignation began to evaporate. 'Maybe you have a point there, Don. So let's just hope all these precautions of keeping the USSF in their own sealed-off hangar can be relaxed as each side proves itself to the other.'

'I won't be holding my breath that your boundless optimism about human nature is proven right anytime soon,' Niki replied.

'You'll see,' I said, hoping that my gut instinct was on the mark here.

My smartwatch warbled and I looked down to see Jack's face gazing back at me from its screen.

'Hey, you're a face for sore eyes. Talking about going dark on me, mister.'

'Yes, sorry about that, but I sort of disappeared down the rabbit hole with this expedition.'

'So, did you find anything interesting hidden away in the depths of *Tempest*?'

'Actually, we did, hence the call. Are you free to join us, Lauren?'

'I can probably move things round in my schedule, which is

pretty flat-out with the USSF arrivals and all the logistics that involves, but can't you just show me what you've found?'

'I could, but I think for the full dramatic effect you'll want to see this with your own two eyes. I'll send a transport pod to collect you. Maybe bring Lucy, Erin, and Ruby too.'

'Okay, now you've got me more than a little intrigued. I take it this is good news, though?'

'Potentially, but we'll discuss it all when you get here.'

Jack smiled at me, looking far happier than he had in weeks, before my watch's screen went blank. Something told me that whatever he'd found was going to be a very big deal indeed.

The transport pod flew along the partly darkened tunnel with exposed panels revealing the guts of piping beneath the surface. It was similar to the others we'd flown down for the last ten minutes. This whole region of *Tempest* was very much a work in progress.

Lucy was studying a holographic map of *Tempest* that was hovering before her in the pod. 'Whatever it is that Jack and Poseidon have unearthed, I can tell you is that it's towards the stern and near the outer hull.'

'And without stealing their thunder, you still have no idea what it could be?' I asked.

'None whatsoever. Although, looking at the large energy conduits connected to it, whatever it is, it's drawing almost as much power for reconstruction as the ion engines.'

'Sounds like something major,' Erin said. 'But why does he want me and Ruby to see it?'

'Hopefully, you're going to find out the answer to that particular question any moment now, as the end of our ride is coming up according to navigation,' Lucy said gesturing ahead through the glass blister-dome of the transport pod

Through it, I could see that the wide tunnel ended at a massive round closed door that had to be a good klick wide.

Parked before it was another transport pod with portable arc lights set up around it to illuminate the gloom. As we began to descend, I noticed there was an open hatch at the base of the massive round door where a blue light emanated.

'Looks like the end of the line,' Ruby said stretching her legs.

As we came in to land next to the other pod, I felt my heart lift as I spotted Jack emerge from the open hatch and wave up at us. A short while later, we were all standing on the surface of the tunnel and I gave Jack a hearty hug before I finally pulled away from him.

'Missed me, then?' he asked with a wry smile.

'Of course. Just tell me it's all been worth it.'

'Absolutely. What we've discovered could change everything.'

'Okay, enough with the buildup already,' Ruby said, popping her gum. 'Just show us.'

'If you'd all like to follow me,' Jack said, taking my hand and leading us to the hatchway. 'Poseidon is waiting in the next chamber to do the big reveal.'

Lucy ran her hand over the walls of the massive doorway closing off the end of the tunnel as we walked. 'This is one of *Tempest's* pressurised blast doors, by the look of it.'

Erin shot her a questioning look. 'I thought *Tempest* didn't need pressurised doors thanks to its gravity shielding?'

'It doesn't, strictly speaking, but this is a secondary safety system in case *Tempest* was ever to lose power,' Lucy replied. Then her eyes widened. 'Hang on, as far as I'm aware these are only built around the exits from—'

'Hey, don't blow the surprise, Lucy,' Jack said interrupting her.

A smile filled Lucy's face as she made a zipper motion across her mouth.

'I hate surprises, just tell us already,' Ruby said.

'I promise, it won't be much longer,' Jack replied as we headed towards the end of the corridor that was filled with inky blackness.

Our breath clouded the air as a distinct chill began to take hold.

'Just give your eyes a minute to adjust,' Jack said as we stepped into the darkness.

What, at first, had been a featureless blackness began to slowly resolve itself into a vast chamber. Faint points of light were pulsing around a gigantic elongated object sitting before us.

'Okay, where are we and what exactly are looking at here, Jack?' I asked.

'This is what I first saw when I entered this chamber, a whole lot of nothing,' he replied. 'Of course, Poseidon with his enhanced vision could see exactly what this was, as you probably can too, Lucy?'

Lucy was already grinning. 'Oh, yes. What an incredible find, Jack.'

'Will someone please spill the beans already?' Erin said.

'Alright, I think I've kept you in suspense long enough,' Jack said. 'Poseidon, can you please hit the lights?'

'At once,' Poseidon's voice replied from somewhere in the darkness ahead of us.

I had to squint as the darkness was suddenly transformed by a bank of blinding lights blazing into life to reveal the area before us.

A huge rectangular room stretched out before us. Gantries criss-crossed it, but it was what was sitting in the middle that stole my breath away. Held in a large metal cradle was a partly constructed ship with flowing surfaces and a hull covered in hundreds of blister domes. Sweeping fins radiated round its hull towards the pointed nose section.

I turned to stare at Jack. 'You've discovered another Angelus ship?'

'Exactly,' Poseidon replied as he approached us. 'A partly constructed battle cruiser.'

Jack nodded. 'You see, this is *Tempest's* shipyard and subject to available resources, and with enough power from the E8 sphere, it can crank out a finished warship at the rate of one per week.'

I stared at him. 'You mean that we can basically create our own battle armada?'

'Exactly,' Jack said. 'Poseidon, tell them what you found in the dock's databanks.'

'Blueprints for building thirty different variants of this ship, from fighters to the human equivalent of a corvette, which you can see partly constructed before you. And it goes all the way up to a heavy cruiser with a crew of a hundred. Obviously, crew is a loose term in this context as they can be partly made up of AIs.'

Erin gestured towards the corvette. 'Does that mean we can use this in the battle with Kimprak?'

'That's the million-dollar question,' Jack said. 'But before we get to that, I suggest that you have a tour of the ship first, because that may partly influence the answer.'

We stood in an elongated crew compartment, and like everything Angelus, there was a sculpted elegance to the interior with walls that flowed seamlessly into the floors and ceiling. The cockpit was lit with a soft-blue light offset by the jewelled lights of the displays lining the compartment.

Erin had already found the equivalent of a pilot's seat and was sitting in it surrounded by multiple control panels and complex-looking multi-axis joysticks. Behind her was a second seat with its own array of screens that Poseidon had just explained was the weapons officer's seat. Ruby had immediately dropped into that and was already looking very much at home.

'Exactly what armaments does this have?' I asked.

'The main weapons are particle beam cannons and gauss gun torpedo launchers,' Poseidon replied. 'Then, like *Tempest,* it also has lasers for point defence.'

'Oh, let me at them,' Ruby said.

'I'm afraid that's not possible, at least not yet,' Poseidon replied.

'Why, what's the problem?' I asked. 'We should be cranking battle-ready ships out of this space dock as fast as we can.'

'It's a question of priorities,' Poseidon said. 'Right now, most of *Tempest's* resources are being directed to bringing the ion drives online. If you switch those same resources to this shipyard we could probably build about six Angelus warships before the Kimprak get here, but then that will mean engaging the Kimprak in near-Earth orbit.'

I groaned and shook my head. 'There is no way we can risk cutting things that fine. And just when it seemed like all our Christmases had come at once.'

'Yes, sorry about being a Grinch, but worst-case scenario, at least you'll have this to play with,' Jack said. 'Apart from anything else, it is flight-ready and could be put through its paces by a competent pilot. The rest of its systems, including weapons, can be worked on in between.'

'Then it sounds like that's our only real option here,' I

replied. 'So, Erin, fancy taking her out for a spin when she's ready?'

'Do you really need to ask?' she replied.

I laughed. 'No, not really.'

But Lucy was holding up her hand. 'Actually, I may have a better idea. This corvette needs a crew of ten and less than an hour ago we were talking about building bridges with our new allies.'

'New allies?' Jack asked me. 'You mean the meeting with the USSF delegation went well?'

'Much better than expected. I'll fill you in on the details later,' I replied. 'Anyway, you were saying, Lucy?'

'How about this for an idea? We let Don captain this ship and be responsible for drawing his flight crew from both USSF and Eden flight teams. With a bit of PR spin, we could make Don the poster boy for the new cooperation between our two sides.'

'Oh, now, I like the sound of that,' I said. 'Sorry, Erin, you're going to have to stick to *Ariel* for the time being.'

'That's not exactly a hardship,' she replied with a smile.

'Then it sounds like we have a plan, and in the spirit of this new cooperation, I'm going to go let Commander Hamilton know.'

'It sounds like I have a lot to catch up on,' Jack said.

'You really do,' I replied, taking in all the lines around his eyes. 'And when exactly was the last time you slept?'

Jack waved a dismissive hand in the air. 'Enough to get by on.'

'In other words, not enough. Let's get you home, fed, and tucked up in bed for some serious rest.'

He gave me a slow smile. 'You won't get any argument from me.'

As we headed out of the cockpit, I took one last lingering look. Within our reach, we now had a major way to tip things in our favour against the Kimprak. The problem was, we just didn't have the time to make better use of it. But if we did manage to win the war, having the ability to turn out our own warships gave us a distinct advantage in being able to defend ourselves against any other threats that might take a fancy to our planet in the future. I just hoped that we, as a species, lived long enough to realise what an incredible gift the Angelus had given us.

CHAPTER SIXTEEN

AFTER SEVERAL DAYS of frantic activity, I sat in the captain's chair again as my flight crew buzzed around me. The Citadel had been raised to its flight position ready for *Tempest's* imminent departure, if everything went to plan.

Through the windows, the beautiful blue crescent of Earth hung behind us. There were two steady trails of shimmering points of light rising into orbit to rendezvous with us. One was from Area 52, the home of the USSF forces, and the other was from Eden on the Mexican peninsula. Both lines of ships flew in a slow-motion aerial ballet that had been converging on *Tempest* over the last few hours.

The final TR-3Bs and X-craft were being loaded into their respective hangar bays. After some further frantic meetings between the USSF and ourselves, it had been agreed that they would be the foot soldiers of Earth's joint armada.

Although further development of the corvette had gone frustratingly slow, that was about to change because the ion engines had just been completed and resources could now be switched to completing the warship. The other good bit of news was that the

Wolfpack production was rapidly ramping and we were already up to just over a thousand drones in the hold. Jodie had assured me that at the rate they were going, every single one of our X-craft would have around four drones per ship. Combined with Troy's fleet from Psyche 16, that we were heading out to rendezvous with, that would mean we would have around fourteen hundred X-craft in total, to add to the eight hundred TR-3Bs of the USSF. Whatever way you looked at it, that was a significant force that the Earth had been able to mount to defend itself and that wasn't even factoring in the difference that *Tempest* could make during battle.

Jack also seemed to be increasingly confident that we'd been able to change the version of the future where I'd died, as there'd been no sign of a corvette in it. I was less convinced. I still had this nagging worry in my stomach that despite everything we could still lose this. Apart from my own death, I had also seen a lot of broken ships floating around in space.

Lucy headed over towards me. 'We're about five minutes away from loading the last of the ships onboard.'

'How are Mike and Jodie doing bringing the ion drive online?'

'Let's ask the dynamic duo directly,' Lucy replied turning towards the holographic projector display. Then she did her whole hand-waving routine, something that Mike had told me wasn't really necessary as she was always linked to the starship. That little show was strictly for our benefit.

After Lucy finished waving her finger in a figure-eight pattern, two figures bent over control panels appeared in the holographic display. In the background, the ion drive was clearly visible.

'Hey guys, how close to starting the ion engine?' Lucy asked.

'We're just running the final checks now, but we should be ready to leave orbit in just a few minutes.'

'Okay, we'll be back in touch shortly,' I said.

Lucy did her hand-wavy thing again and the hologram faded away just as Jack appeared on the flight deck.

'Isn't this place a hive of activity?' he said as he sat in the seat next to mine.

'Like you wouldn't believe,' I said.

Lucy nodded. 'The amount of tasks on my and the other avatars' to-do list has been immense. The number of things you have to check on a starship before it's ready to head off into space, boggles even my android mind.'

'There's certainly a real sense of purpose onboard now with everyone pretty much flat-out busy,' Jack replied. 'It's just such a shame Alice isn't up here to see *Tempest* head out on her maiden voyage, for us humans at least.'

I nodded. 'She's tied up organising some sort of plan B.'

Jack's gaze focused his gaze on me. 'What's that mean?'

'Apparently, she's discussing what we're going to do if we lose with a few key people back at Eden,' I said.

'There's not a lot anyone can do if the Kimprak defeats our fleet.'

'Well, obviously she thinks there is, because she told me she's looking into contingency plans.'

'I could find out what exactly she means, if you'd like me to hack Eden's systems,' Lucy said.

'No, Alice will tell us when she's ready,' I said. 'If I was in her shoes, I wouldn't want to distract us from our mission, which needs our entire focus right now.'

'Okay, you're the boss, but if you change your mind, just whistle,' Lucy replied.

I nodded. Over her shoulder on one of the monitors, I watched the last X-craft disappear into hangar bay one and the last two TR-3Bs heading towards their hangar on the opposite side of the ship.

Lucy followed my gaze. 'Good, it looks like our passengers have boarded and our cruise liner is ready to depart.'

'Talk about a momentous moment,' Jack said. 'Maybe one day they'll write about this in the history books.'

'If we all survive and Earth isn't reduced to burned-out husk,' I replied.

'Hey, what's with the dark attitude?' Lucy said. 'A bit more confidence is what's called for.'

'Sorry, I didn't mean to actually say that aloud,' I replied regretting my decision not to tell her about the Hall of Dreams vision.

'All part of sitting in that chair,' Jack said giving me a look that said he knew exactly what was going through my mind. 'Anyway, it does rather suit you.'

'Well, I feel like an absolute fraud, if you want to know the truth.'

Lucy shook her head. 'I'm going to have to book you in for a self-belief therapy session sometime, Lauren. Also, the other avatars and I have run the coming battle in our simulations, factoring in the latest number of ships in our combined fleet and in ninety-nine percent of all confrontations, we come out on top. Especially since we also have the new Hammer and Lightning torpedoes to throw into the mix. I promise you, this won't be anything like the previous conflicts.'

'You do realise that won't stop me from fretting about the one percent chance where things go catastrophically wrong for us, right?' I replied.

'Yes, once a worrier, always a worrier,' Lucy replied. 'Anyway, the last ships have now landed and we're ready to head out. And John sends his regards.'

'I still can't believe Niki considered John a security risk and insisted he stay sequestered in the hangar bay with his men,' I said.

'At least he's begrudgingly allowed John and his ships onboard, so let's take that as a win for now and hope his attitude eventually softens,' Jack said.

I nodded and returned my attention to the engine room view on the main hologram display. 'Mike, are we good to go from your side?'

Mike's hologram image held up both thumbs. 'Push the pedal to the metal whenever you're ready, Lauren.'

'Hang on a second there,' Jack said. 'As this is such a momentous occasion, maybe you should make an announcement to the entire ship, to go boldly or whatever that jazz is?' Jack said.

'Just when I thought I had you indoctrinated in all things *Star Trek*, you blow it,' I replied. 'It's the most famous split infinitive in sci-fi history, namely *to boldly go.*'

'That's you schooled then,' Lucy said with a smile. 'So how about it, Lauren, any motivational words to give the crew?'

'If I'd realised it was necessary, I would have prepared a speech.'

'Then just say it from the heart,' Lucy said. 'That strategy has rarely let you down in the past.'

'If you say so. Okay, put me on the Tannoy or whatever it is that *Tempest* has, so that the whole ship can hear me please, Lucy?'

'We can do better than that. We can broadcast a live hologram to all parts of the ship including the USSF forces in their hangar. And just for good measure, I'll also relay it to Serenity Base on Psyche 16.

'Are you deliberately trying to give me stage fright here?' I replied.

Lucy smirked as my 3D image appeared on the main hologram before us.

'Knock them dead,' Jack said as he squeezed my shoulder before stepping well out of shot.

A fluttery feeling filled my chest as I took a deep breath. 'This is Commander Lauren Stelleck and I'd like your attention for a moment,' I said, my voice slightly amplified and appearing to come directly from my very own holographic selfie.

Every single person on the bridge turned their attention towards my image now floating before them as Jack gave me an encouraging look.

I cleared my throat desperately trying to gather my thoughts.

'After all these years of effort and preparation, we are finally ready to take the fight to the Kimprak. In a moment we'll be departing Earth's orbit, but I just wanted to thank each and every one of you whose combined efforts have made this day possible. Many of you have already put your lives on the line countless times and will be asked to do so again in defence of our home-world. You are the best of the best, and I am honoured to be your commander.

'As for the crews of the USSF force who will be joining us in this fight, I may not be your commander, but all those sentiments hold true for you too. So I say to you now, let us find common ground as we prepare to fight side by side in this coming war with humanity's true enemy, the Kimprak.' I took a mental breath to inject as much confidence as possible into my next sentence. 'And together, we will head out to meet a ruthless enemy that is coming to destroy everything that we love and hold dear. I promise you now, that we will do whatever it takes to beat them. Good luck to us all.'

Every single person on the bridge including Jack and Lucy began to clap. Feeling self-conscious, I nodded at them all. That feeling was considerably amplified when I saw that the screens on some of the consoles around me were relaying views from around the ship. The most excruciatingly embarrassing of them all included what had to be a hundred-metre-high version of myself that had been projected in the parkland, like some sort of colossal god from an ancient legend.

But what caught my eye most of all, was the reaction from hangar bay two where the assembled USSF flight crews had been watching my broadcast. Unlike all the other views where there were Eden people who knew me clapping and cheering, there was a very muted response from the USSF flight crews. If I was under any illusion about just how hard bridge-building was going to be between our two forces, it was being sharply underlined by what I was witnessing.

I nodded towards Lucy who, with an eye-blink this time, turned the hologram off. I slumped back into my chair as the applause rippled away and people returned their attention to their workstations.

'You see, you're a natural,' Jack said.

'I'm not so sure about that. I could do with a good strong cup of coffee though.'

'I'll have one of the drone bots rustle one up,' Lucy said.

'Thank you,' I told her. 'Did you spot the reaction of the USSF crews?'

Jack nodded. 'Yeah, not great. It would seem Hamilton's enthusiasm for this treaty doesn't fully extend through the ranks yet. But I'm sure we can win them round.'

'I certainly hope so,' I replied. 'Anyway, it's time to get this road trip to the stars underway, Lucy.'

'Okay, the nav is already programmed to set a course for Psyche 16,' she replied as she turned to the hologram. 'Mike and Jodie, time to fire up that ion drive.'

'On it,' Mike said, turning to a control panel. 'Where's that metaphorical big red button when you need it?'

'I can always have one rigged up for you, if you like,' Lucy said. 'Although, it does make me shudder that a highly sophisticated propulsion system would be reduced to a simple on-off button.'

'No, we're good, but thanks for the offer,' Mike said grinning.

'Anything for you, cutie-pie,' Lucy replied, which elicited an eye-roll from Jodie standing next to him as she operated the control panel.

'Increasing the electric field generators from the E8 to the ion drive,' Jodie said.

Mike was looking at the displays too. 'The xenon gas generator in the propulsion chamber and the ion drive is online. All systems check out here. Slaving all controls to the flight deck.'

On one of the monitors with a rear-view of *Tempest's* engine cluster, I saw a bright blue light flare into life in the middle of a large bell-shaped nozzle that was easily four klicks wide.

I glanced out the window half expecting to see Earth suddenly recede into the distance, but of course in reality, since we're talking an ion drive here, without any other visual references, it didn't appear that we were moving at all.

'Um, is it actually working?' Jack asked.

In answer, with a wave of her hand, Lucy pulled up a speed indicator overlaid in the main hologram. It was currently displaying three knots that, as we watched, ticked up to four.

'Not exactly fast, is it?' Jack quipped. 'I'm pretty sure we could walk there faster than this.'

'Give it time,' Mike replied over the hologram link. 'Thanks to the incredible power and advanced design of *Tempest's* ion drive, it will get there eventually. Even so, it will only take us three weeks to get out to Jupiter with it. Granted, that's slower than our X-craft could manage with their helical drives, but this way we'll at least be able to get *Tempest* and the USSF fleet involved in the battle too.'

'If only *Tempest* had its jump drive, then we could make that trip more or less instantly,' Lucy said with a wistful tone.

'Sadly we haven't, so this will have to do,' I said as I watched our speed indicator tick up to a nosebleed-fast ten knots. 'Anyway, congratulations you two, it looks like all your hard work has paid off.'

'It really does,' Jodie's hologram replied. 'We'll finish up here and then head off for a well-earned celebratory sleep. We're both wiped out.'

'You deserve it and make sure you leave the "do not disturb" sign on your door,' I replied.

Mike snorted. 'You better believe it.'

'Okay, catch you on the other side of some serious R&R.' I pressed a button on my chair and their hologram faded away.

'Right, things to do and people to bother,' Lucy said. She turned and headed over to a group of avatars and engineers who were monitoring the ion engine's readouts.

I stood and walked over to the window to gaze out at Earth. It was, as ever, an endlessly changing magical view that would never grow old.

'Beautiful, isn't it?' Jack said as he joined me.

'Oh, it's most certainly that and more,' I replied. 'And certainly worth putting all our lives on the line for.'

Jack cast me a sideways look and without saying anything, hooked an arm around me and drew me in a little closer. Sometimes there really wasn't a need for words. We continued to gaze out at Earth in silence as we imperceptibly began moving away from it.

CHAPTER SEVENTEEN

'WHAT DO you mean I can't lead the exercise with the USSF onboard *Ariel?*' I said shooting Niki a challenging look across the meeting room table three days after we'd departed Earth's orbit.

'I mean, commanders shouldn't be on the front line because they're exposing themselves to unnecessary risk,' Niki replied. 'That's something you simply can't do when all of our fleet will be looking to you for leadership. And before you say anything else, this is something that Troy also understands, and as much as he dislikes it, will also be doing something similar with the Sol fleet.'

'In other words, you've already browbeaten him into it,' I said.

'Actually, I didn't have to. He's an experienced soldier and understands how important it is to protect the command structure during any battle.'

I looked over at Jack, Mike, Lucy, Erin, and Ruby. 'And you agree with this too?'

'I'm afraid it does make sense,' Erin said.

Ruby nodded. 'I don't much like it either, Lauren, but Niki's right. But even if *Ariel* isn't involved, Erin and I can still get our hands dirty.'

Erin nodded. 'I can take over commanding the squadron of Wolfpack drones and Ruby can cover the torpedo fleet that isn't under the direct control of our X-craft.'

I fixed my gaze on Mike. 'And where do you stand on this?'

He sighed. 'Lauren, you may not want to hear this, but you are way too important to lose in battle.'

'Before you ask,' Lucy piped up, 'I'd rather have you onboard *Tempest* with me. For all we know this ship may be pulled into the frontline fight and if that happens your place is absolutely in the captain's chair of this starship.'

My gaze pivoted to Jack. 'And how about you?'

'You can probably guess, so there really isn't any need to ask.'

I ground my teeth together. Of course Jack would support the others, because anything that made that vision of the future that we'd glimpsed less likely would always get his vote. The problem was that if things carried on like this, there was a real danger that it could open a rift between us where we were pulling in separate directions.

I fixed him with a hard stare. 'So you really expect me to let others take all the risks whilst I sit on my arse in this far too comfortable chair, is that it?'

'Trust me, it won't be anything like that,' Jack said. 'You know full well that Battle Command has been patched into the Citadel. You can be as involved as you have been in any previous conflict, with the notable exception that you won't be onboard *Ariel*.'

'So, if I were to put it to a vote, basically you're all telling me that I would lose?'

No one said a word, and with the exception of Niki and Lucy, they wouldn't meet my gaze either.

'What if I made it an order?'

'I'd prefer that you didn't,' Niki said, way too calmly.

A bubble of frustration rose inside me and suddenly I wanted to be anywhere but here. As I stood up, Jack reached for my arm but I shook him off. 'No offence, but I just need to go and clear my head. Sorry.'

He nodded and let go of my arm.

Painfully aware of everyone's eyes on me, I headed out of the meeting room to try and cool down.

I had been wandering fairly aimlessly for a good hour through *Tempest's* corridors and rooms trying to cool my heels. To say I felt embarrassed by my juvenile reaction in the meeting would have been a serious understatement. But what I hadn't readily been able to admit to the others was that, more than anything else, the idea of sending everyone else into battle whilst I stayed safe onboard the starship, filled me with an utter sense of dread. At least when my own life was on the line too, it made sending others into harm's way a lot easier to stomach. The thought of staying behind made me feel like a hypocrite.

I was pulled out of the churn of my thoughts by the sound of Ruby's voice coming from round the corner.

'You damned cheat, Alex!' she shouted. 'I'm so calling you out on that!'

Thinking that something was about to kick-off, I quickened my pace and turned the corner to see the last thing that I was expecting.

Ruby was sitting at a crate with a set of playing cards on it next to the transparent blast door to hangar bay two. Four Tin Heads were standing guard either side of it, along with a couple of security guards shaking their heads at her.

But far from the fury I'd been expecting to encounter, she was now laughing her head off and the reason why wasn't hard to spot.

On the other side of the krine blast door, one of the USSF marines was currently mooning her with his naked bum pressed against the krine glass on the other side. Ruby spotted me approaching and quickly banged her palm on the glass. The man turned round and seeing me, quickly hauled up his trousers, much to the amusement of the small group of USSF crew who'd gathered round to watch.

Ruby quickly stood and of all things, snapped me a salute. 'Ah, sorry about that, Commander.'

I gestured towards the guy smirking at her on the other side of the transparent door. 'Would you like to explain to me exactly what's going on here, Ruby?'

She gestured towards a similarly set up crate on the other side of the glass where the pilot had obviously been sitting a moment before, and had a similar stack of playing cards on top of it. But rather than a game of poker, these cards appeared to have weapons on them.

'I was playing Weapon Top Trumps with my old mate Bob here, an ex-special forces guy that I used to hang out with back in the day. He's a good guy, but a bit of an arse, as you can see.'

I tried to suppress a smirk. 'Quite literally.'

She snorted. 'Yeah. Anyway, we made this game up back in the day, creating our own cards with all the stats for different weapons on them,' Ruby continued. 'But Bob used to cheat and he cheated now. Bastard.' She cast an amused look at Bob who was now making a heart-shape with his hands. 'Anyway, I'll pack these away.'

I looked at her and then at the group of men on the other side of the glass who looked relaxed and were chatting to each other.

Even our own security guards seemed quite amused by what had just happened.

'No, you're good. Carry on as you are, Ruby. We need to build some bridges and that's exactly what you're doing right here.'

'In that case, it's time for a rematch.' She knocked on the glass and pointed down at the card pack.

Bob nodded, patted his mates on the back, and sat back down at his crate and started to shuffle his cards.

The one unexpected consequence of that little interaction was that, as I headed away, I felt a lot lighter than when I'd first rounded the corner.

Of all the people that I might have imagined acting as an ambassador between us and the USSF people, I would have put Ruby near the bottom of that list. But in a situation like this, soldiers were more likely to respect someone that they had served with it. And maybe, just by playing some sort of weapon geek game, arses and all, Ruby had done more to thaw relations between our two forces than anyone else had in the short time that the USSF crews had been onboard.

By leading by example and just being her, Ruby had even taken the edge off my own frustration about being stuck onboard *Tempest* during the coming battle. I needed to think more big picture, be the commander that people needed me to be, and keep my emotions out of it. And in that spirit, I had a good idea about what we could do next to build on what Ruby had started here.

I held my watch up and selected an icon. A moment later Lucy's face was peering out at me from it.

'Are you okay, Lauren?' she asked me with genuine concern.

'Yes, I've got over myself, if that's what you mean. Anyway, I want to bring forward that joint training plan. Would it be possible to get it organised for later today?'

'That shouldn't be a problem and probably a good idea anyway, to do it sooner rather than later, whilst we're still in the early days of acceleration. We also already have about eleven hundred Wolfpack drones that can stand in for the Kimprak.'

'Then let's do it,' I replied. 'And let's also see if we can't thaw things out a bit between our two sides.'

CHAPTER EIGHTEEN

I SAT in the captain's chair as the Citadel buzzed with conversations among people, and avatars worked with each other at their consoles. Jack had been true to his word and was sticking to my side. He was absorbed in his console looking at all the database entries about the finds he'd made with Poseidon during their expedition. Mike was at one of the engineering stations that had been fully linked into the engine room now that the ion engine was up and running, but Jodie was down there keeping an eye on it just in case.

The band reunion was complete with Ruby seated off to one side, a hologram in front of her with tactical info for the torpedoes, whilst Erin was next to her controlling the enemy fleet, AKA the eleven hundred and forty-three Wolfpack drones that would be standing in for them. Their laser strength had been dialled down so they wouldn't do any actually damage, but the hits would still be registered.

The one key person who was missing, who strictly speaking should have been there was John, the irony being that he'd insisted on being onboard his own ship. He'd argued that only one of us needed to be on the bridge during the training exercise and it was useful to see the battle from a first-hand perspective to help us learn from anything that didn't go as well as planned.

Niki had raised his eyebrows at that during the pre-training briefing session and had made a point of looking anywhere but at me, as John had then said, '*I prefer to lead from the front line in a battle.*' The irony wasn't lost on me, especially when our head of security didn't launch into the extended lecture that I'd received. Yes, it seemed it was one rule for Commander Hamilton and another for me and Troy.

We were, at last, approaching the end of what had become a full-on training exercise but which, so far, had proved to be a resounding success.

I'd ordered the Astra TR-3Bs and our Pangolins to form into a perfect square formation but had to suppress a surge of jealousy when I spotted John's ship among the lead vessels. Behind them had been our second line of X103s and the laser variant of the Astras to mop up any simulated Kimprak who got through our first line of defence.

Erin had begun her simulated Kimprak attack run with over a thousand Wolfpack drones. But despite everything she'd tried, and she'd tried her very best, the combination of the USSF and Earth fleet had proved to be a deadly combination, especially when Ruby had thrown our new torpedoes into the mix.

But the unexpected star of the simulated battle had been Don and his new ship. He'd called it *Sriracha,* and much to everyone's amusement, we'd learned he'd been inspired by the hot chilli sauce he loved with the same name. He and his crew had continued to kick arse throughout the battle, and *Sriracha's* particle beam fire and gauss gun accelerated torpedoes had been highly effective at dealing with the enemy.

Much to my relief, it turned out that our combined fleet was good, really good, and poured fire at the Wolfpacks, as Erin tried to keep her handful of drones left well out of range. Now she was coming for an all-in, desperate attack run with her Wolfpack, whose numbers were cut from a thousand to just over sixty-five.

'Do you fancy trying the Battle Command control interface update for the last part of the training exercise, Lauren?' Lucy said.

'It will be as good a test as any,' I said, intrigued to see whether it was as effective as Lucy promised me it would be.

I stepped into the hologram and immediately the control windows moved to the side and tracked with me as I moved through it. I headed towards *Tempest* first and moved my fingers towards it and then felt a solid surface under my fingers as they touched the 3D render of our ship. I couldn't help but grin.

'Okay, that is ridiculously impressive, Lucy,' I said.

'Oh, that's not even the best part,' she replied. 'Try selecting any of the ships in the fleet and see what happens.'

I did as instructed, standing just to the side of the USSF fleet and tried the control function that Lucy had told me about beforehand. With a finger raised in the air on each hand I drew them apart and immediately the view zoomed in on what I was looking at, thanks to some eye-tracking software now built into the system.

'Now that looks very cool,' Jack said.

I glanced over my shoulder and grinned at him before returning my attention to the second phalanx of torpedoes launched by Ruby in the holographic display. They were speeding straight towards the Wolfpack drones marked with grey markers and then detonated a short distance ahead of them. Almost instantly, a vast cloud of simulated shrapnel exploded from the torpedoes and raced towards the Wolfpack. Dozens of Erin's drones winked out of existence on the simulated attack before she could do anything.

'Like shooting fish in a barrel,' Ruby said as she cracked her knuckles.

'You're certainly not making it easy for me,' Erin muttered as ten of her drones came back online after an EM pulse from a barrage of Lightning missiles. Seizing her opportunity, she immediately powered up the Wolfpack drones to catch up with the thirty that had already made it unscathed through the barrage.'

'That's the general idea,' I said not being able to suppress a smile myself.

'And your day is about to get a lot worse, Erin,' Lucy said. 'Railgun barrage opening up now from our Pangolins and TR-3B ships.'

Almost in unison, a swarm of green points appeared from the line of our lead ships, racing forward. I drank my third mug of coffee during the long, eight-minute wait, underlining just how vast the distances were between the two opposing forces.

'How are you feeling not being out there?' Jack asked me during the lull.

'Much better than I expected. I really do have a clear overview of what's going on.'

'So you don't miss being on the front line, then?'

'I didn't say that, but I sort of see Niki's point now.'

'You have noticed where our head of security's ship is, right?'

I raised my eyebrows at him. 'Yes, *Thor* is at the front of our X-craft fleet. Yet again, talk about one rule for him and another for me.'

'That's the way he obviously rolls,' Jack said, his smile widening.

'Heads up,' Lucy said coming over to us. 'Our railgun rounds are about to reach the Wolfpack that's still powering towards us at maximum speed.'

'Then let's go and watch the final act,' I said as I headed back down the steps towards the hologram.

I stepped back into it to watch as our railgun rounds raced towards the last fifty Wolfpack drones.

Once again, Erin was doing everything in her power to make this a difficult fight for us.

Multiple explosions began to rip through the Wolfpack drones, taking out at least half of them in the blink of an eye.

'Booyah!' Ruby said as she punched the air, which elicited a frown from Erin as her remaining Wolfpack drones sped past the Pangolins and TR-3B railgun ships that had moved aside, pouring fresh fire at the drones and whittling the enemy numbers down even more.

As the last twenty surviving drones raced away from them, my gaze skimmed down the list of tactical options floating next to me in the hologram.

'Okay, releasing the Kimprak ball bearing drones so let's see how you deal with those,' Erin said with more than a hint of frustration in her voice.

Then, the three remaining Wolfpack drones unloaded at least a thousand little canisters that Jodie had designed to mimic the Kimprak swarm-bots.

If the firefight had been intense before, it was nothing compared to what was displayed by the Battle Command system now. Tracer fire seemed to fill the hologram, and then to really add to the fun, *Tempest's* point defence system finally opened up after some of the canisters made it past the combined might of our ships.

The space between *Tempest* and the canisters tumbling towards it was filled with a rainstorm of violet, high-powered laser fire that scythed through the enemy's ranks.

My gaze kept flicking to the tactical summary on Battle Command that had been wired into the main hologram display, as the Kimprak bots were quickly annihilated by our starship's formidable point defence grid.

I was just thinking how good this training exercise was going to be for morale, when the comm suddenly kicked in on the bridge.

'Mayday, mayday, we've had a collision,' Hamilton's voice said over the radio link. 'The other TR-3B should be able to make its way back to the hangar, but we're had injuries and are venting plasma from our drive and our escape pods are offline. We're spiralling towards *Tempest* for an almost certain impact in less than three minutes.'

'Bloody hell,' I said. 'We'll do whatever we can to rescue you, John. Just hang in there.'

'Roger that. Out.'

I turned to Lucy. 'Cancel the training practise immediately and show me John's ship.'

She nodded and the view zoomed in on the hologram. One TR-3B was slowly moving away from the other, a large gash in its hull. But it was the other ship, *Astra,* that was of far greater concern. Most of the bottom section of the craft had been sliced clean off, and just like he'd told us, plasma was venting straight into space.

'Lucy, can you get *Tempest* out of its way? They'll all be killed if they slam into us.'

'Not in time. This ship doesn't exactly have a tight turning radius and the emergency manoeuvring thrusters will take too much time. Normally, I'd suggest a tractor beam to catch it, but that's still being rebuilt.'

Before I could reply I spotted the silver-finned *Sriracha* appear in the display, rapidly moving into position alongside the stricken, tumbling TR-3B.

'Did someone around here need a tow,' Don's voice said over the comm channel.

On the hologram, we all saw a shimmering lance of energy

reach out from his ship and latch onto the TR-3B. Within moments it began to stabilise.

'Is that a tractor beam, Don?' I asked.

'Damned right it is. *Tempest's* tractor beam may be offline, but it turns out it's a standard fitting for Angelus warships.'

'Now you tell us,' I replied as my heart lifted as the tumbling of Hamilton's TR-3B gradually slowed to a stop.

'Now to get your ship back safely onboard *Tempest*, Commander Hamilton,' Don said.

'My crew and I owe you a debt of gratitude, son,' John replied over the link.

'Well, for the record, it was very much a joint effort by the crew, but if you want to single anyone out for your rescue, you should probably thank Harry here. He's a member of the Earth fleet who was operating the controls and managed to grab you like a catcher in a baseball game.'

'Then I'll buy him, and the rest of you, a drink when I see you, which unfortunately may have to wait. It seems I have quite the chest wound that's going to need urgent attention.'

I looked at Jack.

'How bad is it, Commander?' he said.

'I'll live, but I'm going to be out of action for a while.'

'Okay, we'll meet you with a medibot when you land and take you straight to surgery,' Jack replied. 'Lucy, can you assist me?'

'Of course,' she replied. 'I'm prepping medical bay three now.'

'Okay, John, just take it easy, we've got you covered,' I said.

'Thank you, Lauren, I will leave it to you to bring my fleet in and debrief them. Out.'

As Lucy and Jack headed for the door I called out to them. 'Can I help?'

Jack turned. 'No, we've got it covered. Your priority will be reassuring the USSF pilots that their commander is going to be alright.'

'When they hear that John's been injured it's going to go down like a lead balloon,' Mike said shaking his head,

'It could have been a lot worse if it hadn't been for Don's swift actions,' Erin said. 'I realise he may technically be USSF, but a lot of the crew on the *Sriracha* are ours and that will count for a lot. You were looking to build bridges, and I don't think that gets much bigger than saving the life of the person who's in charge of their fleet, Lauren.'

'Yes, you may have a point there,' I replied.

But it wasn't until I headed back into the hologram that the implications began to fully sink in. Although this could have easily ended in tragedy, it hadn't. And maybe, just maybe, along with the small examples like Ruby seeing the USSF guys as people rather than an enemy combined with this incident, perhaps we really did have a chance to thaw things out between our two forces. I also had an idea about how to accelerate that, but Niki wasn't going to like it one little bit.

CHAPTER NINETEEN

I stood in the middle of the holographic display examining the 3D map, drinking a Lapsang Souchong tea out of a *SpaceX*-themed mug. According to a green dotted line marking our progress towards Psyche 16, where we'd be loading up with the Sol fleet, we were already two-thirds of the way there.

I spotted Niki coming through the doorway and instinctively looked for somewhere to hide but it was too late because he was already striding towards me.

He gave me a decidedly frosty look as he approached. 'Lauren, I need a word.'

'Yes, I thought you might.'

'When exactly were you going to tell me that you had authorised the transfer of USSF personnel from hanger bay two into the habitation zone to live alongside our people?'

'Ah yes, that must have slipped my mind.'

He glowered at me. 'The hell it did. You deliberately made sure I was kept out of the loop until it was too late for me to do anything about it, didn't you?'

I squirmed inside, but forced my spine to remain ram-rod straight.

'"Deliberately" is a bit of a strong word, more like an active strategy to avoid conflict, but it's done now, Niki. Besides, even you have to admit there has been a major thawing between our two forces. The training exercises have continued to build bridges. Working together was one thing, living and even playing together was the next natural step. If you want to get rid of any lingering suspicion between our two forces, I can't think of any better way but for them to move into the habitation zone.'

Niki gave me a piercing look. 'And what about the security issues, including the possibility of an attempted mutiny where they try to seize control of *Tempest*?'

Ruby, who'd obviously been earwigging our conversation, turned from one of the tactical displays that she'd been studying. 'Oh, come on, Niki! You know we have that one more than covered. *Tempest's* built-in security systems are the stuff of your wet dreams. One of the USSF pilots wouldn't be able to fart without you knowing about it.'

He gave her a stony look and then the hint of a smile curled the corner of his mouth. 'True, but I want it on record that I'm really not happy, Lauren.'

'Duly noted, and my apologies for not keeping you in the loop.'

'Right.' He gave me a headshake as he walked away.

Ruby raised her eyebrows at me. 'Remind me who's in charge here?'

'Yes, once again Niki manages to make me feel like the equivalent of a naughty child being told off by their dad.'

'Well, don't let him get to you because he's wrong on this one,' Ruby said. 'This is absolutely the right call, Lauren. If you want to get rid of the "us versus them" vibe, this is the best way to go about it. Well that, and getting Leroy to open a bar onboard *Tempest*.'

I laughed. 'I'll talk to him about franchising the Rock Garden and opening another branch up here.'

'Now that would make for a lot of happy campers,' Ruby replied grinning.

Niki passed Jack on the way out who made a beeline straight for me.

'Hey, you're a sight for sore eyes,' I said. 'So, how's the latest expedition going?'

'Really well, actually. Poseidon and I have pretty much finished mapping the whole interior of *Tempest*, although there are a few corners we may have missed. We've uploaded everything we've found to help rebuild *Tempest's* databases.'

'So, did you discover any more shipyards on your travels?' Ruby asked with a hopeful expression.

'Sadly no, although we did discover a garage of funky-looking vehicles for planetary use.'

'Nice,' she said giving Jack a fist bump.

'So, have I missed anything whilst I've been away?' Jack asked.

'John has been making a great recovery after the reconstruction of his crushed rib cage by the medical nanobots and is demanding to be allowed to return to duty,' I replied.

'Always a good sign,' Jack said.

'Exactly. Oh, and I seemed to have pissed Niki off by moving the USSF crew into the habitation chamber.'

'Yes, I saw the look on his face as he passed me. But for what it's worth, I think it was a good call, Lauren. I even saw some evidence on the way here, a USSF pilot had busted out a frisbee and was playing with a group of Niki's security guards in the park.'

'See, just like I said, it was the right call,' Ruby said.

I was just enjoying my moment of relief that my instinct had been right, when Lucy hurried over from one of the computer consoles that she'd been working at with a couple of the other avatars. The look on her face told me that my day was about to take a sharp turn for the worse.

'Lauren, we've just heard back from one of the Guardian probes trailing the Kimprak asteroid,' she said. 'It's now drawn close enough for a more detailed sensor scan and we may have a serious problem.'

'How big a problem?' I asked.

'Potentially an enormous one. Let me show you why.' She headed into the hologram and beckoned us to join her.

With a wave of her hand, the view was transformed and suddenly we were standing in a large constellation of asteroids. According to the scale markers around each of them, some were tens of metres across, but others were easily several klicks wide, some monsters among them were even bigger.

'That looks like part of the Oort Cloud,' I said, peering at them. 'But that can't be right because that's way beyond the edges of the solar system.'

'I wish they were there, because that's a long way out. Unfortunately, that particular swarm of rocks is heading towards Jupiter right now and let me show you why exactly.' With another wave of her hand, the view zoomed into the middle of the rock constellation towards a giant cigar-shaped asteroid.

Jack stared at it. 'Is that Kimprak mothership?'

'Correct, and as you can now see it appears it's not coming for Earth alone.'

I stared at Lucy. 'But how can this even be possible, Lucy?'

'Let me show you.'

With another wave of her hand, the view zoomed in on the mother ship. Just visible in the hologram were fine lines radiating out from it, towards the rocks surrounding it. Then Lucy zoomed the view in again on one of the lines for a tight close-up.

It was at that moment that everything fell into place because I could see the chain was actually made out of thousands of Kimprak who were partly unfurled into their familiar trilobite-like form, their bodies hooked together. Then the view pulled all the way back out as the chains were highlighted with green to make them easily visible, the spiderweb of lines connecting the mothership to each and every one of the asteroids around it.

'You're saying that damned thing is towing all those?' Jack asked.

'Exactly,' Lucy replied.

I switched my attention back to the mothership for a closer look. According to the digital scale being displayed next to the mothership, it indicated that it was over fifty klicks long. That was bigger than *Tempest* that stood at thirty-five. By any measure, not even counting the asteroids our opponents had, it was a vast ship.

The massive solar sail that propelled this monster of a craft from Alpha Centauri to our own solar system, appeared to have been folded in upon itself by the tethers that connected it to the main body of the asteroid. The gossamer silver sail was slowly being drawn into a massive tunnel that ran through the length of the asteroid. When I squatted by the tunnel for a closer look I could actually see the large articulated lens that had been used to refocus the laser beam that had been fired from a megastructure that the Kimprak had left behind on the planet it had harvested back in the Alpha Centauri system to power their ship's solar sail. Small squat structures lined the outside of the asteroid. I could also see a series of large holes ringing the mouth of the asteroid.

'What are those?' I asked pointing to them.

'Our guess is that they're the mass drivers that they've been firing those Kimprak-infected meteoroids at us with,' Lucy said.

Jack was already looking haunted and kept casting me sideways looks whenever he thought I wasn't looking. And I knew why. The asteroid ship that we were seeing now, looked exactly like the version we'd both seen in the Hall of Dreams.

'Is this a live view of the ship?' I asked trying to ignore him and the fact this was another step towards making that prediction even more likely.

'Yes, thanks to the quantum entanglement that our QEC radio system uses, this is very much a real-time view,' Lucy replied. 'Also, thanks to that, there should be no danger that the Kimprak can listen in to our communications and tipping them off that we even know that they're here. Needless to say, the Guardian tracking it is in full stealth mode.'

My mind was racing, trying to process how this was going to change things as I stood up to look at the asteroids all around the mothership.

'I'm guessing that the Kimprak have infected these other asteroids as well?'

'Correct, and based on what the activity the Guardian has picked up, we're probably looking at an invasion force of a hundred million Kimprak,' Lucy replied.

I gawped at her, barely able to mentally process what she had just said.

'You mean we're going to be facing a force a thousand times greater than we were expecting to take on?' Jack said underlining the point for me.

'That's exactly what I'm saying,' Lucy replied, her expression grim.

'But are we anywhere near equipped with enough ships and drones to take on a fight that big, even with *Tempest*?' Jack asked.

Lucy spread her hands wide. 'I have no idea, Jack, but this obviously isn't good news in any way.'

'Okay, then we need to hold an urgent meeting with Alice,

Troy, and John. Lucy, also ask Mike and Jodie to attend. We're going to have to brainstorm this to see what, if anything, we can do to counter this.'

She gave me a grim look and nodded. 'Leave it to me, Lauren.'

The glass walls of the briefing room in the Citadel had been turned opaque to give us some privacy for the crisis meeting. Lucy had already assured me that no one would hear anything that we going to be saying on the other side of the glass. If the outlook looked as bad as I thought it did, I didn't want word getting out to the rest of the crew just yet and endangering morale, especially as we'd worked so hard at raising it.

Until now, with everything that we had in our fleet, including the Wolfpack drones that were proving surprisingly effective in the training exercises, there had been an unspoken, increasing confidence among everyone that we really could win this. Now, just like that, all that optimism had been swept away and I could see it reflected in everyone's faces

John joined us looking surprisingly good considering the medical ordeal he'd just been through. Niki was also in attendance, because as far as I was concerned, the more minds to brainstorm this the better. But Lucy wasn't doing anything to disguise just how worried she was and had even taken to the very human action of chewing her lip. Alice and Troy looked suitably grim-faced on their video hologram screens that were currently floating at the far end of the table. There was no question that everyone gathered realised just how catastrophic this news was.

'Okay, we'd better get to it,' I said. 'There's no way to dress this up, other than say it exactly as it is. The odds have suddenly shifted heavily against us winning this war, so I've had Lucy gather us together to discuss if there is anything we can do to change that outcome.'

John sat up and steepled his fingers on the table. 'There's no question that our fleet is going to be facing overwhelming odds, but military conflicts are littered with examples of where a far smaller force defeated a larger army.'

Niki gave him a thoughtful look and nodded. 'The Battle of Thermopylae springs to mind. That's the battle the movie *The 300* is based on. Legend has it, the Spartans had just three hundred men who fought the entire Persian army of a million to a standstill for seven days. Mind you, scholars dispute those numbers now and think the Persian army was actually closer to a hundred and fifty thousand.'

'*The 300* is a great movie and everything, but weren't all the Spartans killed in it?' Mike asked.

'They were, which makes it maybe not the best example,' Jack replied. 'But it also shows how effective a far smaller force can be when taking on a much larger one.'

'But if memory serves me correctly, wasn't geography on their side?' I said.

John nodded. 'Yes, the Spartans took up a defensive position in a very narrow pass that the Persian Army was forced to march through. That meant they could never bring their full might to bear.'

'The Spartan's raw courage aside, that was definitely a major factor,' Niki replied.

'Unfortunately for us, that example doesn't work well here when we're talking about a battle taking place in space,' Alice said.

'There is one thing on our side here, they're all in one place. That concentrates them as a target,' Troy said from his video link. 'Surely, we can use that to our tactical advantage?'

'You mean like firing a bunch of nukes at them?' Jack asked.

'That could work to an extent, but there's one major problem there,' Lucy said. 'We've already detected that some of the chains connected to the outer asteroids in the swarm have detached. They have small thrusters that are slowly manoeuvring them away from the rest of the constellation of asteroids. As the Kimprak prepare for the invasion, it seems that they're aware that they present a bunched-up target for us to strike against, so are taking steps to spread out their invasion force accordingly.'

Niki looked thoughtful and then clicked his fingers. 'Okay, I have another historical reference that might be useful. In 1588 there was a famous naval battle, one that I've war-gamed with you, Lauren.'

My eyes widened. 'You're talking about the English defeating the Spanish Armada, aren't you?'

'I am indeed. Sir Francis Drake famously used fireships packed with combustible materials and set them loose between the Spanish Armada. Their ships were at anchor and the blazing fireships managed to create absolute havoc and the Spanish fleet was forced to cut their anchors to escape. Then just to make matters even worse for the Spanish, a storm blew in wrecking many of their anchorless ships along the Scottish and Northern Ireland coasts. So here's my idea, I was wondering whether we could use torpedoes equipped with nuclear warheads to act as the equivalent of Drake's fireships.'

My pulse quickened. 'Bloody hell, Niki, that could actually work.'

Lucy was now nodding. 'That could certainly do a lot of damage, guys, and cut the Kimprak down to a more manageable number. Unfortunately, the Kimprak-infected asteroids won't be bunched up for much longer based on the intelligence that the Guardian has been able to gather and *Tempest* is simply too far away to reach them in time.'

'But we can't just sit here and do nothing,' Troy said.

'I'm afraid you heard Lucy, there's no way we can reach them in time,' John said.

'Correction, *Tempest* might not be able to reach the mothership by then, but the Sol fleets Pangolins with their helical drives could, if we launched them now.'

'That's just not an option as you haven't got enough ships to defeat them by yourselves,' I said.

Troy held my gaze. 'We won't know that for sure unless we try, Lauren.'

'No, I'm sorry, as tempting as that idea is we need alternative strategies. We both know that you would be throwing away the lives of your fleet if you attempted it.'

Troy didn't respond.

It was Alice who stepped in to fill in the silence. 'Look, there're no easy answers here. Lucy, I assume you'll be running simulations of potential strategies through the Battle Command Centre?'

'Some of the other avatars have that underway, but I can already tell you that it doesn't look promising.'

'Then, as I feared, we need to start looking at contingency plans,' Alice replied.

'What exactly do you mean by that?' I asked.

'I mean, what we're going to do if we're defeated by the Kimprak. Lucy, just how many people could *Tempest* comfortably support for a prolonged space flight?'

'Around twenty-thousand, although most would have to travel in suspended animation within E8,' Lucy replied.

'Hang on, you're not saying what I think you're saying, are you, about turning *Tempest* into some sort of ark ship?' I asked.

'That's exactly what I'm saying,' Alice replied. 'Anyone working in Eden would be eligible if they wanted to go and they could even bring their families with them. John, you could likewise coordinate with the US government and ideally other nations around the world to nominate individuals who could be put forward to travel onboard *Tempest* out to the nearest habitable M-class planet.'

We all stared at her, our combined shock tangible as a charge in the air.

'Bloody hell, Alice, you're talking about this as though we've already lost,' I said.

'I didn't say that, but what I am saying, is that the time has come to look at fallback plans where we at least can take some of the best and brightest of our species and start over again on a new planet somewhere the Kimprak can never reach us.'

A thousand arguments roared through my mind at the same time, but the shock of what Alice was suggesting made it impossible for me to even begin to vocalise them all.

'Does that mean I should be factoring in keeping *Tempest* out of the main battle during any future simulations?' Lucy said.

Unfortunately, it was John who found his voice before I could. 'If you're seriously suggesting that *Tempest* may eventually be used as a lifeboat, then that makes sense.'

I gawped at him. 'It sounds like you agree with Alice on this?'

'I'm a pragmatist, Lauren. Just because we don't want something to happen doesn't mean that we shouldn't factor it into our planning.'

'Oh, bloody hell. And what about you, Troy?'

'I'm as unhappy as you are, Lauren. Even if *Tempest* doesn't have her full weapons compliment, I think it would be a serious tactical mistake to leave her out of this fight...' His words trailed away as he seemed to become lost in his thoughts and he stared past the camera.

I could feel my anger flaring. 'At least one person round here is talking sense,' I said. 'Look, we're in danger of throwing the baby out with the bathwater here. At the very least, we should include *Tempest* in some of the simulation scenarios.'

Alice nodded. 'You make a strong point, Lauren. Lucy, could you do that?'

'Of course, and for what it's worth, I think that's the best compromise here,' she said meeting my gaze.

I felt the hard ball that was filling my chest beginning to soften a fraction. 'Thank you.'

'Then, unless anyone else has any ideas, I suggest we all go and sleep on it and see if we can come up with some fresh ones,' Alice said. 'Is everyone happy to reconvene this meeting tomorrow?'

We all nodded, but the shock was still visible across many of the faces around me and I couldn't help but notice that Troy possibly looked the most haunted of all. A moment later his and Alice's holograms faded away as the meeting room walls turned transparent again. As the meeting broke up Lucy and John began out of the door onto the flight deck, heads bent together in conversation.

I gazed at Jack, Mike, and Jodie who were still sitting with me.

'I can't believe they're seriously considering giving up,' I said, shaking my head.

'Me neither,' Mike said.

Jack took my hand in his. 'I think that goes for all of us. So, who's up for sharing a drink or three?'

'God, yes,' I said. 'Time to break out that twenty-year-old bottle of Highland Park I've been hanging onto.'

'Actually, if you could excuse me, there is a germ of an idea I'd like to explore,' Jodie said.

'Something that could help our current predicament?' I asked.

'Possibly,' Jodie said. 'There's something that I've been looking into that I need to throw some more time at.'

'Do you need any help?' Mike asked.

'I could certainly do with the moral support. I suspect it's going to be a long night.'

'Then I'll be right by your side,' Mike replied.

They both nodded at Jack and me, then disappeared out of the door.

'We'll find a way, Lauren, because we have to,' Jack said when they were gone.

'I'm not so sure there is a way. We're facing overwhelming odds and I have a really bad feeling about it.'

'Because of that Hall of Dreams prediction?'

'Maybe. All I know is that what we've just learnt has made the worse possible outcome far more likely, but also that we could lose Earth anyway.'

Jack didn't say a word, because what could anyone really say? Instead, he drew me into a tight hug. I hung onto him as though he might evaporate as a hundred dark thoughts spun through my mind.

CHAPTER TWENTY

A WEEK LATER, I was woken from my bed by the bleeping of my watch. Blearily, I raised Jack's arm that had been draped over me so I could accept the incoming call from Lucy.

'Lauren, you need to get to the Citadel right now.'

Her urgent tone made any lingering grogginess instantly evaporate.

'Why, what's wrong?'

'It seems that Troy has taken matters into his own hands and the Sol fleet of Pangolins departed Psyche 16 several days ago.'

A chill instantly filled me as Jack began to surface from sleep, his eyes blinking open.

'You're not saying he's launched Sol fleet to take on the Kimprak by themselves?'

'I'm afraid that's exactly what I'm saying,' she said. 'He deliberately had his ships' transponders turned off so we wouldn't know what he was up to. He'll be in range of launching an assault within the next twenty minutes.'

'Oh, shit. I'm on my way, Lucy.' I jumped out of bed and started pulling my clothes on. 'Have Battle Command powered up and open a comm channel directly to Troy. I'm going to try and talk him down off the ledge before it's too late.'

Jack was wide awake now and, hearing my conversation, was rapidly getting dressed too.

'Okay, I'll get back to you as soon as I have Troy on the line,' Lucy said.

As the watch face went dark, I glanced over at Jack as I pulled on my shoes. 'I can't believe Troy would do something so reckless. He's basically going to throw away the lives of most of Sol fleet by attempting this.'

Jack pulled on his t-shirt and frowned at me. 'Okay, this is certainly him going rogue on us, but as to the second part, let's hear what he has to say for himself before we start judging him. I also have to say it sort of reminds me of exactly the sort of thing that a certain woman might come up with, rushing in with a *seat of her pants* plan if she believed it was for the greater good.'

'You're seriously saying this is the sort of thing I'd do in his situation, Jack?'

'A chance to save everyone else with a totally crazy, if not heroic, first-strike action against the Kimprak? 'It sounds exactly like the sort of stunt that Lauren Stelleck would pull.'

I held Jack's gaze with mine for all of three seconds before my shoulders slumped. 'Yes, I know, and you're almost certainly right. But there are absolutely no guarantees and there's so much that could go wrong.'

'I know.' Jack sighed. 'So like you said, let's just hope we can just talk him down off the ledge before it's too late.'

As we headed for the transport pod, I could see that there was a tactical argument for Troy taking this step. This was a last wildcard-gamble before it was too late. But a bigger part of me realised that if this went badly we could easily lose around forty percent of our total ships. That could make an already difficult conflict almost impossible for us to win.

Jack and I both fell silent as we boarded the pod from our docking platform and we were soon heading over the parkland.

Around us, the illuminated sky panels were turning, simulating the start of a new dawn. Far below us, a group of joggers were running along the edge of the lake and my heart squeezed at witnessing this little bit of normality onboard a starship that the Angelus had intended to be our salvation and that we were in danger of throwing away.

Jack had spotted them too. 'Good to see people starting to look so at home here,' he said.

I nodded, grateful for something to pull me out of the spiral of my thoughts. 'It would be nice to think it might be a mix of USSF pilots and our crews training together. At least that's one thing that's gone well. Despite Niki's misgivings, everyone sharing the same space has all worked out really well.'

Jack smiled. 'Who knew that treating people like human beings rather than cattle herded in one of the hangars would piss him off?'

That almost raised a smile from me, but now my thoughts were stuck firmly in the future. 'If we do end up turning *Tempest* into an ark, that parkland will turn into a massive refugee camp,' I said. 'And now that's much more likely to happen because of Troy's reckless actions.'

'And as I keep saying, let's give the guy a chance to defend himself before we hang him out to dry.'

'Okay, okay...' But inside I was seething. The problem was, part of that anger was projected at myself because Jack had hit the nail on the head. Deep down, I couldn't shake the feeling that this was exactly the sort of stunt that I would have pulled. This must be how Niki and Tom had felt about half of my missions.

Our transport pod rose into a hatch in the ceiling and the iris closed behind us. A short while later, we'd stepped out of our ride and were heading into the Citadel.

As always, the long oval-shaped flight deck was filled with people, the night crew that took over from the day-shift. Lucy was already at the forward bridge section the Citadel with a tactical map of the Battle Command system being displayed on the hologram. On it, a vast fleet of green dots indicating our ships were closing rapidly on the large constellation of rocks surrounding the Kimprak mothership.

Jack and I both took the mugs of steaming coffee from Lucy that she offered us as we approached her.

'Thanks,' I said taking a much needed long gulp to try and sharpen my mind. 'Have you managed to contact Troy yet?'

'No joy so far. Although, I'm absolutely certain he can hear us.'

'Okay, then let me try. Also, could you alert John? I think he needs to be made aware of what's happening, as this affects both of our fleets.'

'On it, and the line is now open to Troy's ship, *Falcon One*,' Lucy replied.

A blank video window appeared floating in front of the hologram of the fleet. I took another gulp of coffee, and as I began pacing round, the hologram kept track of me.

'Troy, this is Lauren. For god's sake, pick up! You've got to talk to me.'

I let a few seconds pass, during which the video window remained stubbornly blank.

I tried again. 'Troy, I know you can hear me. Please respond.'

Again there was no response.

Jack nodded towards me as he took a sip of his own coffee. 'Let me try.'

'Knock yourself out,' I replied.

Jack stepped up to the hologram. 'Okay, buddy, Jack here. This radio silence is doing no one any good. If nothing else, tell us what you're thinking.'

There was a few seconds pause and then the video feed burst into life and at last, Troy was looking out at us, his expression wary.

'As you can probably see from your tactical display, I haven't exactly got long to chat here, people,' he said.

'Then we'll skip straight past the part of you doing this without at least running it past me and the others first,' I said.

'That's because I knew exactly what you would have said, Lauren. But with all due respect to all of you, I actually put it to a vote with my crew and they volunteered to come.'

I felt some of the fire inside me drop a few degrees. 'Even though you all could be throwing your lives away, as well as severely compromising our ability to defend Earth if you lose your ships?'

Troy looked somewhere beyond the camera and nodded to someone. 'Okay, I have just two minutes left to explain the *why* before this mission kicks off. This is all based on Niki's fireship idea, Lauren. We have been running various permutations of it through our own Battle Command and have twenty-one torpedoes with nukes divided among our ships that we've been busy printing since Jodie sent us the plans for them. But here's the crucial part, we're going to launch a wave of Lightning torpedoes first, to create a massive EMP pulse. Our weapon experts have also set the nukes to maximum yield that will create an overlapping destruction zone. Based on our estimates, that should destroy everything but the asteroid ship itself.'

There was a mumbled voice in the background and he nodded again. 'Okay, I have just thirty seconds left,' Troy continued. 'Before you lay into me, the plan is for that to be as far as our engagement goes. Once the torpedoes have done their work, we'll simply turn round and head out to rendezvous with you for the final battle. You see, even a maverick commander like me isn't quite as reckless as you probably thought I was. So please, trust me when I say that I will do everything in my power to protect my crew as far as is humanly possible.'

I narrowed my gaze on him. 'So why all this secrecy? That sounds like a solid plan, one that I would have fully supported had you bothered to confide it with me?'

'Because sometimes it's time for talking and others it's time for action and this is the latter. If we'd discussed this first, you would have had to let the others know and someone somewhere would have tried to stop it. But if we get this right, it will save infinitely more lives than I'm putting on the line today. So please forgive me, and I'll see you on the other side of this. Out.' Troy reached forward and then the screen went dark.

I immediately turned towards Lucy. 'You need to get Troy back because we need to discuss the details of what happens if this first strike of his doesn't work.'

'Sorry, Lauren, I can't. They've deactivated the comms at their end. They are, however, still transmitting transponder and sensor data so we'll have a ringside seat for whatever happens. We also have a live feed from the Guardian that's still tracking the Kimprak ship.'

'You mean all we can do is watch this unfold?' Jack asked.

'That sounds like pretty much the sum of it,' John replied from behind us, having appeared at the top of the steps leading to the flight deck.

'We need to bring you up to speed with what's happening,' I said, turning to look at him.

He waved his hand at me. 'No need. Lucy briefed me during the ride here on the transport pod. Commander Troy Armstrong has decided to go rogue on us, is that about the sum of it?'

'Pretty much,' I replied. 'His intentions are good, but he shouldn't have taken this action without talking to us first.'

'Well, Lauren, I think that as my grandmother once said, god rest her soul, that there's no use crying over a pail of milk that's been kicked over by a truculent cow,' John replied. 'A court-martial, or whatever it is that you people do, can wait. The real question is, whether this strategy can actually work or not?'

'We're about to find out any moment now,' Lucy said. 'The Sol fleet just launched the first wave of Lightning missiles.'

Our attention all switched back to the Battle Command hologram as green markers for the torpedoes appeared among the ranks of the Sol fleet and began racing away towards the cluster of Kimprak-infected asteroids. Reduced to spectators, John and I began to pace.

On the hologram, we watched from every available angle as the Sol fleet's torpedoes slowly closed in on their target across the vast distances between the two forces. Thirty Lightnings led the charge, followed by the six nuclear torpedoes.

No one said a word as the tension ratcheted up. Even Lucy had become uncharacteristically quiet as no doubt the massive computing power of her AI ran through all the permutations of success or failure.

'Okay, there are finally signs that the Kimprak have spotted the torpedoes and have begun to react,' Lucy said after eight minutes had ticked past.

'What are they doing exactly?' Jack asked.

'According to the Guardian's data, the Kimprak have just severed all the tethers to the remaining asteroids closest to them and are beginning to move away from the mothership.'

'Please tell us that it's too little too late?' John asked.

'It certainly looks that way,' Lucy replied. 'It really does seem like Troy's fleet has caught the Kimprak on the hop.'

'I pray that's the case, for all our sakes,' John said.

I'd drained the last of my coffee and was onto my second cup by the time the torpedoes finally reached the asteroids.

A sense of hope was just starting to build inside me when Troy's plan started to go horribly wrong. Red markers suddenly erupted all along the flanks of the mothership and then thousands of red dots began to race outwards towards the closing torpedoes. At least a dozen seem to intercept one of the Lightnings and it blinked out of existence.

'Oh crap, is that some sort of point defence system?' Jack asked.

'I've just been analysing the Guardian's real-time data and that's exactly what it is,' Lucy said. 'Like *Sriracha's* weapon system that uses gauss guns to accelerate torpedoes, it seems the Kimprak are doing the same thing. But in their case, their payload seems to be bots literally shot out of the gauss guns like hypersonic cannonballs.'

'Oh bloody hell. Just how dangerous are those things?' I asked.

'Really dangerous, I'm afraid,' she replied. 'Here let me show you.'

A close-up 3D view of one of our Lightning torpedoes appeared in the hologram. The Kimprak were locked onto it, their mandibles already eating into its core.

'I'm afraid it's even worse than it first looks,' Lucy continued. 'According to the computer systems onboard those torpedoes, the Kimprak are attempting to hack into their systems.'

I put my hands on my head. 'You're not saying they're attempting to take control of those Lightnings, are you, Lucy?'

'That's exactly what I'm saying, and it looks like they're going after the second wave with the nukes... Wait. No. Thank goodness Troy seems to have realised what's going on and has ordered the nukes to turn round which they are doing, and... Oh shit and damnation.'

'Don't you "oh shit and damnation" us, what's happening?' Jack said.

'The Kimprak have successfully hacked past the Lightning torpedoes' firewalls and they are turning them around as well.'

'Turning them round, as in sending them back the way they came?' John asked.

'Exactly,' Lucy replied, her expression full of worry.

Where there had been green dots there were now pulsing red ones, indicating that the compromised torpedoes now belonged to our enemy. The Lightnings were beginning to race back towards the Sol fleet of Pangolins that were considerably closer than they had been when the torpedoes had first been launched.

'Shit, it's getting worse,' Lucy said. 'The mothership appears to be using large mass drivers to now launch asteroids up to ten-metres-wide straight at the Sol fleet. And you can guarantee that they're each stuffed to the gills with Kimprak passengers.'

My blood ran cold as we watched fresh Kimprak projectiles race out behind the captured torpedoes and head towards Troy's ships.

'There must be something that they're able to do,' John said.

The words had barely left his mouth when a fresh volley of torpedoes erupted from Troy's ships and sped out to meet the compromised Lightnings and the wave of small asteroids behind them.

'Sol fleet just launched a massive barrage of Hammers,' Lucy said.

I put my hands on top of my head as the tension became unbearable. Then, with blossoming explosions, the Hammer missiles detonated right in the flight path of the closing Lightnings. The captured torpedoes began to blink out on the display as each of them ran straight into the wall of expanding shrapnel. But Jodie and the Forge team had done too good a job when they'd created the torpedoes' guidance systems.

Out of the thirty Lightnings, three corkscrewed through the shrapnel, avoiding any impacts, made their way through intact and raced straight on towards the Sol fleet. I clutched my hands into fists as they detonated, a bright blue sphere expanding out of each to indicate the EM pulse radius racing towards the Pangolins.

Travelling at the speed of light, the expanding blue sphere on the hologram engulfed the Sol fleet within moments and every single ship went dark on the display as their systems were knocked out by the pulse.

Then it got even worse, because it was then that the asteroids tracking behind the torpedoes, exploded.

I suddenly found it hard to breathe as a vast swarm of red-tagged spheres erupted from the lumps of rock that our Battle Command had already identified as individual Kimprak bots. Worse still, even though their flight systems were offline, their momentum was still carrying them towards the Sol fleet.

Like a slow-motion car crash, I watched the vast Kimprak swarm sweep into the ranks of our ships and begin destroying the Sol fleet.

I was in the middle of the hologram with John and Jack now, watching up close as the alien's mechanised bots ripped into the ships' titanium hulls. Seconds after impact, they quickly began to unfurl from their armoured, ball bearing configuration and burrow into the stricken X104s.

'This is turning into a slaughter,' John said, his voice strained. 'The Sol fleet are sitting ducks after those EM pulses.'

'Not for much longer,' Lucy replied. 'The Sol fleet ships' systems are hardened against electronic attack and secondary systems are also built-in. They should be starting to come back online in the next few seconds.'

Then my heart lifted. Like a ripple, the lights came on as the ships that hadn't been infected by Kimprak bots, powered back up. They immediately began to rapidly manoeuvre, railgun and mini-gun rounds erupting from the fleet and slicing through the hordes of Kimprak bearing down on them.

But I quickly realised it was too little too late. Even as the huge combined firepower of the Sol fleet carved through the ranks of the Kimprak, our ships were quickly being overwhelmed by the sheer number of bots swarming among them. Within six heartbreaking minutes, eleven hundred-plus ships had been cut down to just over five hundred. The remaining ships skimmed around the cloud of glittering Kimprak as they devoured the X-craft, heading towards the markers for the nukes that were coasting at the edge of the battle.

Two X104s had hooked up with two of the nuke torpedoes that floated at the edges of the battle zone and had so far avoided capture. At once they began to escort them, flying either side of the cluster. Them my heart rose to my mouth as the Pangolins and the torpedoes turned and dived straight towards the swarm.

'What the hell are they doing?' I asked.

'I'm pretty sure that's a kamikaze run, and those flight crews are on a one-way trip,' John said.

'You mean they're going to detonate those nukes right in the middle of the remains of the Sol fleet?' Jack said, his expression tight.

Before John could reply the answer came, as two huge pulses of energy ripped through the X103s, destroying Kimpraks and X-craft alike.

Tears immediately beaded my eyes. This couldn't be happening. It was a nightmare come true.

Then I spotted three other Pangolins had picked up the other three nukes and were heading straight towards the asteroid swarm. The lead ship had a metadata tag identifying it as *Falcon One*.

A video window appeared, and Troy's face ashen filled it. 'I'm so sorry, Lauren, they whipped our arses and we didn't see it coming. I've ordered the rest of our ships to head back to the rendezvous point to meet up with *Tempest*. This is all my fault...' He had to squeeze his eyes shut, no longer able to speak.

I tried to find the words too, but nothing came. But what could you say to someone who would be tearing themselves apart over a strategy that cost so many lives? But it was John who came to the rescue.

'You had no way of knowing what their defence capabilities were. None of us did, Commander,' John said. 'And if you hadn't made an advance strike on the Kimprak mothership today, we would have been in the dark when we took them on at Jupiter. Now, thanks to you and your fleet's actions we have a much better idea of what we're up against. That knowledge alone may well have saved the lives of many, many people.'

Troy looked up to meet John's gaze. 'That would be worth dying for, but we're not finished yet. We're going to attempt three nuke special deliveries by shoving them straight down the throat of that fucking mothership.'

At last, I found my voice again. 'But you'll be throwing your lives away.'

'The three Pangolin crews on this special delivery run are determined to see this through, and that includes me. Goodbye, Lauren, and please don't think too badly of me.'

I already knew there would be no arguing with him, so all I could offer in these last moments were words. 'I'll never think badly of you, Troy. You're the bravest person I know. And what you did today will make a real difference, something that we will learn from and adapt our strategies. I promise you, whatever it takes, we will avenge the life of each and every one of your crew.'

'Thank you and may God protect you all,' Troy said. He snapped us a salute that we all returned, before he reached forward and turned off the video link.

My brain went numb as I watched his three ships race into the cluster of asteroids, darting between them and somehow avoiding all the Kimprak fire racing out to meet them. But then their luck and skill began to run out, as three became two, then one.

In those final moments, the last ship, *Falcon One*, was unlike anything I'd ever seen in my life. It jinked around space, seeming to be everywhere at once. Troy's piloting skills were awe-inspiring to witness. But it was still just one lone ship against an armada. Even Francis Drake would never have liked those odds.

As three streams of Kimprak converged on the lone Pangolin, somehow Troy avoided them all, but as he spun the ship sideways it clipped the surface of one of the asteroids surrounding the mothership, probably only by millimetres, but it was enough. *Falcon One* spiralled straight into the surface and disappeared from the tactical display.

Just like that, Troy was gone.

I didn't try to fight back the tears. I allowed them to stream down my face. Jack's arm curled round me and I leaned into him as it felt like the centre of my soul was torn to shreds.

CHAPTER TWENTY-ONE

With just a week left until we reached Jupiter, my hand dug into Jack's as the memorial service got underway. Leaving the running of the ship to the automated systems, literally every human onboard *Tempest* and every single avatar were there to pay their respects. The other major addition were the survivors of Sol fleet, just over twelve hundred survivors from five hundred Pangolins that had managed to make it back to our starship.

We now all stood in a particularly beautiful corner of the parkland under the leaves of a broad, spreading oak that apparently the Angelus had brought aboard when they'd first landed.

On the grass lawn in front of it, stood a massive polished block of granite. Lucy had the nanobots construct it in just one night, complete with an inscription of all the lost crew members.

On the top of it, a five-metre flame burned in slow motion, thanks to the same localised gravity field trick that was also used on the waterfall in the Temple of Transmutation. The effect of the slowly dancing flame was hypnotic, just as it was intended to be. I certainly kept finding myself staring into it, a focal point in the storm of grief that was roaring through me.

And every time my gaze dropped to the names of over fifteen hundred people carved into the stone block, the grief inside me felt like it was growing into a tsunami that would sweep me away.

I stood flanked by everyone most important to me, including Jack, Mike, Ruby, Erin, and Lucy. And I loved every one of them to the core of my being for that. These people were my family, the people who I'd gone through so much with and had forged bonds with like no others.

I glanced across at Ruby who had tears streaming down her face which rocked me almost more than anything else. It would haunt me to the end of my days witnessing the moment that she'd learned that her girlfriend Jane, an engineer who had been on board one of the doomed Pangolins that had been lost in the battle. It was a story I'd heard a hundred times over and was true for far too many standing here.

A procession of priests from every religion had already spoken, a clear representation of the diversity of our crews from all around the world. But I'd barely heard a single word as a thunderstorm of emotion crashed around inside me. Then Jack was squeezing my hand back and gazing into my eyes, almost like he was projecting his love into me, to give me strength for what I was about to do.

Alice had already volunteered to step in via a hologram to give the speech that had to be given, but this was something I knew I had to do for my sake, as much as everyone else's.

As I grasped my notecards that I'd spent hours writing, even though they amounted to just a few hundred words, I forced myself to let go of Jack's hand, my rock in the storm.

Mike reached out and squeezed my shoulder as I passed him. Then with the eyes of *Tempest's* entire crew on me, I stepped away from the support of my friends and headed out towards the lectern that had been set up before the memorial stone.

The thirty-metre walk to that podium felt like thirty miles, with every step my feet felt like they had turned to lead.

I passed John who was flanked by all his senior officers and he gave me an encouraging look. Out of everyone here, he probably most of all knew what it was like to have to stand up in front of people who had lost family, friends, and lovers and try to offer them words of comfort.

I reached the lectern and took hold of it, my knuckles white.

I looked down at my note cards, but the words swum and danced and refused to come into focus as tears filled my eyes. Instead, I made myself look up and out at all the people before me. But all I could see was a blur of faces, a vast expanse of humanity waiting to hear what I had to say.

It was then that I realised that there could be no prepared speech for this, so I dropped my notecards onto the lectern and instead, just spoke from the heart as Jack had encouraged me to do before.

'I honestly haven't got the words to express what I am feeling, what we're all feeling about everyone that we lost yesterday,' I said, my words amplified by some hidden mic and filling the vast space around us. 'The grief is too raw for me to even be able to think clearly and I have way too many tears in my eyes to even read the speech I prepared, so forgive me if I stumble and I come up short because it's all I have right now.'

Then in the sea of faces, I saw the look of love and support on the faces of those who I was lucky enough to call friends, especially Jack, and I took strength from that.

At last, the sea of other faces began to come into focus. Yes, this wasn't about me, this was about every person here and as a commander responsible for so many of their lives, I needed to be there for them right now. And that was exactly what I would do.

I took a deep breath, turned and briefly pointed towards the names on the memorial stone. 'We lost so many souls yesterday who had put their lives on the line to defend Earth. But they went into that battle with their heads held high, knowing the risks but doing it anyway. That is what true bravery looks like.'

Many people in the audience were nodding.

'When Commander Troy Armstrong took the Sol fleet into battle, none of them had any idea just how lethal the defence capabilities of the Kimprak were going to be. No one could have. If he and the Sol fleet had succeeded we would be celebrating them as heroes today, but even in defeat that's exactly what they are.'

'If they hadn't attacked the Kimprak we wouldn't now be aware of just how effective the alien defences are. Now, thanks to their ultimate sacrifice, Commander John Hamilton and I have already been busy analysing the data from that battle and adapting our plans accordingly. We will learn from what happened and we will adapt. Our numbers may be less now than they were before the loss of our sisters and brothers, but we will avenge every single one of them.' I thought of Jane hugging Ruby at the party, and my grief was transformed into a fire and I raised my voice. 'And I promise you now, that whatever it takes, we will avenge every soul that was lost. We will defeat the Kimprak invasion forces coming for Earth and we will destroy them!' I almost shouted. 'What say you?'

'Aye,' Jack said first. Then his voice was joined at first by dozens, and then thousands of others, repeating the same word. And our voices rose together until the chamber echoed with our cry.

The following day, I sat on the bridge gazing at the Battle Command simulation mode on the main hologram, doing everything in my power to make good on my promise to wipe out the

Kimprak. Ruby had joined Lucy, Niki, John and me as we ran through various revised attack options. Jack, Mike, and Jodie were also there to brainstorm. Jodie had set up a blog page where our ideas were being posted to see if anyone could think of a way to improve them. The fact was, the tragic loss of the Sol fleet Pangolins had fused everyone into a single crew. There was no us and the USSF anymore, just a group of people who were absolutely pulling together to make sure that we did whatever it took to defeat the Kimprak.

Out of all of us, Ruby had eyes of steel since the memorial service, using her grief over the loss of Jane to power her laser-focus. She was currently standing before us in front of the holographic representation of a Lightning torpedo, presenting her proposed missile attack strategy to the rest of us.

'Okay, we've all seen how the Kimprak were able to capture our torpedoes and use them against us,' she said. 'And in all the sims that we've run since, we keep running into the same roadblock and they keep kicking our arses after they capture our torpedoes.'

'That's almost certainly how mechanised races like the Kimprak have been so successful in the past, even when taking on technological superior species,' Lucy said. 'They end up simply using that species' weapons against them.'

'So you're saying that we've already lost and there's nothing we can do about it?' Jack asked.

'Absolutely no way I'm saying that,' Ruby replied. 'But we have to be cunning in the way we deliver the weapon payloads to their doorstep. And I've taken some inspiration from you guys always quoting historical battles all the time, so here's my spin. With Lucy's help, I've put together a simulation to show you my idea.'

She pressed a virtual control panel hovering in front of the main holographic display and the Lightning torpedo shrank as the view zoomed out. Other torpedoes now came into view until a dozen were revealed.

'You remember how Niki was originally convinced that the USSF delegation was actually a Trojan Horse strategy to capture *Tempest*?' she asked, then quickly added, 'No disrespect, Commander Hamilton.'

'None taken,' John said smiling across at Niki.

'Well, that gave me something of an idea. In the original story, the wooden horse was built by the Greeks and they left it out outside the gates of Troy, which they'd been trying to capture forever. The Greek army then sneaked away and the following morning, thinking the giant horse was a gift for the gods left behind by the Greeks, the Trojans brought it into the city. But of course, as we all know, there were actually a bunch of Greek soldiers hiding inside it. In the middle of the night they crept out, opened the gates to the city to let the rest of the Greek army in, and then quickly kicked the Trojans' arses.'

'I'm not sure that the Kimprak would fall for a Trojan Horse floating in space,' Mike said with a wry smile.

'Maybe not, but how about this for an idea?' Ruby pressed the control panel again and the view zoomed out to reveal a large asteroid in the hologram display.

John's eyes widened. 'You're saying we turn an asteroid into the equivalent of a Trojan Horse?'

'Damned right we do. We know the Kimprak are always hunting for resources to use, so why not put a nice big juicy lump of rock filled with Lightning warheads slap-bang in the middle of their flight path to Jupiter?'

I felt the tension that had been giving me a pounding headache for the last few days start to loosen its grip. 'That could actually work, Ruby. But even if they swallowed the bait wouldn't there be a chance they'd discover them as soon they started to mine the asteroid?'

'Actually, I might have an idea there,' Jodie said. 'As we are all very aware, there's some very advanced technology on this starship, including the Photonic Mass Projector shielding system that *Tempest* uses. Lucy, is there any reason we couldn't set up a smaller version to disguise a tunnel that we excavated in the asteroid to shield it from view across every electromagnetic spectrum, pretty much like the shield generator does for *Tempest*?'

'I don't see why not,' she said. 'But what about the surrounding rock? Wouldn't it act as a massive barrier and reduce the effectiveness of the EM pulse?'

Mike scratched his neck as he gazed at the asteroid hologram. 'We could plant similarly shielded explosives to blast out channels to the surface just moments before the Lightnings detonated.'

'Yes, but even if that does work, it will only knock them out for a limited time right?' Jack asked. 'That's going to minimise our window that we can use to maximise our advantage.'

'Actually, I have news there,' Jodie said. 'You know that Kimprak bot that we recovered from that crash site in Australia and that I've been studying? Well, so far I've had no luck finding a kill switch in their code, but I have run a battery of tests on it, specifically with fine-tuning an EM pulse in mind, and I've had something of a breakthrough. With a few easy adaptions we can tweak our Lightning torpedoes, not to just knock them out for a maximum of a minute, but somewhere closer to five.'

'That could make a huge strategic difference,' John said.

'I agree, this really is starting to sound like a viable plan,' I added.

'Hang on, surely shielded or not, eventually the Kimprak are bound to discover the torpedoes,' Jack said.

'In that case, the timing will be absolutely critical,' I replied. 'We put the asteroid in their path and leave just enough time for them to draw it into their constellation of rocks, but before they start really digging into it, and we detonate it.'

'This is all fine in theory, but how do you propose we physically get an asteroid into the Kimprak's path in the first place?' John asked.

'Actually, there is an obvious way and that's to use the same ship that saved your craft, John. Especially since the *Sriracha* has the equivalent of a tow hook,' I said. 'She's also by far the fastest ship currently in our fleet and could reach the Kimprak flotilla in just a few days.'

John nodded. 'That sounds like the foundation of a very solid plan. It just needs some more fleshing out.'

'Actually, I'm not quite done yet,' Ruby said. 'I still have one more idea for a revised strategy for the main battle.'

'Then fire away,' I said, 'because you're obviously on a roll.'

'Our torpedoes were only taken over because, apart from being able to manoeuvre, they didn't have any other way to protect themselves. So next time we attack them we could try this approach instead...' She pressed an icon on the control panel and the asteroid was replaced with a close-up of an elongated torpedo.

'This is one of our new torpedoes carrying a nuke warhead,' Ruby said. 'The problem is that some of the ones that the Sol fleet had when they went up against the Kimprak have now almost certainly fallen under their control, so we can expect them to use them against us in the coming battle.'

'In that case, we'll need to keep our fleet as spread out as possible and not present such a tempting target,' Jack said.

'That could definitely help, but I can think of one vast ship that's almost certainly going to be too big a target to resist and that's *Tempest* herself,' I replied.

'Hang on, even if that's true, the nukes are within tolerance of what the Photonic Mass shield generator can cope with,' Lucy said. 'A massive swarm of Kimprak attacking us all at once you can worry about, but a few nukes.' She shrugged. 'No biggie.'

'It's moments like this that I'm starkly reminded just how incredible this starship of yours is,' John said.

'You better believe it,' Lucy replied with a wide smile.

'So, we can all breathe a bit easier about that now,' I said. 'How does that relate to your idea, Ruby?'

'This is how.' She swiped down on the holographic control panel and the view of the Hammer missile zoomed out. Now we could see a cluster of twelve Wolfpack drones around it.

A slow smile filled my face as I realised exactly what Ruby was proposing. 'You're talking about each of our nuke torpedoes having the equivalent of an armed escort, aren't you?'

'Absolutely, Commander. If our torpedoes can't directly defend themselves then we do the next best thing. We surround them with Wolfpack drones armed to the teeth with their rapid-burst lasers. That's obviously far safer than sending any of our crewed ships in to do the same thing. Then, once our torpedoes have done their worst and softened up the target, we attack with our fleet, wiping those sick robotic smiles right off the Kimprak's stupid metal insect faces.'

'You do know they aren't actually capable of smiling, right?' Mike asked, grinning.

Ruby just rolled her eyes at him.

'This is sounding more than positive,' Jack said. 'We may have actually found a way to win this thing.'

'It does, doesn't it?' I replied. 'Has anyone had any other ideas that we can throw into the mix?'

Mike caught my eye and nodded. 'Just a small suggestion, but rather than just calling them nukes, I say that in keeping with the naming convention of Lightning and Hammer, we call those torpedoes, Thunders.'

Everyone nodded with approving looks.

'That gets a big thumbs-up from me,' Ruby said. 'And that way when we go into battle I can sing that Queen song with something about Thunder and Lightning, being very frightening. Not sure how I can weave Hammer in there as well.'

'Knowing you, I'm sure you'll find a way,' Jack said raising his eyebrows at her.

Ruby snorted. 'You better believe it, buddy.'

It was noticeable how the tension on the flight deck had tangibly shifted as I gazed at the people round me.

'I don't know about the rest you, but at the start of this meeting I felt the weight of the world on my shoulders,' I said. 'But now I can see that we have a very real way that we can win this and that's only because of the sacrifice that Troy and the others made. Without them, we would have been going into this battle blind.'

Lucy was nodding when her eyes suddenly widened. 'Guys, you're not going to believe this but we have an incoming transmission from Troy.'

I stared at her. 'Did I just hear you correctly?'

'You did, Lauren. I'm pulling up the transmission feed now.'

We all turned to stare at the video window that had just appeared in the holographic display, and more specifically, Troy's space-helmeted face. Behind him were the forms of at least twenty other people crouching in the darkness of some sort of cave system.

'Oh, thank god, we've finally been able to boost our signal to get through to you,' Troy said.

'But your alive,' was the only thing my stunned mind could come up with at that exact moment.

'Yes, but not for much longer. A number of the escape pods were able to eject before our ships were taken over. We're currently holed up in one of the Kimprak asteroids, but are having to keep our heads down for obvious reasons. It's crawling with the steel cockroaches. We have a total of twenty-six survivors here, but we're running low on oxygen. Our best estimate, even with all our efforts to conserve our supplies, is that we have about thirty minutes left.'

Any sense of elation that Troy and at least a handful of others had survived was swept away by his words. Once again, I felt absolute despair sucking at my heels until Mike spoke up.

'Hang on,' he said. 'Lucy, you still have that Guardian drone tracking the mothership?'

Her eyes locked onto his. 'You mean scoop them up and transport them over to E8?'

'Yep, just like the Guardian did in the Resonancy Generator chamber to save us when it flooded,' Mike replied. 'Assuming that's even possible without a micro mind close by?'

'Please say yes,' Jodie said. 'At least then, we can save some people from that awful battle.'

Lucy looked across at a group of the other avatars crewing the control stations and they all nodded at once.

'Okay, having just discussed it with my brothers and sisters, even heavily shielded and disguised, there is a possibility that the Kimprak will spot the Guardian at such close proximity and destroy it. That aside, it is possible we could actually pull this off. A Guardian hasn't got sufficient power to create a full E8 reality bridge to your universe, but it does have enough power to create the equivalent of an E8 stasis field bubble. That would keep them all alive, effectively in suspended animation, until the Guardian can bring them back to *Tempest*.'

I nodded. 'Then order it to do exactly that, Lucy.'

'Done, and it's on its way. Travelling at maximum speed, it will be with them in forty seconds.'

I turned back to the video link window. 'Did you catch all that, Troy?'

'Roger that. We'll be ready.' Then his eyes locked onto mine.

'Lauren, I just wanted to say how sorry I am about being so bull-headed. We did try everything we could, but they caught us out and so many lives—' He squeezed his eyes shut behind his visor, his jaw muscles cabling.

'I know,' I assured him. 'I know and we can talk it all out when you get back here.'

He managed a nod but couldn't meet my gaze.

'ETA is now five seconds,' Lucy called out.

A fresh video opened next to the live feed from Troy of the Guardian rushing towards one of the larger asteroids on the edge of the constellation. The view of the rocky surface filled the screen.

I just had time to nod at Troy and read the haunted look in his eyes, which told me that he was carrying the guilt of every death on his shoulders, before the video link cut out.

'We have them all safely stored in an E8 stasis field,' Lucy announced.

The footage from the video window swung away from the rocky surface and the view was filled with stars.

'The Guardian is already out of enemy weapon's range and is heading back here at maximum speed.'

'Oh, thank god,' Jack said, squeezing my shoulder.

The strength almost flowed out of my legs as the tension that had been building inside me let go, but like always and without saying a word, Jack was there to steady me.

As relieved as I was, part of me also wondered whether Troy would have preferred to stay behind and die on that rock. Even though the Sol fleet had made a real difference, I doubt he would see it way when he counted how many lives his mission had cost. It was in that moment that I made a silent vow to myself, that I would help him through this as one commander to another, as much as anyone possibly could.

CHAPTER TWENTY-TWO

WITH LESS THAN a day to the asteroid capture mission, a suitable candidate already having been located by Lucy, the Guardian probe had finally made it back safely to *Tempest*. I'd been there to meet and greet, but most of all I just wanted to see how Troy was doing, which in a word was badly. In the debriefing with Troy and the other survivors, even though John, Niki, and I had been as gentle as we could, it had only helped twist the knife as Troy was forced to relive the consequences of his actions.

Even John, who I thought might have been less tolerant of a maverick commander, had been sympathetic to what Troy had tried to do. But even when we'd run through what a major difference our new attack strategies should make, it had little effect in shifting the balance of Troy's mood. Then again, I knew that I would be feeling exactly the same if I were in his shoes—broken to the very bottom of my soul.

On my way to the Citadel to run another training exercise utilising the latest tactics, my transport pod had been flying over the monolith when I spotted a lone figure. Instantly I just knew it had to be Troy. A quick check with Delphi had confirmed my suspicion, and a short while later I'd disembarked the pod and was heading towards him.

On the memorial, some of the names, including Troy's, were in the process of vanishing. Lucy had told me in one of the many briefings that the nanobots were going to remove the names of the twenty-seven rescued crew members. She'd also obviously told Troy, who was here to witness the event for himself.

He stood like a statue before it, his hands clasped behind his back. As I approached I paused because it suddenly felt like I was about to intrude on what had to be a very private moment. But then I saw that he was trembling. It was then, that my emotional autopilot took over and I stepped over to him.

'Troy?' I said gently.

He didn't respond, but just kept staring straight ahead at the names as another one faded back into polished stone.

I moved to his side, blue eyes glittering with tears, but what can you say to someone that felt responsible for every single death on that monolith? So I did the thing that you do when you can't reach someone with words, I wrapped my arms around him and just hung onto him, feeling the tremor running through his body.

We stood like that, me awkwardly holding onto the man as he silently wept, until at last he stilled. Even then I didn't let go, until eventually, he pulled away. I looked at the memorial to see that the last of the names had vanished including Troy's own.

When I looked back, Troy had moved over to one of the stone benches that had been erected around the monolith beneath the shade of the oak. He sat, then hung his head and clasped his hands together as he stared at the ground. The man looked like an island in his grief, but I also instinctively knew that he needed to be left alone. As much as I wanted to take his pain away, to tell him it was alright, deep down I knew it wasn't. Troy needed to find his own way through this to the other side.

So instead of words, I stepped to him, gently laid a hand on his shoulder, then headed back towards my transport pod.

I stood with John on the flight deck of the Citadel gazing out at the vast disc of Jupiter. We'd all watched spellbound as the planet had grown steadily larger, partly because of the awe-inspiring beauty of the vast planet and string of moons that shone like a chain of jewels catching the sunlight. There was also the focal point—the hypnotic, ever-changing famous giant red spot, the storm that rotated into view as the gas giant spun on its axis.

Thanks to my lifelong knowledge of astronomy I knew that the red spot storm had raged for close to two centuries, since it had been discovered by an amateur astronomer called Samuel Heinrich Schwabe back in 1831. That specific piece of astronomy general knowledge had helped my team win the Christmas pub quiz when I'd still worked at Jodrell Bank back in the UK.

But it wasn't just its abstract beauty that made Jupiter the focus of everyone's attention. We all knew that this would effectively be humanity's last stand against the Kimprak. If we failed here, our homeworld would be lost. It was that simple of an equation. And I saw that same certainty etched into the expressions of everyone as we closed in on the gas giant, Jack included, even though he did his best to hide it from me. That's what we were all trying to do, put our best face forward with a mask of professionalism that hid the fear that we could lose this coming battle.

The exception to this was Lucy and the other avatars, who seemed totally unflappable. When you were as ancient as they were, you'd seen it all before and a lot more besides. Despite everything, including the possible loss of *Tempest* in what was coming, the avatars didn't seem fazed in the slightest, which was exactly what the human crew needed from them most.

Lucy headed towards me and waved her hand towards the holographic display which glowed into life. On it was a view of the *Sriracha* towing an asteroid a good few hundred metres wide, the faint tether of its tractor beam connecting them visible as a line of shimmering blue light.

'Don and his crew are ready to release the asteroid on the far side of Jupiter to send it out towards the Kimprak mothership,' Lucy said.

'Can you put him on the line please?' I asked heading over for a closer look.

'Of course.'

A video window appeared in the hologram with Don gazing out at me.

'How's it going?' I asked.

'Very well, Lauren. We arrived at our rendezvous point bang-on schedule. Since then, the avatars assisting us have tried to make sure our flight path makes it look like the asteroid will have just randomly moved into the Kimprak's mothership flight path when released.'

'Then to paraphrase that old saying based on the actual Trojan War, let's hope they don't look a gift horse in the mouth,' Jack said as he joined us from the console where he'd been studying the thousands of photos he'd taken of Angelus artefacts during his exploration of *Tempest*.

'Yeah, that,' Don said smiling. 'All the EM warheads have been safely buried on the asteroid and the Photonic Mass shields are doing an excellent job of masking their presence. They're totally invisible even when you're practically on top of them and don't show up on any standard sensor scan.'

'So, what's the Kimprak's ETA to scoop up their gift-wrapped asteroid?' I asked.

'About twenty-four hours,' Don replied. 'But there's something else that we've been puzzling over and that we need to run past you.'

'Fire away,' I said.

'We've been picking up a long-range signal that seems to have been tracking the mothership as it heads in. Have you sent out another Guardian probe to track its progress that you didn't tell us about?'

Jack and I looked at Lucy who was already shaking her head.

'Nothing to do with us,' she said. 'Are you sure it's not just another natural phenomenon like another asteroid or even an undiscovered comet?'

'That's what has us puzzled. It keeps making subtle course changes suggesting it has some sort of propulsion system.'

I stared at him. 'Please tell me you're not saying it could be another Kimprak ship?'

'We're not sure because it's right at the range of our sensors so we can barely make it out.'

'You don't suppose it's our Grey buddies in one of their Tic Tac craft tracking the mothership as it heads in?' Jack asked.

'It certainly could be and if so it might be worth trying to make contact,' I said. 'They've always had our backs before and they may be prepared to help again in the coming battle.'

'In that case, now that we've done our delivery run it sounds like we should go and check it out,' Don said. 'It should take us about six hours to reach it including a deceleration burn of our fusion engine. We'll obviously go in fully stealthed so either way, whatever or whoever it is, won't know that we're there unless we choose to let them know. Once we've done that, there should be enough time for us to make it back to you before the main battle kicks off.'

'Do it,' I replied. 'Meanwhile, we'll be checking on the progress of the Kimprak towards our Trojan Horse.'

'Then good luck to us all,' Don replied. 'We'll be in touch. Out.'

The video screen went dark and then in its place the large countdown timer to the estimate of the final battle reappeared with thirty-six hours and twenty-four minutes on it. Inspired by Alice's example back at Eden, I'd had the avatar crew install these everywhere where there were people, from the habitation zone to the hangars, all to keep everyone focused on what was coming.

'What's the status of our battle readiness, Lucy?' John asked.

'All ships are being prepared with full armaments and the molecular printers are cranking out the Wolfpack drones and torpedoes, including the Thunder nuke variants, as fast as we can make them. The flight crews are currently concluding sim training before the final battle. The only thing that won't be ready in time is a second corvette class ship that's currently being assembled in the ship shipyard. We've also started work on the main fusion engines, but that's going to take months before they're ready.'

'Then let's hope we have an opportunity to try them out then,' I replied. 'Anyway, it sounds like everything that can be done is being done.'

'It is,' Lucy replied. 'But as always, if you can think of anything else, just let me know.'

John clasped his hands behind his back in exactly the same manner that Troy had done down at the memorial. But in John's case, rather than grieving for the fallen, he was gazing out at Jupiter.

'So here we are, approaching the most important battle in human history,' he said.

'So it would seem,' I replied. 'It's cost a lot of effort and sheer bloody will, not to mention a lot of lives, to get us here.'

He met my gaze and nodded. 'Commander Lauren Stelleck, do you know what's traditional to do at a time like this?'

As I peered into his eyes the answer immediately came to me. 'For a commander to go and talk to their people?'

'You see, like everyone keeps saying, you're a natural military leader. So what do you say to us strolling through the decks and hangars talking to our people?'

'I can think of nothing better to do because ultimately this is all about supporting each other for whatever lies ahead,' I replied.

John nodded as we turned together and headed for the door.

The time had long passed since the two fleets were kept to their two hangars and now both TR-3Bs and X-craft sat alongside each other in hangar bay one. The two fleets had at last, and when it mattered most, become one.

John and I walked together through the hangars, each of us taking the time to talk to the flight crews, pressing flesh, and offering up words of encouragement where we could.

It struck me just how quickly the bonds had developed between the USSF pilots and our own flight crews. More than once we saw them helping each other out, and there was even a game of basketball in progress where one enterprising soul had set up two hoops.

When it felt like my hand was going to fall off after shaking so many hands, John and I parted ways and I headed off to the industrial zone of the ship where Jodie and Mike seemed to be spending all their time in these final days, while John went back up to the bridge.

As I exited the transport pod I stepped out into the control room of one of *Tempest's* molecular printer workshops, which was where Lucy had told me that my two friends had been holed up.

When I saw them it was obvious to me that neither of them had slept. The only person who looked relatively fresh in the room was Asim, an AI who had once been stationed at Petra in Jordan where his micro mind had been buried in the sands of the ancient site.

Mike looked up with bleary eyes as I entered the room.

'Wow, you two look like you could seriously do with some sleep,' I said.

'Which is exactly what I keep telling them, but they keep insisting on staying even though I'm more capable of handling the production of all our printers,' Asim said.

'And as we keep telling Asim, we aren't going anywhere until we've produced as many torpedoes and Wolfpack drones as possible,' Mike said. 'At least until the E8 power feed is directed away from the molecular printers to the weapons and shield system.'

Jodie nodded. 'Our place is right here, nowhere else right now.'

'Has anyone told you that you're both really stubborn?' I replied.

Mike smiled at me. 'It takes one to know one.'

I chuckled. 'Isn't that truth.' I gestured to the window where a succession of E8 spherical molecular printers were blazing with energy that could be seen in the cracks between their hexagonal panels. 'So that aside, how have you been getting on?'

Mike exchanged a smile with Jodie. 'Maybe it's better if we just show you, because I'm not sure words do it justice.'

He headed towards a door at the far end and it slid open.

As I stepped through the air caught in my throat.

We were standing on a raised gantry in a giant warehouse space. Thousands and thousands of Wolfpack drones were stacked in layers across the floor. If that wasn't jaw-dropping enough, in racks on either side countless torpedoes had been built and were being continually ferried away by a fleet of robotic transports out through hatches in the wall.

'As you can see, we've been quite busy,' Mike said.

'Says the king of understatement. This is incredible, guys. So just how many Wolfpack drones have you managed to build?'

'Seven thousand, eight hundred and fifty-eight currently,' Jodie said. 'We're trying to go for a flat eight thousand before time runs out.'

'But that's incredible. It could make all the difference. And what about the torpedoes, how many of those?'

'Five thousand in total, three thousand of which are already loaded onto our ships, we have about another two thousand here that we can either launch from *Tempest* or reload our ships with during the battle. Having said that, we've only been able to produce twenty Thunder torpedoes because we ran out of plutonium and there's simply no time to get any fresh supplies sent from Earth.'

'Hopefully, we'll have more than enough of those already, and what you've produced is breathtaking.'

'So maybe no more lectures about getting enough sleep and maybe just let us go and do our thing,' Mike said with a wry smile.

'Okay, point taken,' I replied shaking my head at him.

My watch warbled and I looked at the face to see Lucy peering out at me. 'You need to get up to the bridge and quickly. There's been a development and I'm afraid it's not a good one.'

'Why, what's happened?'

'The *Sriracha* has just gotten close enough to register what that strange radio source was that they picked up and it's some sort of battleship that has commenced a burn and is decelerating towards the Kimprak.'

'You're telling me that another alien species has been tracking the Kimprak and is about to take it on?'

'Yes. It does appear to be on an intercept course and Don has reported seeing what he assumes are torpedo ports opening. But that aside, our initial analysis indicates that it's anything but alien based on its design, and is in fact human.'

Mike, Jodie, and I all stared at my watch.

'You're telling me someone else is out there trying to fight that thing?' I said.

'Yes, and when I showed it to John, he said he'd seen a proposal cross his desk for that very design a decade ago and that it's actually a USSF designed fleet carrier and heavy cruiser called the *Vanguard*.'

It was then that an astonishing thought rushed into my mind. 'The Overseers, it has to be. They're the only ones with access to that sort of information and also the ability to build it. This might be a stretch but it also explains why Alvarez and the other Overseer agents suddenly disappeared off the face of the planet, because they actually did exactly that.'

Lucy nodded. 'And by the looks of it, they're heading straight into battle with the Kimprak with their shiny new toy.'

'Then enemy or not, we have to stop them, because however powerful the *Vanguard* is, we already know it's going to be no match for the Kimprak by itself. Otherwise, there's every chance that they could capture *Vanguard* and then use it against us.'

'I know, and anticipating what you would say, we're already attempting to make contact with *Vanguard,* but so far they're ignoring us.'

'Oh bloody hell. I'm on my way.'

Mike shot me a look as I rushed for the door. 'This could change everything again, couldn't it?'

'Yes, and not for the better if we don't play our cards right,' I replied.

CHAPTER TWENTY-THREE

JOHN WAS STANDING with Lucy and Ruby in front of the main hologram as Jack and I entered the Citadel. Every console was filled with humans and avatars watching what was happening on the main hologram.

Within the display was what looked like a relayed live feed from the deck of *Sriracha* in a floating video window along with various charts and diagnostic readouts. They were orbiting a blocky-looking 3D black-painted ship that looked like it had been carved from vast slabs of metal. Three large bell nozzle rockets extended from the far end and lay idle. But there was a secondary ring of smaller nozzles around the ship's nose burning glowing orange plumes forward into space. Also around the nose section, there were large scooped-out grooves that reminded me of the torpedo ports on a submarine. The ship's surface was bristling with gun turrets. Also along the craft's flanks were dozens of large, square hatches. In terms of looks, compared to *Tempest*, it was a Brutalist conception and looked very much designed for war rather than to win any design awards.

'Unknown vessel, please respond,' John said.

I listened to the following hiss of static that was being tracked with a sine wave of little valleys and hills.

'Still no response?' I asked as Jack and I headed down the steps to the others.

'None whatsoever,' Lucy replied. 'We're relaying our transmissions via the *Sriracha* and as far as we can tell they're definitely receiving us.'

'Just how far out from the mothership are they now?' Jack asked.

'Not as far as we would like for them to be able to pull back in time,' John said. 'Lucy, can you show us the tactical overview of the situation.'

She nodded and with a finger swipe through the air, the view of the mystery ship zoomed out. A fifth of the size of the mystery ship the *Sriracha* was relatively close to it, just tracking behind in the craft's wake. But of much more immediate concern was the Kimprak mothership and its constellation of asteroids that the battleship was flying towards at a tangential intercept angle.

'Oh bloody hell, how long till they reach it?' I said.

'About ten minutes,' Lucy said. 'And as you can see they've already begun their braking run.'

'That suggests to me that they really think they can go toe to toe with the Kimprak and slug it out,' John said shaking his head.

'They also have no idea what they're up against,' I replied. 'Okay, let me see if our suspicions are correct about this being an Overseer's vessel.'

With a tap of the holographic interface, I pulled up the comm video window. 'This is Commander Lauren Stelleck of the starship *Tempest* hailing the warship currently heading towards the Kimprak mothership, please respond.'

Once again there was just a hiss of static in response.

'If you're not prepared to talk to us, then just listen,' I continued. 'You have no idea of the level of firepower that you're going up against. Those asteroids that surround the mothership are seeded with Kimprak and they are using gauss guns to fire their bots in order to capture ships and anything else fired at them. We found that out to our extreme cost when we lost over five hundred ships which were captured and had to be destroyed. There is no reason that you will fare any better than us. The only sensible strategy is for you to join our fleet so we can attack them together. That way we at least have a fighting chance to stop them.'

I waited as John leant in closer towards me. 'If that doesn't get their attention, I don't know what will,' he said.

Despite this optimism, the sound of static crackled on.

I tried one last time. 'Look, we are almost certain that yours is an Overseer ship and I wouldn't be surprised at all if that bastard Colonel Alvarez is commanding it, because this is so his bloody style.'

This time the crackle softened and as the sine waves started to spike in the frequency window, the video link burst into life.

I found myself staring at the guy I absolutely loathed from the centre of my being, Colonel Alvarez. This was the guy I'd first encountered back at Jodrell Bank when he'd stormed the control room, but now sported extensive burns as well as his eye scar thanks to him being buried alive under the desert sands back at the Richat Structure.

'Well deduced, Stelleck,' he said gazing out at me. 'Ah, and Commander Hamilton. So, you have thrown your lot in with the terrorists then.'

'Lauren and her people are anything but that, Alvarez. Unfortunately for us, the USSF's view was very much distorted by the lies that you and your Overseer people have spun.' Anger flashed in John's eyes. 'Just tell me why your organisation would be so warped as to do that?'

A thin smile filled Alvarez's face. 'The Overseers are the real power behind the thrones of the world, be it governments, militaries or even multi-corporations. Our touch is the silk glove enclosing the hand of steel that has run the world for the last couple of centuries and our control has been absolute. And I can assure you now, that it will be again despite your best efforts to flush our agents out. Our organisation runs the world whether you realise it or not, and we defend what's ours even from an alien invasion such as this one. We need no one's help in this battle and when we have dealt with the Kimprak, we will destroy you. We will not tolerate a challenge from anyone, be it the USSF or Lauren Stelleck and her bunch of terrorists wherever you're hiding out here.'

I just shook my head. 'Once again you're as delusional as ever, Alvarez, and as much as I would love to take the time to settle this once and forever, you have absolutely no idea what you're up against. Didn't you hear me when I said we lost five hundred ships and we barely scratched the bloody thing? So why do you think you'll fare any better?'

'Oh, you'll see, Stelleck, and as much as you think we needed the help of alien races to win this battle, I'm about to prove just how wrong you are. Beyond studying their technology, the Overseers have long-prepared for this day, as you are about to witness. Now, as much as I would love to debate this with you, I have a war to wage.'

We saw him reach forward and press something below the screen. A moment later the video link went dark.

'That guy is utterly delusional,' Lucy said.

'He certainly sounds like it,' Jack said.

John dragged his hand over chin and headed around the screen to the live feed from *Sriracha*. 'Did you hear all that, Don?'

'We most certainly did. What are your orders, Commander?'

John turned to us. '*Sriracha* could try to neutralise the *Vanguard*'s engines.'

Lucy shook her head. 'It would make little difference. I'm afraid the law of physics is at play here. If you took out their reverse thrusters, for example, all that would do is stop the ship's ability to break its momentum and it would crash straight into the asteroid swarm.'

'You mean there's nothing we can do to stop this?' I asked.

'Not from what the battle sim data is telling me. Alvarez's determination to pick a fight with the Kimprak is on the rails now.'

I stared at her, appalled. and was already mentally processing the bloodbath that was likely to play out, not to mention the sheer amount of refined metals in the warship that Alvarez was about to present the Kimprak to feast on.

'So what would you like us to do?' Don asked over the video link.

'Just keep your distance for now and make sure you don't inadvertently get sucked into the engagement,' John said.

'Roger that,' Don replied. 'Hang on, something's happening on that battleship. Those hatches appear to be opening all along its hull.'

I headed into the hologram and zoomed in on the 3D model of the *Vanguard*.

Sure enough, I could see the black rectangular blast-like doors sliding up into the hull, revealing a string of lights inside leading into the depths of the vessel. Then specks started to appear from all of them, as objects began speeding out into space.

I zoomed the view in for a closer look and each of what had been dots resolved themselves into TR-3Bs.

Jack stared at them. 'My god, just how many ships are they launching?'

'From memory, the design enabled that battle carrier to hold up to three thousand ships,' John said. 'However, the cost to build *Vanguard* with a full flotilla was at over a trillion dollars, which was deemed to be too expensive to ever be a practical proposition.'

'Well, despite that hefty price tag, the Overseers have obviously got deep enough pockets,' Jack said.

I crossed my arms. 'Despite this show of strength, no matter how many TR-3Bs they have, I'm not sure that even they will be enough based on the Kimprak mothership's ability to defend itself.'

'They may not need to rely on their fleet alone, because the *Vanguard* was also designed to detonate nukes in a combustion chamber within the ship to power a six hundred gigawatt main forward laser battery,' John replied. 'Needless to say, the crew compartment, which is relatively small for such a huge ship, is heavily shielded.'

'Holy crap,' Ruby said. 'That amount of firepower sounds seriously useful in a firefight.'

'It will be,' Lucy replied. 'If John is correct, it gets it close to the laser power of the main batteries of *Tempest*, but of course, our power comes directly from E8 to power our energy weapon systems so no need to use nasty nukes to power them within our ship.'

'So the *Vanguard's* main weapons system could make a real difference in this battle?' I asked.

'If nothing else, it could certainly give the Kimprak a very bloody nose,' Lucy replied.

'I don't know about anyone else, but I can't help myself rooting for the Overseers in this fight,' Jack said.

I nodded. 'You're not alone. Although, even if they don't realise it yet, we should all be fighting on the same side.'

'The thing I still don't understand is just where did they get all those flight crews from, let alone train them up to use those ships?' Don said from his video window who'd been listening in on our conversation.

'They didn't, according to the *Sriracha's* scans,' Lucy said. 'Her sensors aren't reading any life forms on those TR-3Bs.'

'You're saying they're fully automated?' I asked.

'They certainly appear to be,' Lucy replied. 'But unlike our Wolfpack drones that have AI systems installed so they can think for themselves, all of those ships are directly slaved to the *Vanguard*.'

'That doesn't surprise me,' Jack said. 'The Overseers have always been control freaks and getting messy human beings out of the equation is absolutely the sort of stunt they would pull.'

John sucked his teeth. 'We actually experimented with that approach at the USSF and quickly discovered that automated control systems on a TR-3B were nowhere near as good as a human pilot, certainly in terms of thinking on their feet during a conflict.'

'Well, maybe they don't need to be if they're just effectively turning their fleet into drones and hoping to overwhelm the Kimprak with sheer numbers,' I said.

But Ruby was already shaking her head. 'No way, because those critters can multiply as fast as I can spit. And for every TR-3B they capture, at least another hundred of the metal cockroaches will be replicated.'

'Well, it looks like we're about to see how this all plays out, because they're opening their laser weapon ports in the nose of the *Vanguard*,' Don said over the video link.

'We're about to discover just how effective their main weapon system is in battle against the Kimprak, because according to *Sriracha's* sensors, we're seeing a spike in energy that matches a nuke being detonated,' Lucy replied.

The words had barely left her mouth when three wide blinding blue laser beams burst from the nose of the *Vanguard*.

I didn't have to select anything because with a wave of Lucy's hand she was already zooming the hologram view out. The beams of energy raced at the speed of light across the one hundred thousand klicks that still separated the battle carrier from the mothership according to a scale indicator.

'I'm amazed that they're trying to hit it at that sort of range,' Jack said.

'That would certainly be a problem if you were talking about firing within the atmosphere of a planet,' Lucy said. 'But out here in space, with nothing to impede those laser beams, they will carry on indefinitely, although it will start to be scattered eventually by the fine particulates that float around in space.'

'Ten seconds to impact' Ruby called out, looking at her console.

The three laser beams were heading straight towards a gap between the constellation of asteroids on a path that led straight towards the mothership.

I found myself clenching my hands into fists as it looked like it seemed impossible that the *Vanguard* would miss, willing the Overseers to hit our common enemy. I wiped at my eyes, hoping I was seeing things, but no. The asteroid was moving around the mothership.

'Damn it. It seems like the Kimprak have another trick up their sleeve,' Lucy said. 'They've reconnected the asteroids back to the mothership with their tethers and are using them to manoeuvre those rocks into position to form a shield wall.'

Sure enough, where there had been a gap a few seconds before, there was none now, and the lasers burned into the asteroid that had been moved into position. With blazing fire, the lasers burned into it, sending huge gouts of molten rock into space before the beams cut off.

But then the asteroid field was moving again, pulled by their tethers, and gaps opened again in what had become a shield-wall made of rock. A moment later, a trail of meteoroids were being fired out through the gap by the mothership.

'Scans show every single bloody one of those rocks is stuffed to the gills with Kimprak,' Ruby said peering at the metadata tags already assigned to them. 'Let's just hope their TR-3B fleet has some success, because they're beginning their attack run now.'

I could see that she was right. In the hologram, the vast robotic TR-3B fleet was diving towards the enemy, firing thousands of railgun rounds marked in green in the display that raced ahead of them towards the stream of Kimprak meteoroids. Flashes appeared throughout the swarm of rocks as the Overseers began to thin them out.

'We're detecting another energy pulse in the *Vanguard*,' Don said through the video feed.

Once again, three pillars of blue energy lanced out of the battleship's nose-gun ports as the gap dropped to fifty thousand klicks and the *Vanguard* continued to brake with its forward thrusters that were now slowing the vast ship rapidly. This time there was still a gap in the asteroid shield that the mothership had been firing bots out through. With deadly precision, the lasers zipped straight through it and hit the cigar-shaped asteroid vessel midship. Multiple explosions rippled along the hull as for the first time a human weapon found its mark on the enemy craft.

Cheers and claps broke out among those who'd been watching the spectacle unfold on the hologram with even Ruby joining in. Yes, the Overseers might be our sworn enemy, but this single act of defiance lifted my heart like nothing else could right now.

But then, when it felt like the balance in the battle was shifting towards the Overseers, it pivoted back again in an instant.

The asteroid field was moving again and this time it made a convulsing movement briefly contracting like a person sucking in a lungful of air. Then a lone three-klick-wide asteroid was spat out of the middle of the pack and sped directly towards the *Vanguard*.

Immediately the TR-3B fleet began to pour their weapon fire down into it. But the rock was too big and the railgun rounds just took lumps out of it, their laser fire only scorching lines across its surface. I could already tell that it was barely enough to dent the massive rock let alone slow it down.

'The *Vanguard* needs to blast that damned thing out of the sky before it slams into them,' Ruby said.

'As I seem to remember that was one of the technical limitations of the laser firing matrix,' John said. 'It takes time for the nuclear chamber to cool down sufficiently before they can use it again.'

Ruby shook her head. 'Damn, they need that weapon online right now.'

'Come on, come on, Alvarez,' I found myself saying aloud.

The asteroid had closed to a shockingly close distance in space warfare terms, just ten thousand klicks, when at last the forward laser battery fired again. It raced out and struck the asteroid dead centre, slicing through it. Cracks cascaded across the rocky surface like a sheet of glass being hit, and then it seemed to detonate, fragments shooting out from it.

Again there were whoops from the rest of the crew on the flight deck, but Ruby was already shaking her head.

'The Overseers don't realise it yet,' she said, 'but the Kimprak are just getting started.'

Vanguard rear engines lit up with blue plasma and it began turning away. The problem was it was happening too slowly as the asteroid remnants had closed to less than five klicks now.

Then, as Ruby prophesied, things suddenly got far worse for the Overseers.

Even as the *Vanguard's* weapon batteries opened up, targeting the boulders that were still hurtling towards it, each of them suddenly blossomed thousands of Kimprak bots that darted away like chrome seeds heading straight towards the warship.

But Alvarez and his crew weren't taking it sitting down either. At once, their swarm of TR-3Bs were on the Kimprak, the laser variants of their ships blazing fire into every single one that their targeting computers could identify.

'Just how many damned Kimprak are the remnants of that asteroid packing, Lucy?' Jack asked.

'At least two hundred thousand based on the *Sriracha's* sensor estimates.'

My blood ran cold as a fleet of three thousand TR-3Bs suddenly didn't seem like enough. Everyone fell silent as we watched the battle play out, the whoops and clapping already a distant memory.

A meteoroid that had made it through all the warship's defences impacted near the tail of the battleship and sliced through two of the bell engine nozzles of the *Vanguard*. Further out in space, the individual Kimprak had started to link together into one of their metallic nets and the fleet of TR-3Bs that flew straight into it were snared like flies in a web as it closed rapidly around them.

The vast warship was hit again by another meteoroid even as its weapon batteries blazed out at almost zero range towards the incoming storm of death.

The view zoomed in briefly to show the Kimprak erupt from the crashed meteoroid that was glowing like a hot coal in the hull near the stern of the *Vanguard*. The bots escaping immediately began to unfurl into their trilobite form and burrow into the hull. A single engine continued to blaze and *Vanguard* began to limp away.

Over his video link, Don broke the terrible silence that had filled the Citadel as the disaster unfolded before us. 'Permission to head in to help.'

Before I could respond, John jumped in first. 'As much as it pains me to say, Don, permission denied. There's nothing you can do to help them. That ship has been infected, and before long it will be overrun with Kimprak. However, the *Vanguard* is equipped with plenty of escape pods. So, for now, we need you back here for the final battle and then if we survive that, we can look for their survivors.'

Don closed his eyes briefly and when he opened them again he nodded. 'Roger that, Commander.'

Dozens of the TR-3Bs were wiped out by a series of explosions, probably belatedly initiated by their self-destruct systems kicking in.

I traded a grim look with John and nodded. 'Lucy, try contacting Alvarez, please.'

'I already have, and true to form, he's not responding,' she replied.

'So much for the Overseer's grand plan,' Jack said shaking his head. 'For a moment there, I really thought they had a chance to take that Kimprak mothership down.'

'We all did, Jack,' I said in a quiet voice as I turned away from the death throes of the battle playing out on the holographic display in all its awful, 3D glory.

CHAPTER TWENTY-FOUR

JACK and I laid in the grass of the parkland looking up at Jupiter through the crystal panels that had been set to transparent. Thanks to that, the habitation zone was brushed with the sunset colours of the gas giant we were now orbiting, the distant spires of the city gleaming with golds and reds of Jupiter's light. Also, rather disconcertingly, the lake was acting like a giant mirror to reflect the planet above us. This was definitely a, *"we're not in Kansas anymore,"* moment.

Jack squeezed my hand. 'So has dragging you away from the Citadel helped at all?'

'If you mean has it distracted me from the imminent battle? Then not really. I already feel burned out before it's even begun for us.'

'Anyone would be feeling rung out by what you've been going through as commander. Especially after the two previous defeats for our species, defeats that were in no way you're doing, by the way. Worse still, you were forced to watch what happened with *Vanguard* play out, powerless to intervene, which in many ways just makes the stress even worse.' Jack sat up and gazed down at me. 'And I wish I could take it all off your shoulders. But in the same way that you probably feel powerless, so do I. Forced to watch the woman I love go through all of this and unable to do anything practical to help.'

I turned my head to look at him. 'That is quite the speech, Jack.'

'Yeah, it's been rattling around in my head for a while now.'

I gazed into his deep blue eyes and felt a huge surge of energy in my abdomen almost like a physical cord of energy, snap towards Jack connecting me directly to him. 'Oh, Jack, I've been so caught up in my own head that I've barely seen you properly. I mean, really seen you.'

'That's only because you're suffering from the weight of all this responsibility on your shoulders.'

'True, but I'm surfacing from that for a moment to ask, how you are?' Jack started to turn away, but I grabbed hold of his chin and made him look at me again. I could sense that there was something he needed to say even if he didn't want to tell me. 'Just talk to me, Jack, please.'

He let out the longest sigh and nodded. 'To be absolutely honest, I'm doing badly, Lauren, because there's nothing I can really do to help anymore. When we were away on missions recovering micro-minds, that was different. Then you needed my expertise both as an archaeologist and even as an ex-soldier. But now, apart from mapping this ship with Poseidon, I don't really have a real role anymore. To be blunt, I feel like a spare wheel and I can't even do anything to help relieve some of the stress that you're going through.'

Now I was staring at him. 'Oh bloody hell, this just proves how wrapped up in myself I've been. You are a huge part of how I keep going each day, Jack. You are my rock, and I honestly couldn't do any of this without you. You've been carrying round the weight of that damned vision, which can't have been easy. If our positions were reversed, I would almost certainly be feeling exactly the same as you.' I took his hands in mine, caressing them with my thumbs. 'From now on, I want you by my side. I need your instincts now more than ever. But more than that, I need you, Jack Harper, to be with me until the end of this battle, however it works out. Apart from anything else, if this isn't a time for surrounding yourself with the people you love, I don't know when is.'

A slow smile filled his face. 'Wow, that's quite the speech back at me.' Then he gazed into my eyes and that tingle of energy ran through my abdomen again as that cord of energy drew us together.

I placed my hands on either side of his face and kissed him, just allowing myself to lose myself in his love and warmth for a moment. After all, this moment right here of tenderness between two people, was exactly what we were fighting for.

I don't know how long we'd been clinging to each other when my watch buzzed. Reluctantly I pulled away from Jack and checked it. Lucy's face greeted me.

'I hate to interrupt, but it's time, Lauren. Our Trojan Horse will come into range of the Kimprak mothership in about ten minutes. I've already sent a transport pod to pick you guys up.'

'Okay, we'll be straight there.' I pressed an icon on the watch to end the call. As I stood, I took Jack's hand. 'I need you by my side.'

'Then, I'll be there for you any way I can,' he replied as we headed towards the transport pod that was already coming in to land on the lawn next to us.

Jack and I stood in the middle of the hologram display along with Lucy and John. Displayed within it, thanks to another Guardian probe that had moved into position and was tracking the Kimprak mothership heading into orbit round the far side of Jupiter, we had a live view. The mothership and its constellation of rocks were slowly but surely moving ever closer to our Trojan Horse asteroid.

'It looks like all the calculations were spot on and our Trojan Horse is bang in the middle of their path,' Jack said.

'*Tempest*'s systems can navigate a million objects all at once, even factoring in orbital mechanics, which are always fun, but it's still a thing of mathematical beauty when it computes a trajectory like this,' Lucy said.

'We'll have to take your word for it,' I said.

'Do,' she said as she took a sip of black coffee from a thermal mug.

'Since when have you been drinking the hard stuff?' John said gesturing towards it.

'I'll have you know I've developed a real taste for it. Probably due to spending way too much time with Lauren and Jack.'

'Glad to be a bad influence then,' I replied, grateful for the bit of banter to distract me from what was happening on the hologram, where the fate of our world was potentially hanging in the balance. 'So have we had any more news about what happened to *Vanguard*?'

'The last thing that *Sriracha*'s sensors showed was that the battle cruiser had been caught by Jupiter's gravity well and didn't have enough power to escape with its single functioning engine,' Lucy replied. 'Eventually, it will be dragged down into the atmosphere where it won't last long.'

'And what about survivors?'

The Guardian drone that was sent to scour the area found nothing, but then, if they did eject there's a good chance they would have been captured by the Kimprak too.'

I grimaced. 'Right...'

Partly to distract myself from imagining the fate of anyone who had fallen into the robotic species' clutches, I studied the markers in our Trojan Horse asteroid for the position of the payload that it was secretly carrying buried within it. The Thunder torpedoes had been positioned according to *Sriracha's* survey of the asteroid, in what had appeared to be the least interesting location mineral-wise to the Kimprak. Hopefully, that would mean they would leave those areas well alone for the time being, but any moment now, we were going to find that out for sure.

The other members of the flight deck, human and avatars alike, briefly stopped what they were doing to watch as the countdown timer to the mothership reaching our Trojan Horse ticked down to the last two minutes.

'It looks like something is happening among the swarm of asteroids around the mothership,' Jack said.

When I looked closer at the hologram 3D model I could see he was right. The asteroids were beginning to move and reorientate themselves so that a large gap had emerged. Then fine filaments were reaching out like the tentacles of a Kraken towards our Trojan Horse. A quick zoom-in by Lucy revealed the strands to be chains of Kimprak stretching out to our asteroid.

'This looks promising,' John said as he headed into the hologram so he could examine what was happening up close.

My mouth was growing dry as we watched the swarm close to less than a klick. There was so much that could still go wrong. Then, without saying a word, because he absolutely knew how anxious I was feeling, Jack took up a position right next to me as my wingman for whatever was about to happen next.

The strands of Kimprak chains began latching onto our asteroid. One by one the strands became hundreds, all tethering our Trojan Horse into the web that now directly connected it to the other asteroids. Gently they adjusted its trajectory as they drew it into the gap, until it was just another large lump of rock moving with the rest of the constellation.

It was Ruby who finally broke the silence. 'Well, thank the actual fuck for that.'

Just like that we were all laughing and clapping and Jack was right there for the hug I threw his way.

'You see, today has been a good day after all,' he said pulling away from me.

'It's certainly been a good start to our battle plan, but there's still plenty of time for the Kimprak to discover our present before it gets here tomorrow morning.'

'You really are prepared to look our gift horse in the mouth, aren't you?'

I laughed. 'When you put it like that, maybe you have a point.'

'Exactly,' he replied, grinning.

'Actually, for once, I'm afraid it's going to be me that's going to rain on your parade,' Lucy said. 'Thanks to the sensor suite that we buried in the asteroid, we now have a better view of the mothership and its bad news. Let me show you why.'

The 3D view zoomed towards the mothership, the asteroids skimming past us, and then I saw them, easily a thousand triangular-shaped craft attached to the craft's stone hull.

'Bloody hell. You're not saying that the Kimprak captured a third of the Overseer's fleet?'

'That's exactly what it looks like,' Lucy replied, her expression pinched.

'Crap,' Ruby said shaking her head. 'As though the odds wouldn't have been bad enough with the loss of the Sol fleet.'

John drew in a deep breath. 'This does feel like one step forward and two steps back yet again.' He glanced at the counter hanging over the hologram, which read twelve hours and fifty-eight minutes.

I knew exactly what he was thinking, that wasn't exactly a lot of time to factor this increase in enemy units into our battle plans.

'Okay, it's going to be a long night, so we need to load this new data into the Battle Command's systems to see just how bad the news is,' I said.

'I'll go and get a fresh brew of coffee going,' Jack said as he squeezed my shoulder and headed off.

With a wave of Lucy's hand, the view of the mothership faded away to be replaced by the 3D model of *Tempest*. It struck me then, more forcibly than ever, that our starship contained humanity's last best hope of stopping the Kimprak invasion force from reaching Earth. I knew then that if the vision of my future was true that I would definitely sacrifice myself if it meant I could stop the mothership from ever reaching our precious world.

In the small hours, when at last I'd finished brainstorming revised tactics with John in the Battle Computer sim, I grabbed the opportunity to find a piece of paper and a pen. There was one last that thing that I absolutely had to do before everything kicked off.

Now I sat in the Temple of Transmutation listening to the waterfall's murmur quietly echoing around me and doing my best to let the tranquillity of this place soak into my bones. I breathed in the scent of the midnight orchids now at their most intense to try and steady myself after the emotional trauma of what I'd just put myself through. That had resulted in the letter that I was slipping into an envelope with Jack's name on it. Every single word in it had been dragged from the centre of my being, every single one of them fretted over. But somehow, after many attempts, I'd finally found the right words to tell him just how much I loved him.

It was the one thing I knew I had to do because there was every likelihood I wouldn't make it through it. As for the other practicalities, like a final will, there was no point because I had very little in the way of possessions to give away. It seemed my world had totally been transformed over the last five years into a pure life-experience one rather than possession-based.

As I held the envelope in my hand, Jack's name on it swam in my vision as tears filled my eyes.

I'd sometimes dared dreaming of our future together if we defeated the Kimprak, the one where our destiny looked like a timeshare between me working back at Jodrell Bank and Jack back at whatever dig site he wanted to explore. I'd even imagined us having children one day, a girl and a boy who we would, of course, both adore with all our hearts as they flourished and grew into exceptional adults. It was a future that was meant to be filled with so many happy memories. But all that had been swept away since seeing the vision of my own death. Now I all saw was Jack's life without me in it, and that made me want to sob.

Of course, I tried my best to really think about how Jack would cope after I was gone so there was a lengthy lecture in the letter that once he'd had a chance to mourn that he shouldn't close himself off from the idea of building a new life with someone. I just wanted him to be happy. Yes, it might be an ending for us, but that didn't mean it couldn't be a new beginning for him and whoever was lucky enough to fall into his orbit, just as I had done on that windswept beach back at Skara Brae.

I looked at the sculpture of the Angelus before me and breathed in. The beauty of this place was exactly what I needed and despite my tears, I felt a pressure valve releasing inside me. For the first time in a long time, I actually felt a sense of calmness building inside me.

Yes, I was going to die and yes, it would almost certainly

232 of this 232

break Jack's heart, but the important thing was that there would be a life for him afterwards.

It was then that I heard footsteps approaching and I knew without looking round exactly who it would be.

'I thought I might find you here,' Jack said gently as he sat down next to me. But then he saw my tears and immediately took my hands in his. 'What's wrong, Lauren?'

As he looked at me with such tenderness and concern in his eyes, it nearly undid me all over again, but summoning my courage, I handed him the letter.

'You have to promise me that you won't open it until after I'm gone,' I said.

Jack gazed at the letter and then at me and he instantly knew what it was. 'You mustn't talk like that. We both know what we saw is only a possibility not a certainty.'

'But we both need to be prepared in case it does work out exactly that way.'

'Well, you'll have to excuse me if I do everything I can to make sure it doesn't.'

I cupped his face in my hands. 'I know you will, but that aside, basically this letter tells you, Jack Harper, just how much I damned-well love you, although you probably already know.'

'I do.' He rested one of his hands on mine. 'You, Lauren Stelleck, are the absolute love of my life. And whilst you're still breathing, there is still hope.' He wiped away my tears with his fingers and then he kissed me.

My heart roared with yearning for him. Then Jack was standing and holding out his hand. 'So let's go make love and catch what sleep we can.'

'Sometimes you really do have the best ideas,' I replied smiling as I took his hand in mine. Then together we headed out away from the waterfall to head back to our room to make the most of whatever time we had left in the universe together.

CHAPTER TWENTY-FIVE

As THE COUNTDOWN ticked down to twenty minutes, we could see the grey, pitted surface of Jupiter's moon, Metis, through the windows of the Citadel. Metis was one of the inner moons of Jupiter, a lump of rock roughly fifty klicks across that was leftover from the formation of the solar system and had long ago been captured by the gas giant. More importantly, tactically speaking, it was just big enough for *Tempest* to hide behind. Even though our starship was fully stealthed, Lucy had told us there was still a remote chance that the mothership's sensors might spot any electromagnetic disturbance caused by our E8 field slightly distorting local space-time. Of course, once combat was underway and we were throwing absolutely everything at the Kimprak, they would quickly realise we were here.

Beyond Metis, Jupiter was a partial crescent with its dark side occasionally lit up by flashes of lightning from its never-ending electrical storms that raged through its gas clouds. At any other time, it would have been a mesmerising view, but right now, I barely had the headspace to even register it.

Around me, the flight deck was fully staffed. Erin had already slid the head sensor on that would enable her to control our Wolf-pack fleet that had grown well past the eight thousand that Jodie and Mike had been hoping to build, to what turned out to be nearly nine thousand. After some much-needed sleep, Mike and Jodie had joined us for the big battle to help monitor all technical systems alongside the avatars.

Ruby sat at her weapon's console and was pulling on a mind interface headset like Erin's that she would be using to control *Tempest's* torpedo arsenal. As she finished adjusting it the built-in sensors on the headband lit up in a string of blue lights and all sorts of diagnostic screens flared into existence before her on her holographic console.

'How does the brain interface feel, Ruby?' Jack asked.

'Like you wouldn't believe and quite the head rush. It can do everything too. For example, if I just wonder what our current torpedo inventory is...' On the holographic screen in front of her appeared graphics for each of the torpedo types and how many there were.

A grin filled her face as she turned to face Mike and Jodie who were seated opposite her at two engineering stations. 'Wow, you guys have been busy building torpedoes as well the Wolf-packs, by the look of things. According to these inventory stats there are 5,360 Hammers, 2,801 Lightnings, and 24 Thunders.'

Jodie nodded. 'And that's not counting all the ordinance already loaded onto the fleet. But it's a shame with the power drain on the E8 from the weapons and defence systems that we won't be able to produce any more during the battle.'

'I think what you've already built is more than enough,' Ruby said with a wide grin.

'Talking of numbers, what's our final ship tally?' Jack asked.

'We managed to build quite a few X-craft in the molecular printers, but obviously nothing like the number of Sol fleet ships that we lost. Including the Sol fleet survivors who will be under your command, Lauren, we have a total of 1,187 X-craft and of course the 843 USSF TR-3Bs.'

'So what does the battle sim say that our odds are now with all that thrown into the mix?' Mike asked.

I exchanged a frown with John. 'I'm afraid it's not looking great thanks to all those Overseer ships that the Kimprak captured. But if it comes to it, we're prepared to throw the kitchen sink at them.'

'What's that mean?' Jodie asked.

'We'll ram the mothership with *Tempest* and drive it into the gravity well of Jupiter.'

This was the fallback plan that, until now, I'd been keeping to myself after looking at all the various likely outcomes in the sims we'd run and that had been gnawing away at me. I hadn't even told Jack. Now, as expected, everyone was gawping at me.

'You'd seriously sacrifice this starship, not to mention everyone on it, to bring that mothership down?' Erin asked.

'Only as a last resort,' I replied. 'We would eject the majority of the crew in escape pods programmed to take them back to Earth.'

'But what about Alice's idea of turning *Tempest* into an ark ship?' Mike asked, pale-faced.

'To be frank, in that extreme scenario, Lauren's idea is a better one and would get my vote if it ever comes to it,' John replied. 'Much better that Earth survives, even if it is at the cost of this incredible vessel.'

So there it was, laid out for them all to see, my awful last throw-of-the-dice idea to save our world.

My gaze swept over everyone. 'That's our absolute worst-case scenario so let's do everything we can to make sure it doesn't come to that.'

Everyone nodded, but there were haunted looks on many of the human faces around me.

However, Lucy looked at me with something approaching pride.

'As much as it grieves me to say, it's the right call and you have the support of every avatar on this ship, if it comes down to that being the only option,' Lucy said. 'Anyway, I thought you'd like to know that our sensors indicate that the Kimprak mothership will appear from around the planet in five minutes. We should put *Tempest* into full battle mode now and power up our photonic mass shield and bring the point defence grid online.'

'Then, please go ahead with exactly that,' I replied as I sat down in the captain's seat next to Jack and he squeezed my hand.

'Ah no, I would if I could, but for anything that isn't a sim, it needs to be the captain of the starship who does that by saying, "*Commence battle stations.*"'

'Seriously, the Angelus used that command?' John said.

Lucy grinned at him. 'No, they didn't, actually, but I thought it sounded so damned cool I tweaked the control protocols. Mind you, I also showed considerable restraint because I also wanted to add a rapid drum-beat, like when they activated battle stations in that old show called *Stingray*, but Poseidon talked me out of it saying it would be too distracting.'

That raised a smile from me. 'Sometimes you even out-geek me, Lucy.'

'Oh, I try my best. Anyway, who's going to issue the order?'

John gestured towards me. 'This is your ship, you should do the honours, Lauren.'

'If you insist,' I replied with a small smile. I cleared my throat. 'Delphi, please commence battle stations.'

'Commencing battle stations,' the AI replied.

There might not have been rapid drums, but immediately a klaxon sounded and the lights dropped to a red glow. As the Citadel began to descend into the hull, the view of Jupiter and

Metis slipped away and the vast blast plates slid into place overhead.

The main hologram projector automatically powered up the Battle Command Centre. Around the edge of the bridge were different floating video views of key points of interest that included live views of flight bays, and the middle showed views of the mothership that was being tracked by the Guardian probe.

'Time to get our birds in the air,' John said.

'Agreed,' I said. 'Delphi, launch all ships.'

'Launching all ships,' Delphi replied.

There was immediate activity in hangar bay one as TR-3Bs and X-craft all started to rise from their pads, their crews already strapped in and ready for the launch order. The ships then began to make their way to the hangar exit falling into a perfect line formation thanks to the hangar control system manoeuvring the individual craft whilst they were still inside our starship.

'Damn, I wish we were going with them,' Ruby said.

'Me too,' Erin said casting a wistful look towards the video view.

'As much as a big part of me agrees with you, our place is here,' I said.

John nodded. 'I know exactly how you feel. It's hard to remain behind when others head into battle. However, look what happened to me when I was bullheaded and did exactly that. As much as I don't like it, my place is here alongside you, Lauren. If it's any comfort, I fully expect that *Tempest* will end up taking a full role in this battle before it's over.'

'In other words, be careful what you wish for,' Lucy said.

'Exactly,' John replied giving me and Ruby a pointed look.

I knew he was right, but part of me would never feel good about remaining in what amounted to the safest place in this battle. Somewhere on my journey to this specific day, I'd become a true soldier in every sense, one who was used to putting their life on the line. Although John might have had an epiphany in the training exercise, it was still hard for me not to feel my place was on the front line.

Jack gave me a sideways glance as though he knew exactly what I was thinking, but of course, he probably did. I also knew for a fact that he would be much happier with me being here—anything that made the Halls of Dreams prediction less likely to come true.

The view tracking our combined fleet had begun moving into an inverted cone-shaped formation as they departed *Tempest's* hangars.

'That's an interesting arrangement for our fleet,' Mike said.

'It's a defensive pattern that John and I came up with that's proved to work really well with the battle sim experiments we've been running,' I replied. 'The TR-3B railgun ships and our Pangolins are positioned towards the rear of that cone, but still have a clear line of sight for shooting out from the formation. The X103s and the laser variants of the TR-3Bs are arranged round the leading edges of the cone. There they can protect the other ships and also be able to engage any threats headed their way.'

'Let's not forget the Wolfpack's role in this,' Erin said.

'Absolutely,' John said. 'Until now, we haven't been able to use them against the Kimprak. Hopefully, thanks to their considerable numbers they will make all the difference.'

'I will certainly do everything in my power to make it a major one,' Erin said as her headset began to glow more brightly as she concentrated. 'Launching now...'

On the holographic representation of *Tempest,* hundreds of ports opened up. Wolfpack drones began bursting from them by the hundreds, and screens lit up in front of Erin as she took control of them. Around a fifth of the drones drew up in an outer ring around the leading edge of our fleet but the majority slid into position in groups of four around our ships.

'This is new,' Jack said leaning forward in his seat to look at them in the hologram.

'It's that loyal wingman strategy that we've been working on,' Erin replied. 'Each of those Wolfpack drones will be slaved to the individual ship's weapon's officer. It will give the X103s an extra level of firepower and protection and also effectively increase the number of ships.'

'So why not slave them to the TR-3Bs as well?' Jack asked.

'Because unfortunately, their flight systems are incompatible because they were always designed to work with X-craft,' John said.

Jack nodded. 'I'm sure the other Wolfpacks will have our backs as well.'

Lucy turned to us. 'The *Sriracha* is launching now,' she said.

I turned my attention to *Tempest's* rear space dock to see the *Sriracha* emerging from it. I toggled a channel to it and Don's face filled my video screen.

'How's everything going?' I asked.

'All weapons systems are online and we're ready to rumble,' he replied with a grin. 'Ah, and I should also probably tell you about our wingman.'

'What, you mean you have a Wolfpack drone tracking you?' I said peering at the schematic display in the hologram but seeing no evidence of one.

'No, I mean literally an actual wingman who should be launching any moment now.'

Mike made a *hmmm* noise in the back of his throat.

When I glanced across at him he immediately tried to avoid my gaze, raising my Spidey senses. Jodie was looking anywhere but at me too.

'You both know something about this, don't you?' I said.

'We do,' Jodie replied, but didn't elaborate.

Before I could respond, I noticed a small wing-like ship

shooting out of the space dock and taking up position alongside the *Sriracha*. At the same moment, an incoming message flashed up on my screen marked with the metadata tag of *Falcon One*. With a growing sense of confusion, I pressed the comm button to see Troy's face appear before me.

'Is that you, Troy, flying whatever that craft is?' I said.

'It is indeed, Commander,' Troy said.

'And where exactly did you get that particular vessel?' John asked.

Mike shot me a guilty look. 'That would be down to me and Jodie. We found the schematics for a single-person space fighter in the shipyard schematics that we've already nicknamed Raptor, because the Angelus name was just way too out there. Anyway, we only had time to print one before the battle.'

Jodie nodded. 'We just happened to mention to Troy in passing that we needed a test pilot, and before we knew it he'd volunteered.'

'"*Just happened*" to mention it to him,' I said, using air quotes. 'So, the fact that Troy is probably the best test pilot in our whole fleet had nothing to do with it, I suppose?'

'Well, if you put it like that, what a coincidence,' Mike said pulling a face.

'Don't be too hard on them,' Troy said. 'I needed a pair of wings for this battle and after a lot of soul searching, I realised there was absolutely no way I was going to sit this out on the bench. Lauren, I needed this. You of all people should be able to understand that.'

I held his gaze. Of course he needed this, just as I would have in his position. I didn't need to be a psychologist to know just how much he would be tormenting himself over what had happened to the Sol fleet, and this was him trying to make amends. Once again he was acting just as I would, if I'd been in his shoes.

I nodded. 'I totally get it, Troy. So, what can your new ship do?'

'We're about to find out, but it's extremely fast with its fusion drive and is armed with what in the operating manual is referred to as a *turbo laser*.'

'That sounds like something straight out of *Star Wars*,' I replied.

'Which is exactly what I'm hoping. Lucy tells me it should prove pretty lethal taking out those damned Kimprak bots.'

I shot Lucy a look. 'You knew about this too?'

She shrugged. 'Hey, who am I to bust up a party?'

I raised my eyebrows at her before returning my attention to Troy. 'Well, you actually have my blessing in this. So, my orders for you are pretty much the same as for the *Sriracha*. You, Don, and his crew are basically free agents who are free to mix things up a bit, offer support to the rest of the fleet where you can, and strike our enemy where you see opportunities.'

'Roger that, Lauren, and thank you for supporting me in this. Out.' Troy's face disappeared from my console.

John, who'd been analysing his own tactical screens, gave me an approving look. 'Basically, you're thinking that they'll be skirmishers, free to harass the enemy?'

'Exactly, it was yet another thing I studied in wargaming with Niki.'

But the thing we both left unsaid, was that we both knew that Troy was looking for some form of redemption and this might actually help him in a small way, by taking an active role in the battle. I just hoped he didn't end up throwing his life away in the process.

'Okay, all that's left to do is to launch the first wave of *Tempest's* torpedo arsenal and move them into position,' Ruby said. 'Permission to launch, Commander Stelleck?'

'Whenever you're ready,' I replied.

'As always, born ready.' Ruby cracked her knuckles and then popped in a fresh stick of gum. As she concentrated, her mind control interface glowed and her screens filled with data. According to the stats, also now being displayed on my console, two hundred Lightning torpedoes, and the same again of Hammers, and five of our precious Thunder nukes launched. These would be the first wave of *Tempest's* torpedoes with the rest held in reserve.

The specks of torpedoes flew out on the tactical display and away from the fleet, arching around Metis and heading out towards the designated staging area from where they would be launched the moment we issued the order to begin the attack.

'Okay, the torpedoes are in coasting mode, waiting for your orders,' Ruby said a few minutes later as they reached their designated navigation marker in the main hologram display.

I nodded and took a centring breath as I gathered myself for what was about to come. This was it, after years of preparation, what happened in the next few hours would almost certainly seal the fate of humanity and our world.

Jack glanced across at me. 'How are you feeling?' he whispered.

'Terrified, anxious, but now also weirdly exhilarated.'

He gave me a smile. 'Yes, I know exactly what you mean, I feel exactly the same. I also think that's probably true for every single person on board and across the fleet.'

I took in the tense expressions of everyone round me as they gazed at their consoles, but also of pure focus and sheer determination to get this thing done. Then I looked at the countdown timer, the timer that had been counting down for years at Eden and now here onboard *Tempest*, with literally sixty seconds left to go until the battle would begin.

A tsunami of emotions should probably have been rolling through me in these last moments, but all I felt was a desperation for the pressure of waiting to finally be over and for this all to be underway.

In the last twenty seconds, John toggled the fleet-wide comm on. 'Good luck to each and every one of you. Fight for those you love, fight for your world, and deliver your A-game to this fight. No one can ask any more of you than that.'

It was a simple speech, but it hit the mark perfectly and I found myself wishing that I'd given it myself. Even our most seasoned pilots and crew must have been feeling more than a little bit apprehensive by now.

In the last few seconds, the view on the hologram started to zoom out from *Tempest* and our assembled fleet until the whole of Jupiter came into view.

As the countdown hit zero an adrenaline rush pulsed through me and my heart clenched as a large pulsing red dot surrounded by a constellation of smaller ones appeared around the edge of the gas giant on the main hologram. But there was also a green dot among the red ones with a metadata tag that identified it as our Trojan Horse.

'We have confirmed sensor lock on the Kimprak mothership,' Lucy said.

'Here we go,' I said. 'Ruby, please launch your first wave of torpedoes.'

'Roger that, torpedoes are away. Time to impact, twenty minutes.'

I nodded to John. 'Time to use our new unified fleet identifier that we agreed on.'

He smiled. 'It is, indeed.' He toggled a comm channel. 'Earth Fleet, you are to proceed to the engagement zone.'

This was another marker moment where, at last, humanity had fully put aside its differences to fight as one. Just as it should always have been.

Then, almost like one living entity, our fleet began their

rocket burns, moving away, accelerating hard straight towards Jupiter. They would build up maximum speed so they could pull out of the atmospheric dive and be able to catch up with the mothership as it drew parallel to Metis, and *Tempest* lurking behind it.

'Estimated time till we're in combat range is twenty-five minutes,' Lucy said as she looked at a dozen tactical screens that she had open before her.

Jack gestured towards the countdown timer that had been the metronome for so long. 'It's begun ticking up.'

'That's because it's now marking the duration of the battle,' Lucy replied.

'Always a useful detail for the historians when it comes time to document this battle one day,' Jack replied.

I didn't give him a reality check that there was a good chance that there might not be any historians left to record it. But then again, I knew that Jack was just trying to stay positive for my benefit.

So, keeping my thoughts to myself instead, I used my control panel to zoom in for a closer look at our Trojan Horse held in place towards the front of the pack. It had been agreed that we would detonate it a few minutes before the first wave of our torpedoes reached the target.

I got up from my seat and headed into the hologram so I could examine our ships, drones, and torpedoes from every angle, watching events unfold so far, exactly as they had in the sim. The only exception to that was the addition of the *Sriracha* and *Falcon One*, who were tracking our fleet off to one side. I hoped for Troy's sake, he really did find some sense of peace in whatever was about to happen.

The mothership was growing steadily closer as it used Jupiter's gravity well to scrub off a huge amount of its interstellar speed. According to the stats, it had already reduced its velocity by eighty percent and it was still decelerating hard.

We watched the orbital mechanics play out over the next twelve minutes, as the mothership drew level with Metis. The Kimprak vessel was glowing a dull red, as were many of the asteroids between it and the gas giant, as it scrubbed off its remaining speed in the upper atmosphere of Jupiter. One more full orbit of the gas giant and it would have done enough to begin its slingshot straight towards Earth. That was our window of opportunity to make this plan work.

'Okay, time to power up our ion drive so we don't get left behind,' Lucy finally said.

'Are you ready?' I asked Mike and Jodie.

They both nodded.

'Powering up the ion drive now,' Mike said.

'And the Photonic Mass shield is set to maximum,' Jodie added.

A large glowing blue light appeared at the stern of the 3D model of *Tempest* in the hologram as our ion drive lit up and our vast ship began to move away from the moon, slowly accelerating towards the mothership in the distance. Like the rest of our fleet, we were also using the gravity pull of Jupiter to assist our acceleration.

'Let's just hope that the Kimprak don't notice any spatial distortion caused by *Tempest* until it's too late, so we don't lose the element of surprise,' Mike said.

I nodded. 'If you hadn't realised already, I'm keeping everything crossed here.'

He smiled across at me. 'We all are.'

We all watched our fleet reach the end of its dive-flight, with Ruby's torpedoes having already done the same just ahead of them. Now they were all pulling up hard to catch up with the mothership that had sped past below them as it continued to skim through Jupiter's upper atmosphere.

As John and I'd agreed during the battle sims, our faster X103s were keeping their speed down to match the slower pace of our Pangolins and TR-3Bs. They were also relying on their rockets rather than their helical drives, because apart from the fact the TR-3Bs didn't have the equivalent, John and I were both determined not to split our fleet.

I resisted the urge to start gnawing on my nails as our torpedoes and ships began to reel in the mothership.

'Any indication that the Kimprak know we're here yet?' John asked.

'None at all, so it seems that all our ships' stealth systems are working as hoped,' Lucy replied. 'However, as they draw closer there is every chance they will start to notice the gravitational distortions in the local space. You can't fly that many ships through space without creating a few ripples and they're bound to notice them eventually.'

'Hopefully, by that time our Trojan Horse will have done its job and it will be too late for them to do anything about it,' Mike said.

'We won't have much longer to find out,' Jodie said. 'We're about to send the detonation code in the next ten seconds.'

The hologram display started to zoom in towards our asteroid.

'In five, four, three, two, one...and signal sent,' Jodie continued.

My heart was thumping hard as I watched for the pulse that should be bursting any moment. One second stretched to two, then three and still nothing. My gaze swivelled back to Jodie who was now frowning.

'That doesn't make any sense, the warheads should have definitely received the signal by now and detonated.'

'Oh hell, you don't think despite all our precautions the Kimprak discovered them?' Jack asked.

Jodie grimaced. 'That's certainly a possibility.'

I was already feeling a tightness in my chest as I turned towards Lucy, because this could blow a huge hole in our battle plan. 'Can your Guardian probe give us any clue as to what might have happened?'

Lucy nodded and a live camera view appeared in the window, zooming in tight on the surface of the asteroid. I could see the glints of metal snaking across the surface of our Trojan Horse where the Kimprak had begun burrowing into the surface as they mined it for materials. Then the view closed in on a particular crater where an antenna lay broken in two as several Kimprak trilobites devoured it.

'Damn it, they discovered the relay station on the surface even though it was heavily stealthed,' Mike said.

I stared at him. 'Please don't tell that means they've discovered the Lightning warheads as well?'

'Not necessarily, they're buried pretty far beneath the surface.'

'But even if they're still intact, we have no way of detonating them?' I asked.

'Well, there might be a way as the warheads themselves also have a low-powered transmitter, which is how they communicated with the base station on the surface,' Lucy said. 'If we managed to get a ship close enough we could use its transmitter to activate a manual timer. The only problem is that the Kimprak are extremely likely to detect even a single ship's presence at that close a range, and unfortunately, a Guardian drone hasn't got a powerful enough transmitter.'

'Hang on, what about *Sriracha's* transmitter?' I asked. 'Surely, that Angelus ship has a powerful one and is more stealthy than the rest of our craft.'

Lucy was already nodding. 'Yes, by quite a margin and it also has gravitational engine dampeners which can very effectively mask any gravity vortexing from her fusion rockets that the Kimprak might be able to pick up even at that range. The same goes for *Falcon One*.'

'But this is sounding risky,' Mike said. 'Shouldn't we consider turning the fleet round and waiting till we can be sure this will work?'

'Unfortunately, we don't have the luxury of that sort of time,' Erin replied. 'If we turn the fleet around now, they won't be able to stop the mothership as it slingshots towards Earth on its next orbit.'

'Orbital mechanics is a bitch like that,' Lucy said. 'This is our only window to launch a full attack, as opposed to some sort of harrying option or chasing them down as they head to Earth. But whatever you decide, make it quick because we literally have a three-minute window left to do this.'

'Then it sounds to me like we have no option but to send the *Sriracha* in ahead of the fleet, with *Falcon One* on escort duty,' John said. 'What do you think, Lauren?'

'I agree,' I replied. 'We need to contact Don and Troy and let them know the plan and then let's make this happen.'

John nodded. 'And let's pray this actually works.'

CHAPTER TWENTY-SIX

THE VIEW of the *Sriracha* and *Falcon One* flying next to each other seemed so real in the hologram that it felt like I was actually looking at the two ships from another craft trailing them. But of course, I wasn't actually there. I felt a huge stone of guilt in my stomach weighing me down, that I was safe onboard *Tempest* whilst Troy, Don, and all his crew were all putting their lives on the line.

Around me, people's tension was palpable as we all waited for the five minutes that felt like an eternity. Both ships pulled ahead of the fleet, and then had overtaken Ruby's torpedoes that had been throttled back, as they sped towards the constellation of asteroids around the mothership.

The delay of detonating the Trojan Horse had put us on the back foot. But the one thing tactically still in our favour, was that the asteroid had now been placed in the rear of the constellation around the mothership, which would make it a little easier for Don and Troy to sneak up on it.

'Okay, we're boosting our transmitter and will be in range in sixty seconds,' Don said over the video link from the bridge of the

Sriracha as we all listened in. '*Falcon One,* stay sharp. As far as we know they haven't detected either of our ships, but they could also just be luring us in.'

'Don't worry, Don, if I see so much as a glint of metal heading our way I'm going to melt it to slag,' Troy replied.

For a man who I'd seen utterly broken only a few days before, he sounded focused and very much together. But then, sitting in a cockpit would always feel like home to him. I also wouldn't be surprised if there was a certain sense of sanctuary from his own thoughts whilst flying that fighter. That would probably be especially true during combat.

'So far so good,' John said to me as he watched their progress.

'I won't relax until they've made a clean getaway,' I replied.

'If anyone can pull it off, it's Troy and Don,' Jack said. 'They are two of our best.'

'I know, I know,' I replied as I reached out and squeezed his arm before returning my attention to the hologram as Don started speaking again.

'Okay, we're beginning our braking manoeuvres so we don't fly past the target,' Don said. '*Falcon One,* on my mark, in three, two, one...'

Both ships flipped over a hundred and eighty degrees in the hologram display as they reversed directions, their fusion engines throttled to max as the speed indicator began to drop.

'According to *Sriracha's* sensor readings they are beginning to scrape through the upper atmosphere of Jupiter,' Lucy said. 'On the plus side, that means that they can start to use their ant-grav drives for high-speed manoeuvres within the planet's gravity well.'

'Good, because they need every advantage they have on their side until those warheads are detonated,' John said.

We watched the two ships decelerating fast to match the speed of the mothership and its herd of asteroids. At last, the distance had closed to a toe-curling two klicks, when the radio comm crackled into life again with Don's voice.

'Okay, we're amplifying the signal and broadcasting to the warheads now,' he said.

Absolute silence fell on the flight deck as we all listened in.

Then there was a long whoop. 'Yes, Lightning warheads have received the arming codes and the timer has been set for two minutes, thirty seconds.'

Troy responded over the radio. 'Then it's time for us to get... oh crap! I'm reading at least a hundred compromised TR-3Bs taking off from the mothership and heading straight towards us. They must have picked up our boosted signal.'

I immediately activated the comm. 'Which means they must also know that something is now buried in our Trojan Horse asteroid and are probably already tunnelling towards our warheads.'

'Then let's just hope we buried them deep enough for them not to get to them in time,' Don replied. 'Two minutes coming up on the timers and we're commencing full-burn away from the asteroids.'

On the display, both ships surged back the way they'd come as their engines throttled to max.

'Damn it, those enemy ships are on our tail and opening fire,' Troy said.

We saw the squadron of the TR-3Bs clear the asteroids' constellation and race towards *Sriracha* and *Falcon One*.

I drove my fingernails into my palms as our ships raced away from them and the imminent explosion.

'Lucy, can you please overlay a radius for the EM pulse when the warheads detonate?'

She nodded, and with a wave of her hand, a blue transparent sphere appeared, centred on the mothership with *Sriracha* and *Falcon One* about halfway towards the edge of the boundary.

'Please tell me they're going to make it in time, someone?' I said.

'It's looking touch and go, I'm afraid,' Lucy said.

I drove my fingernails into my palms so hard I could feel welts take shape as our two ships dodged and dove around the rail shots being fired at them from the pursuing TR-3Bs.

It came down to the wire when, during the last ten seconds, a railgun round came so close to *Sriracha* that the point defence system on the corvette was forced to take it down with a blaze of laser fire, vaporising the hypersonic projectile on impact.

'Okay, here we go,' Don said over the comm. 'The detonation of the surface charges are just about to kick off before the main event.'

A series of pre-detonations erupted across the surface of our Trojan Horse's 3D model, revealing vast shafts in the asteroid just as had been planned.

'Just three seconds until the detonation of the Lightning warheads,' John said watching a new timer in the hologram tick down.

I chewed my lip as a flash of intense light blazed out of all the shafts in our asteroid. Then a blue transparent sphere on the 3D display was racing outwards and overtaking the TR-3Bs which began spiralling as their systems shut down, a few crashing into each other.

The *Sriracha* and *Falcon One* had almost reached the boundary as the blue sphere started to fade indicating the weakening strength of the EM pulse as it overtook them. Then, just like that, the view of Don blinked out.

Lucy was already turning towards me, her palms up. 'Before you panic, both those ships are heavily shielded and their systems will have automatically shut down to prevent them from getting fried. At that range from the epicentre of such a large EM pulse, they should be coming back online with a couple of minutes.'

'How long for those enemy TR-3Bs to reboot?' John asked.

'They haven't got as much shielding as the Angelus ships and were closer, so we're probably looking at close to five minutes for them,' she replied.

My attention immediately switched back to the mothership. 'Okay, the most important question right now is, did that EM burst knock that bloody thing out?' I said pointing at it.

Lucy paused, and then a wide smile filled her face. 'Yes, the Guardian is registering zero electrical activity from the mothership, although as we both know, that won't last forever.'

I spun round to look at Ruby. 'How far out are your torpedoes?'

'Already burning in at maximum speed and on the home-straight now, contact in two minutes.'

'And the main fleet along with my Wolfpacks are another three minutes behind them,' Erin said.

'Okay, everyone pray that these are big enough knock-out blows to take that damned enemy ship down,' John said.

The view zoomed out to show a large-scale tactical view as the Battle Command system took over so we could see exactly how the battle was unfolding. On it, the first wave of Ruby's torpedoes were hurtling towards the mothership and the asteroids clustered around it.

I retreated to my captain's chair so I could follow specific aspects of the battle from my console. I had just reached it when the comm crackled back into life and the metadata tags next to *Sriracha* and *Falcon One* turned green.

'And we're back, did anyone miss us?' Don said.

That almost raised a laugh in me. 'Like you wouldn't believe.'

'In that case, do we have your permission to engage all those targets just sitting there begging for us to shoot them, before they have a chance to reboot?' Troy asked.

'With our blessing,' John replied.

'Roger that,' Don replied. 'Engines are online and weapons are hot, time to go and kick some butt.'

'Did you mean to make that sound like a rap song?' Ruby asked smirking.

Don laughed. 'Of course, but please excuse us whilst we shoot some fish in a barrel. Out.' The comm light blinked off beside his name on the display.

The *Sriracha* and *Falcon One* were reduced to simple green dots on the tactical map as they raced towards the TR-3Bs that had pursued them and were now tumbling slowly through space. I zoomed in on my console for a closer look and saw both ships open fire almost at the same time.

Falcon One's turbo laser spat out streaks of fire-like bullets that punched holes straight through the hulls of the Kimprak ships and made two of the craft explode almost immediately. But it was the firepower of *Sriracha* that took my breath away. Her particle beams burned through the enemy craft and split them in two like the proverbial hot knife through butter. At the same moment, a full flotilla of its gauss launchers opened up in her nose and according to the metadata tags, at least a dozen Hammer torpedoes launched out of them and raced towards the Kimprak fleet. With a rippling series of explosions at least a quarter of the formerly pursuing ships were blown apart.

'Holy crap, I need myself one of those ships,' Ruby said, shaking her head as she watched the action play out on the main hologram.

'And I promise that you can have one gift-wrapped if we make it through this,' I replied.

She grinned at me. 'You do know that I'm going to hold you to that, Commander?'

'I do,' I replied, allowing myself a brief smile despite all the tension that was sloshing around in my stomach.

Lucy's expression grew pensive. 'Bother. I knew it would be

only a matter of time, but the mothership is starting to come back online.'

Ruby's eyes tightened on her display. 'Okay, my first wave of torpedoes are only forty-five seconds out now.'

'Concentrate your fire on those asteroids and the mothership,' I said.

'Already planning to,' she replied.

Red markers started to erupt all over the mothership as its remaining slaved TR-3Bs lifted off and sped away to meet our torpedoes, which had just raced past the *Sriracha* and *Falcon One* and were hurtling towards them.

But then the asteroid pack convulsed and a dozen huge lumps of rocks, each several klicks wide, were spat out, racing out straight to meet them. At the same moment, streams of metallic fire lanced out from the asteroids towards our torpedoes, quickly forming into nets and rapidly expanding outwards.

'Bloody hell,' Mike said. 'They've mounted Kimprak launchers to those rock projectiles.'

'If they think that's going to stop me they have another thing coming,' Ruby muttered.

The markers for her torpedoes began to move apart spreading into a wide ball, the Lightning missiles moving to the front of the formation.

As the first asteroid tumbled towards her swarm of torpedoes streaming Kimprak bot-fire, Ruby sent ten Lightnings straight towards it. With pulses of blue light, each of them detonated, killing the streams of fire from the giant rocks. Next, Ruby flew one of our precious Thunder nukes straight into them, blasting them apart with a blinding explosion that blazed for a moment, then rapidly dimmed as it expanded through space. The rest of the torpedoes were curving around it to avoid the shockwave. But the Kimprak nets had already joined together to form a structure so vast—easily a hundred klicks wide—that even a combination of

Lightning and Hammer detonations only took out a small fraction of it.

But the second wave of Ruby's torpedoes had made it past and were weaving through the streams of Kimprak fire straight towards the mothership with the rest of the Thunder nukes towards their tail.

'Come on, come on,' Jack said, leaning forward in his seat, his hands clasped together.

A small seed of hope was starting to build in my chest when one of the asteroids around the mothership suddenly exploded.

'Did you do that, Ruby?' John asked staring at her.

'That was nothing to do with me, and my second wave of torpedoes are still a minute out,' she replied.

'I'm afraid that was all the Kimprak's doing, they seem to have deliberately detonated it,' Lucy replied.

'But why?' I asked.

'Because of that,' Jack said, gesturing towards the main hologram where countless-thousands of tiny objects were racing outwards in an expanding cloud. 'It looks like they're deliberately seeding the whole area with Kimprak, like limpet mines ready to latch onto anything getting too close to them.'

'Oh bloody hell, out of the frying pan and into the fire,' Jodie said.

I nodded, my mind racing. 'This has definitely shifted the odds in the Kimprak's favour for now. Ruby, can you still clear a path for the fleet coming in hot on your tail?'

'Working on it,' she said. Her hands were flying over her screens as they rapidly opened and closed.

On the battle map, the rest of us watched the torpedoes hurtle straight towards the thousands of Kimprak that had already started to form a second net.

Explosions and pulses started to detonate right across the battlefield as *Sriracha* and *Falcon One* did everything they could to pick off the Kimprak at the edge of the fight. Ruby had her jaw set, beads of sweat breaking out on her forehead.

'Die, you bastards,' she muttered as the brain control interface's blue lights blazed an intense white as she issued a continuous stream of commands at the speed of thought.

The odds might have been against her, but Ruby was slowly but surely opening up a hole in the enemy's defences as she threw Thunders into the mix too, to thin out the denser patches of bots.

'How far out is our main fleet?' John called out.

'Just two minutes away,' Erin replied.

'Then time for the Wolfpack to earn their keep,' I said. 'Accelerate any that aren't assigned to our ships, to build on Ruby's work and blast a way through.'

'Roger that,' Erin replied.

Like Ruby, dozens of windows opened up in front of Erin. The speed of commands she was issuing, thanks to the mind control interface, was breathtaking and within moments the Wolfpack drones designated with blue markers, were speeding ahead of the fleet. They began darting through the ranks of the Kimprak's nets, strafing it with laser fire and vaporising any bots that they hit, to burning droplets of molten metal.

But the reinforcement enemy-TR-3Bs were on the case too, racing out to meet torpedo and Wolfpack alike. It wasn't long before there were so many explosions erupting across the battlefield that it was almost impossible to make out what was happening.

'This is what I call the fog of war,' John said, shaking his head at the tactical display.

'Then it's time to hand full control over to the Battle Command,' Jodie said. 'It was designed for exactly this sort of intense conflict. It will filter out all the excess information so we only need to concentrate on the high-level stuff, as it deals with the rest. The strategic options it throws up will be constantly adapting to the changing situation.'

I nodded. 'John, are you happy to take this step?'

'Absolutely, things are happening faster than I can blink right now.'

'Okay, Delphi, turn over control to Battle Command.'

'Turning control over to Battle Command,' Delphi replied.

The thousands of contacts within the hologram began to have multiple flight paths plotted out from each one as the system started to take over.

The dedicated AI behind the Battle Command system began sifting through each and every option for the Wolfpack drones and quickly listed options for Erin, complete with full stats.

The transformation was almost immediate. Even though Erin had been doing an incredible job of controlling all of the drones, there was now a sense of extra order kicking in with the AI offering up deliberate strategies that even included sacrificing drones if it was tactically for the greater good.

One example I spotted in the high-speed dogfights, was a lone Wolfpack drone deliberately slowing and presenting an easy target for three TR-3Bs chasing it. As it was intercepted, at least six other Wolfpacks swooped in and all three TR-3Bs were taken out with blasts of laser fire.

Slowly, a hole started to be nibbled out of the Kimprak nets, with that now expanded to a multi-level spider web of lattices.

All this seemed to happen in a whirlwind of action that only lasted a minute. The next thing I knew, the markers from our fleet of ships were rapidly approaching the battlefield in the hologram.

'Okay, here we go, Lauren,' John said as both of our consoles lit up with dozens of tactical options.

I nodded. 'Let's hope we can deliver that knock-out punch.'

This was the moment that John and I had been training for. It had already been decided that he would take command of our railgun craft, namely the Pangolins and TR-3Bs, whilst I took control of the X103s and the laser variants of the TR-3Bs.

'Good luck,' Jack said to me as he gave me an encouraging smile.

I nodded and managed a faint smile as I breathed deeply trying to calm the spin of my nerves. Then, as John and I had planned, I selected the *Alpha* option.

As our fleet raced towards the hole in the enemy defences that had been opened up, the X103s under my command began to move towards the edges and began picking off individual Kimprak that were floating in space with blasts of their mini-guns.

Then, John's Pangolins and TR-3Bs drew closer together and fired railgun volleys in perfect synchronisation.

On the tactical map, the projectiles raced out as an enormous swarm of green points shredding the sections of Kimprak nets directly ahead of the fleet that had already started to reform. The ships under John's command fired again and again, until a clear channel had finally been opened up, also throwing their ships' torpedoes into the mix to help.

'Okay, the remainder of my second wave of torpedoes will try to blast a way through,' Ruby called out.

'Understood,' John replied.

His ships moved aside to create a corridor for the torpedoes to pass through, and the *Beta* option on my console started to blink and I quickly selected it.

At once the X103s and laser variant TR-3Bs under my command started to speed forward, as their crews began engaging the last five hundred or so enemy TR-3Bs.

My X103s weren't alone either as their wingman Wolfpack drones that had formed up around each of the ships added considerably to their killing firepower. The ships blazed through the ranks of infected TR-3Bs and quickly began to thin their numbers. I selected fresh tactical options as Ruby's final wave of torpedoes began to streak towards the mothership.

'Damn it,' Ruby said. 'It looks like the Kimprak aren't going to take this lying down.'

A glance towards the main holographic tactical map revealed exactly what she was talking about. The mothership had shot out at least ten asteroids towards the flotilla of torpedoes racing at it. To make things even worse, the Kimprak chains connecting them were drawing them together into a solid wall.

'Can you manage to dodge those asteroids?' John called over to Ruby.

'Doing my best, Commander Hamilton,' she replied.

The outer torpedoes were already curving away, but the closing speed was too great and the asteroids crashed straight into the middle of the pack, wiping out the bulk of them.

But there were still several hundred that managed to dodge them, the Battle Command map showing a trajectory that would take them around the asteroids and straight on towards the mothership.

Before there was even a chance for any fresh hope to take root, five asteroids in the shield-wall detonated. At once an enormous swarm of Kimprak ball-bearing bots raced out from them and sliced through the torpedoes, destroying all of them instantly, whilst others took out several dozen of the ships under my command that had been attempting to clear a path. Even then, the Kimprak were far from done as the fresh reinforcements were linking up with the other nets and had begun to rapidly expand.

My blood ran cold as I witnessed what was happening.

Options were flashing all at once as John and I hit them as fast as we could, our fleet doing everything it could to take out as many of the Kimprak as possible before the net closed around them. Erin whirled the Wolfpacks through the chains, destroying thousands, but quickly began losing drones too.

I knew in that instant that the battle was slipping away from us.

'They are literally trying to capture all our ships in a bloody great net,' I called out as beads of sweat broke out on my forehead. 'We've got to get *Tempest* into the fight, or at least distract the Kimprak long enough so we can do some serious damage, before they wipe out our entire fleet.'

John nodded. 'I don't think we have a choice, we need to finish off those damned metal cockroaches.'

'Bloody right we do,' I replied. 'Ruby, launch *Tempest's* remaining torpedoes, and Erin, prep all our remaining Wolfpacks for launch. Lucy, power up our point defence grid because we're going in.'

Lucy snapped me a salute with a broad smile. 'It will be my absolute pleasure, Commander.'

The tactical map zoomed out as our vast starship began to track towards the mothership. Pure adrenaline coursed through my system making my blood sing. Whatever it took, we would stop those bastard machines, right here, right now.

CHAPTER TWENTY-SEVEN

ALREADY TRACKING through space at the same speed as Metis, *Tempest* didn't so much surge forward, as gradually increased her momentum towards the alien mothership as the ion drive, with a gravity assist from Jupiter, accelerated our starship towards it and the battle raging in its wake.

The problem was, I could feel my anxiety increasing by the minute as we watched more Kimprak strands link together to close any holes that had been blasted in the net. It was growing steadily denser despite everything our ships were doing to keep them at bay. My heart had already clenched a number of times as several of our craft had deliberately detonated their self-destruct programs after being captured.

But somehow the *Sriracha* and *Falcon One* had avoided being ensnared with the rest of our ships and drones. They were blazing fire into the links, along with our ships on the inside caught like a shoal of fish and doing everything they could to escape.

'Erin, time to launch *Tempest's* reserve Wolfpacks to form a protective shield around us, because once they spot this starship we'll be far too tempting a target to ignore,' I said.

'Roger that,' Erin replied.

On the tactical display, another couple thousand Wolfpack drones burst from the launch bays and began to head out to their designated coordinates.

'How is your final wave of torpedoes doing, Ruby?' John asked.

'Just a few minutes out now, but there's no way we can risk using Hammer or even Thunders against that net, unless we want to wipe out our own ships too,' she replied. 'Even Lightnings are risky. At that range, there's a good chance that it will take our ships longer to recover from an EM pulse and that would leave them sitting ducks.'

'That's why I want you to concentrate your fire on taking out those asteroids,' I replied. 'It's becoming obvious that the Kimprak have used them to constantly reinforce their lines. If we take them out and also use *Tempest's* point defence laser battery system, we should be able to significantly reduce their numbers. Do that well enough, and we should be able to shove a nuke down that mothership's throat and blow it apart.'

'Now that sounds like a plan to win once and for all,' John said giving me a nod.

'It's certainly a desperate one, but when everything is at stake, that's exactly what we have to try,' I replied.

Lucy gave me a look heading towards real pride, just like my aunt might have once done. 'Absolutely, Lauren.'

Ruby swallowed her old gum and stuck in a fresh stick. 'Okay, sending the Lightnings in first, to knock out as much as we can around that mothership. That will hopefully soften up their defences long enough for us to take out those damned lumps of space rock with ten of our remaining nukes. Meanwhile, I'm going to keep the Hammers in reserve for now.'

'Do it,' I replied.

She nodded and on the Battle Command display about half the torpedoes accelerated hard away from the others in curving arcs, the trajectories of which were already being displayed, with each hitting one of the asteroids.

Slowly, like a giant leviathan, *Tempest* was closing in on the battle zone too.

'How long until our weapon batteries are within range of that Kimprak net?' Mike asked.

'About five minutes,' Lucy replied. 'But the moment our weapons open up, stealthed or not, the Kimprak will know for sure we're here and will probably throw everything, including the kitchen sink at us.'

'Good, because our role in this is to draw enough of the enemy's fire to let our ships do their jobs,' I replied.

We all watched the distance gradually countdown as we headed towards the battle zone that was still flashing with weapon fire. But I could also see a number of our ships, both TR-3B and X-craft had been caught before they'd had a chance to self-destruct and were being absorbed by the Kimprak to create more of their kind. Instantly, I was thinking of the crews that were being killed, the terror they were feeling as the Kimprak devoured their ships around them before finishing them off. A cold fury filled me and I made a silent oath to myself, whatever the cost, I would make them pay for what they'd done and destroy every damned one of them.

'Okay, we're in weapons range, permission to fire, Commanders?' Lucy asked.

John traded a look with me and we both nodded.

Immediately, violet-coloured laser fire started to streak out from our point defence battery towards the Kimprak net, burning the robotic creatures that had unfurled into their trilobite forms to link together to create the net. Within moments, large sections of their net was glowing molten-red as the *Tempest* maintained her fire.

'E8 power grid is holding steady,' Mike called out.

'That's the good news, the bad news is that the mothership's sensors have now locked onto our position,' Lucy said. 'Oh shit.'

None of us needed to ask what, because on the holographic display we saw the last ten remaining asteroids convulse and then were hurled out straight towards us.

'Ruby, hit those bloody things with everything you've got!' I shouted.

'Accelerating the Thunder nukes ahead of the main pack,' she replied. 'Contact in three, two, one...'

Multiple explosions ripped through the asteroids shattering them into fragments that had already begun spewing their poisonous payloads of Kimprak bots.

'Ruby, send the remainder of your Hammer and Lightnings straight at the mothership and hit it now!' I shouted as I leant forward in my seat to watch how this played out.

Hundreds upon hundreds of Lightnings and Hammer missiles raced towards the mothership. Multiple explosions impacted along the surface of the cigar-shaped asteroid breaking huge chunks of it away and disintegrating large swathes of machinery along its length. The overlapping ECM pulses completely engulfed the enemy vessel

Lucy was already scanning the readouts and then punched the air. 'Yes, the mothership's systems are offline again!'

There was a brief series of whoops and cheers, including from me, before John raised his hands. 'This is far from over. We need to finish it off while we can. How long till that mothership reboots, Lucy?'

'About five minutes.'

'Okay, how many nukes have we got left?' I asked.

'None already deployed, but we have at least five left onboard

Tempest and four warheads, but there isn't any way of using those.'

'Then five it will have to be,' I replied. 'Let's finish that thing off, fire them all now.'

Ruby nodded and pressed an icon on her holographic screen. At once, five Thunder torpedoes leapt out of the launch tubes along the side of *Tempest's* hull. They all turned and sped straight for the mothership and the swarm of debris from the remaining asteroids, including what had to be hundreds of thousands of Kimprak floating around them.

'What's the status of those Kimprak bots floating in space, Lucy?' John asked.

'I'm afraid, they were far enough from the EM pulse not to be offline,' she replied.

'In that case, Erin, time to make your Wolfpack really earn their keep,' I said. 'Clear a corridor for the nukes to pass through.'

'On it,' Erin replied, her eyes screwing up as she concentrated and got to work.

Her Wolfpack surged ahead of the nuke torpedoes, their lasers blazing through the Kimprak and incinerating them.

The problem was, the space between them was also littered with fragments of rocks and as the Wolfpack drones flew through it, for all the skills of the AIs controlling the individual flight paths under Erin's guidance, there was no clear easy route through. On the tactical display, one by one the drones started to wink out of existence, either taken out by the rock shards or captured by the Kimprak nets that were already growing again within the debris field.

'Darn it!' Erin said as the number of Wolfpack drones started to be rapidly depleted.

'Do everything you have to do to get your nukes through to the mothership, Ruby,' I called over.

'Working on it,' Ruby replied as her hands almost became a

blur. Then she cursed as first one Thunder torpedo was rapidly taken out, followed by a second.

The last three torpedoes were corkscrewing through the debris field as the Wolfpack drones danced and spun round them, Erin, doing absolutely everything she could to keep the flight path clear for them.

I was out of my seat with John now, as we both headed closer to the hologram to examine the action from all angles as the view tracked alongside the torpedoes.

'Crap!' Ruby said as another Thunder was captured.

Erin threw at least a dozen Wolfpack drones straight at a dense tangle of Kimprak, losing them in the process but also punching a hole through their defences.

'I owe you one,' Ruby called over to her as she raced the two nukes straight through the gap before the Kimprak closed it again.

My pulse thumped in my ears as we watched them race towards the mothership, not a bot to be seen anywhere.

'This is the home run,' Ruby called out, sweat pouring down her forehead.

My gaze shot to the timer showing how long left till the mothership started to reboot. Just twenty-eight seconds.

'Come on, come on,' Jack said through a clenched jaw as he watched the two Thunders speed towards the enemy vessel.

There were three seconds left on the clock when the first nuke hit towards the nose of the mothership and the second slammed into the mid-section of it.

Two massive pulses of light raced out, followed by a shockwave that tore through the debris field.

'Brace yourselves,' Lucy called out as the shockwave raced out towards *Tempest*, throwing Kimprak and the remaining Wolfpack drones aside as it passed through them.

John and I both dropped back into our seats, hanging on as

we watched the shockwave roar towards us. A moment later, a violent shudder shook the ship hard enough to make every bone in my body shake and make the hologram flicker briefly. Then, the vibration was quickly dying away.

'The inertial dampers are compensating, we should be in the clear now,' Lucy said.

I craned my neck forward to stare at the hologram as the massive explosions began to thin, expecting to see the shattered remains of the mothership. But then I made out what was left of it, and I let out the gasp along with nearly everyone else on the flight deck. I had to fight back nausea because the mothership was still there.

The only visible significant damage was that a massive hole had been gouged out of the nose and tail sections, destroying a number of its gauss gun launchers but otherwise the vessel was intact. Worse still, the hologram was now displaying lots of activity, including a fresh stream of Kimprak bots being fired straight towards *Tempest* from the remaining weapons systems. Lights were flickering along the surface of the mothership and my eyes shot to the reboot screen that had already expired.

'Damn it, we need more bloody nukes to lob at the thing but we're all out,' Ruby said.

'Then maybe the time has finally come to ram that bloody thing with *Tempest* to finish this,' John said.

But even as my stomach started to clench, Lucy was already shaking her head.

'It appears that there's no need,' she said. 'Someone is going to beat us to it.'

I shot her a look. 'What the hell do you mean?'

With a wave of her hand, the tactical map zoomed out to reveal a large slab-shaped ship heading along an opposite orbital path, straight at the mothership.

Raw shock slammed into my mind as I instantly recognised

the *Vanguard*. The ship's hull was crawling with Kimprak that had already eaten away vast sections of the warship, but somehow the craft was still flying.

Lucy shook her head, her eyes wide. 'The *Vanguard* appears to be on a direct collision course with the mothership. Even though it's limping along on a single engine, its closing speed is huge.'

My mind scrambled to come to grips with this new reality. 'Are you saying that they are going to deliberately ram them?'

'That's certainly what the orbital mechanics model suggests,' Lucy replied.

'Okay, this could change everything, but let's try and find out for sure,' I said. 'Lucy, can you see if you can raise Alvarez?'

Lucy nodded and a blank floating window opened at the front of the hologram. A moment later it crackled into life with an image of Alvarez himself that was partially breaking up with digital static.

'Alvarez, are you really going to attempt to ram that mothership?' I said.

'Correct, Stelleck. After all, we can't let you have all the glory of defeating the Kimprak.'

John stared at him. 'But you'll be throwing your lives away, man.'

'Much better to do that and save our world,' he replied.

'Hang on, that's on the verge of being downright heroic,' Lucy said as she raised her eyebrows at him.

Then, impossibly, in the middle of that awful battle, the man that had always been my sworn enemy, actually laughed.

'So it would seem,' Alvarez said smiling. 'But at the end of the day, I'm just a soldier trying to fulfil his duty. Our ship is badly crippled anyway, and we're only just holding off the Kimprak that have already burrowed deep into our hull and have compromised many of our systems. It's just a matter of time before they seize full control and I just can't allow that to happen. Much better to go out in a blaze of glory and take that bastard ship down with us.'

Jack joined me to gaze at our old enemy. 'But there's no need for you to be onboard, Alvarez. You must have some sort of escape pods you could use and then we can pick you up afterwards when this battle is all over.'

'So we can all become your prisoners? I think not. Besides, I can imagine just how insufferable you all would be if I allowed that to happen.'

'But you'll be throwing your lives away unnecessarily,' I replied.

'Lauren, we don't have a choice. Some sort of Kimprak computer virus has already infected most of our flight computers so we've had to take manual control of them. If we leave this ship now, there is still time for the Kimprak to divert *Vanguard's* path.'

I slowly nodded, unbalanced by the fact he'd just used my first name and there was even tenderness in his voice. A torrent of contradicting emotions ran through me. I might have always loathed this man, but here he was doing something entirely honourable.

Finally, I raised my hand and saluted him. Then Jack did the same, followed by Ruby, John, Mike, and many others on the flight deck, even Lucy.

It was one of the most poignant things I'd ever witnessed in my life. In the final moments of a vicious battle, Alvarez was no longer our enemy. When it really came down to the wire, he turned out to be just another human trying to protect our homeworld.

'Good luck and good hunting, Colonel,' I said.

He nodded and returned our salute as the video feed blinked off. Then, of all things, I felt a lump in my throat as we all turned to watch as the *Vanguard* raced towards the alien ship.

The mothership had already switched its fire of bots from the *Tempest* towards the rapidly closing Overseer ship.

'Lucy, do whatever you can to help the *Vanguard* make it to their final destination,' I said.

She nodded and *Tempest's* laser batteries began to fire into the stream of Kimprak now racing to meet *Vanguard*. My gaze briefly pivoted to our fleet who were still battling to escape the Kimprak net. So much now depended on the *Vanguard* hitting its target.

We watched as the huge ship powered straight towards the mothership that had travelled between the stars to wage war on Earth, but who no longer had any asteroids left with which to defend itself.

The *Vanguard* flew stubbornly on with the single engine powering it, its hull glistening with thousands of Kimprak, as plasma and debris vented from multiple holed sections.

The mothership, more than alert to the danger, was now firing everything it had straight at the Overseers ship when *Vanguard's* lone engine finally spluttered out. But nothing could stop the warship now, and carried by momentum, it raced on.

I covered my mouth with my hands, my stomach crunching into a ball as the *Vanguard* smashed straight into the nose of the enemy vessel.

We had a last brief glimpse of the *Vanguard* as explosions detonated along its hull before it split apart and we lost sight of it in a pulse of blinding light that engulfed both it and the mothership. Then, a vast shockwave was rushing out towards us.

'Here we go again!' Ruby shouted as she braced herself in her seat.

'This is going to be much worse than the shockwave we caused,' Lucy shouted. 'Whatever you do stay in your seats, as I'm initiating personalised gravity dampeners to protect you all.'

I immediately felt the gravity beneath me in my seat let go

and I was briefly weightless as the localised gravity field built into each of the flight seats did their best to cocoon us from the worst of the shockwave.

Next to me, Jack had his hands clawing onto his seat arms as Jodie, Mike, and John looked pale-faced at the hologram display as the shockwave boiled through space towards *Tempest*. Only Ruby and Erin were still scanning their screens up to the last moment, along with the avatars around them who, like Lucy, didn't seem to be batting an eyelid.

Beyond the gravity shield around each of us, I saw every surface shake violently as the shockwave hit our starship like an avalanche. All the lights and the hologram went as the ship vibrated like my old tuning fork had when I'd used it to strike the Empyrean Key. But then, slowly, the vibration began to die away and the lights flickered back on. Suddenly, gravity grabbed hold of me again and pulled me down into my seat.

I sucked in a breath as my heart hammered in my chest. 'Is everyone okay?'

A lot of affirmatives came back.

Jack shot me a relieved look. 'That was quite the ride.'

I nodded and I returned my attention to the hologram as it powered back up.

The remnants of the *Vanguard* were buried in the nose section of the mothership that had been split, a fissure running down most of the length of the alien ship. The markers on the holographic display indicated that there was absolutely no activity on the front third section of the mothership. But then bile rose to my throat when I saw that the rear section of the craft appeared to be very much operational. Already, like a stream of silver water, a swarm of Kimprak so dense that there barely appeared to be a gap among them, were scurrying along the surface of the mothership and enveloping what remained of *Vanguard*.

'What's the status report on that alien ship, Lucy?' John called out.

'According to our sensors, the integral structure of the asteroid has been severely compromised. It's also been knocked into a lower orbit. That's the good news. The bad news, is that bloody thing is still operational. Worse still, as we can already see for ourselves, they've begun processing the remains of the *Vanguard* to produce more Kimprak.'

'We can't let that happen or we'll be back to step one,' Mike said.

'Absolutely,' I said. 'So what tactical options have we got left, Lucy?'

'If we had any nukes left, I'd say hit it hard with them and we could finish the job that the *Vanguard* started. Unfortunately, as well all know, we're out of those.'

'There is one other option and we all know what that is,' John said with a grim face, his gaze sweeping over everyone on the flight deck.

'Once again you're suggesting we ram them, aren't you?' Jodie said, her face pale.

'That's exactly what I'm saying. That way we can finish this once and for all.'

I gazed at all the people around me, so many I called close friends and loved dearly. These were my family. I certainly wouldn't let them throw their lives away because I had an appointment with destiny.

But I already had a *plan B*. From the moment that the spare nuclear warheads had been mentioned, part of my brain had been racing ahead with my biggest seat-of-my-pants plan of all time. Especially as I had already seen a certain group of warheads in a certain vision of the future. But to carry this off, I needed to use my best poker face now to protect my friends from themselves, especially Jack, who I knew would do whatever he could to stop me from trying this.

'Okay, how long do we have to ram the mothership with *Tempest*, Lucy?' I asked.

'If we are seriously going to use this starship as a battering ram, we need about five minutes to increase our current ion engine thrust to beyond the safety thresholds, which will be a moot point if we are going to destroy this starship anyway.'

Everyone's eyes were on me as I slowly nodded.

'John, do you agree that's our best course of action?'

He nodded with a solemn look. 'I most certainly do.'

'In that case, I want an evacuation order issued and for everyone to make their way to the escape pods. We can at least try to save as many lives as possible and it sounds like we have no other choice.'

My gaze travelled to the net still enclosing the X-craft and Pangolins that had been continuing to try to fight their way out of the Kimprak's clutches.

Lucy had followed my gaze. 'The one good thing is that once we take the mothership out, that Kimprak net should fail. Then, when our fleet escapes, they should be able to pick up the survivors.'

John nodded. 'At least that will be one small blessing.'

'Okay, I'm going to leave you to get this organised, John, because I'm absolutely bursting to have a comfort break after all that coffee.'

That raised a small smile from him. 'Of course.'

I then made absolutely sure I didn't catch Jack's eye as I quickly headed up the steps of the flight deck and raced towards one of the exits that led to a transport hub for my rendezvous with destiny.

I was already feeling sick at the thought of what I was about to do, but I had no choice if I was going to save everyone I loved.

CHAPTER TWENTY-EIGHT

THANKS to my commander authorisation codes, a short while later, I stood in hangar bay one as Tin Heads loaded the warheads into *Ariel's* cargo bay on my orders. I had already got Delphi to prep the ship for flight and I was going to rely on her to fly me to the target.

I was drumming my foot on the flight deck by the time the Tin Heads had finally finished and closed the hatch. I was about to race up the ramp to board *Ariel* when I heard a cough behind me.

I grimaced as I turned to see Jack standing there with Lucy, Erin, and Ruby.

Lucy crossed her arms and shook her head at me with the expression of a very disappointed parent. 'Seriously, you were just going to try and sneak off without saying anything?'

'I take it you've seen past my little ruse then?' I said.

'You mean the one where you load *Ariel* up with those nuke warheads and take her to do a Kamikaze run in an attempt to take that mothership out?' Ruby said as the others nodded.

'Bloody hell, you all know me way too well.'

'We do,' Erin said. 'And there is absolutely no way we're going to let you try it alone.'

'Nice attempt trying to distract everyone with evacuating the ship though,' Jack said.

I pulled a face. 'Sorry, that was a necessary deception to make my plan work. Anyway, Lucy, can you rescind that order as soon as we're clear of *Tempest*?'

'Of course, but what makes you think I'm not coming with you?' she replied.

I thought of the vision that seemed determined to unfold just like I'd seen it. But that also meant I was about to win this argument.

'Because *Tempest* needs you, especially if there is any chance that we don't make it out of this alive.'

Lucy scowled. 'But my place is with you, my little sunflower.'

'Please, you need to do this for me. Just promise me you do nothing to stop us.'

'Is that what you really want?'

'Yes, with my whole heart.'

Lucy nodded and dropped her head to stare at the floor for a moment.

'Hang on, you said *stop us,* so I'm guessing that you're not going to try to stop the three of us from coming with you?' Ruby said.

'I have about as much chance of that as trying to hold back the tide with some harsh words. I mean, would *you* try arguing with you lot?'

'Probably not,' Erin said grinning.

The time had finally come to reveal my last throw of the dice, especially to Jack's ears, to hopefully avoid dying, although I'd already realised it was very likely not going to work out.

'Here's the deal, we need to get *Ariel* as close as possible to the mothership before we let Delphi takeover and we eject in the safety pods.' I said. 'Then Delphi will fly *Ariel* straight into the breach in the mothership's hull. Hopefully, the nuke warheads that I've just loaded onboard will be enough to finally crack that ship wide open like an egg.'

Lucy raised her gaze back to me. 'It most definitely will be, and even if it isn't, it should be enough to knock the mothership far enough down into Jupiter's gravity well for it not to be able to make it out again. But if you don't make it out of there alive, then I'm going to give you hell.'

I made sure to avoid Jack's gaze that had tightened on me. There was still every chance I wouldn't be in that escape pod, I knew it and so did he. It certainly seemed that, so far, the way everything had unfolded the more that events were propelling me towards my imminent death. But even if that still happened, as long as I got the others to safety first, then I could cope with that. One life to save so many was a fair trade that I would take any day of the week.

But a storm of emotion was now brewing inside me and I held my arms out to Lucy who stepped into my embrace and hugged me.

'I am so flipping proud of you, Lauren,' she whispered into my ear.

'I certainly couldn't have done this without you, and I thank the day that you came into my life.'

I gently kissed the side of her head and when I pulled away I was shocked to see tears in her android eyes. But that was the thing, she'd stopped being an AI a long time ago and had very much become a real best friend to me.

'See what you've done?' she said flapping a hand at her face. 'Now get out of here because John is already starting to ask too many questions up on the bridge, especially after so many of us disappeared at once. Poseidon telling him that we're all on a comfort break will only pull the wool over his eyes for so long, especially when it comes to me.'

I laughed, which helped push down the tears that had been threatening, because even if Lucy didn't realise it, there was still a strong chance that this would be the last time we would see each other.

I quickly turned on my heel and headed for the ramp. 'Come on, team, let's get this bird into the sky.'

I felt so much more at home sitting inside the cockpit of *Ariel* than I ever had in the captain's chair of *Tempest*. After so many missions with this original prototype X103, I realised now that this cockpit, complete with the faint whiff of hydraulic fluid and hot metal, actually felt more like my home than anywhere else, even Earth.

The current view on *Ariel's* virtual cockpit was spectacular. *Tempest* was falling rapidly away behind us, her stealth field rendered invisible by the cockpit system so we could see exactly what was going on. The deltoid-shaped sweeping lines of the silver starship were illuminated by the continuing barrage of violet laser fire that was now focused back on the vast Kimprak net still surrounding our fleet, and that was at last beginning to fail. Thankfully I could already tell that it was only a matter of time before our ships broke free from it.

The Wolfpack drones were still zipping round the battlefield, Erin told me that she'd handed over control of them to one of the avatars. They were certainly doing a good job, because they were taking out Kimprak wherever they found them floating free. But it was what was directly before *Ariel* that stole most of the attention.

With Jupiter as a backdrop, the mothership, the underside of which was blazing with fire as it skimmed the atmosphere at a lower altitude, had become a living tide of metal as the Kimprak feasted on the bones of the *Vanguard*. I couldn't help but shudder as I thought of the fate of Alvarez and the others, and just hoped for their sakes, that the impact had been enough to kill them outright.

Then, as I knew it would eventually, the comm light started flashing.

'We have John on the line for you, Commander,' Ruby said.

I pulled a face. 'Put him through.'

John's face appeared on the monitor. 'What the hell do you think you're doing, Lauren? Turn that ship around and head back to *Tempest* right now!' he demanded.

'We both know that's not going to happen. This is, by far, the best play here and we both know it. Besides we're all going to eject at the last moment, because heroism only goes so far,' I said hoping beyond hope that Jack might even buy that story too.

'Bloody hell, you're so stubborn,' Mike said as he appeared on the video feed. 'And how come you didn't ask me? Was my invite for this special party lost in the post or something?'

'No, your place is with Jodie, especially if something happens to us.'

He stared at me. 'Bloody hell, don't talk like that, Lauren.'

'Just being a realist. And if something does go wrong, you give Jodie a hug from me and tell her to look after you or else.'

Mike's eyes were shining, but he nodded as he smeared away tears with the back of his hand. 'You've got it, boss.'

'Okay, if you really are set on this, and you obviously all are, then let's see what we can do to help,' John said. 'Lucy, can you use the laser battery to thin out the Kimprak between *Ariel* and the target? And please do the same with the remaining Wolfpacks.'

'It would be my absolute pleasure,' Lucy's voice replied in the background.

Almost immediately, violet laser fire speed past, vaporising the Kimprak scattered before us. Then, swooping into position like an escort came the Wolfpack drones, their turbo lasers blazing.

'Thank you, John, we appreciate the help. When we get back I have an excellent Highland Park whisky to celebrate our victory.'

'Then I look forward to it. Good hunting, Lauren. Out.'

As his image disappeared off the virtual cockpit, I couldn't help but notice the little head shake that Jack gave me, which immediately made me feel guilty. But my little speech to John had also been deliberately intended for the ears of Ruby and Erin to reassure them that everything was going to be okay. The one person who knew the likely outcome was now staring straight ahead at the mothership and not saying a word. So much for him buying my spin story. I just hoped that one day when Jack was safe, he would find it in his heart to forgive me.

'Okay, we're about to head into a dense patch of Kimprak, so hold on everyone,' Erin said.

The words had barely left her mouth when *Ariel* started spinning round us in every direction as Erin used our REV drive to its full effect. As the ship rolled, the gyro gimbal mechanism did everything it could to keep the flight deck level. But the effects of inertia couldn't be compensated for, and it felt like my body was pulled in every single direction by the extreme manoeuvres.

Part of the remains of the *Vanguard*, a slab section of riveted hull that had floated away from the impact, tumbled past us. I just had time to register the Kimprak burrowing like maggots into the metal.

The Wolfpack drones were just blurs further out ahead of us

now, darting everywhere like dragonflies as they took out anything that looked like it might be a threat to our ship.

Tempest's point defence system was also doing an incredible job of clearing the way and it struck me then that if she had its full armament of weapons how even more formidable she would have been in this battle. Unfortunately, I would never get to see just how powerful our starship really was, because with every passing second as we closed on our target I somehow knew for certain that my life was about to end.

Ruby blazed away with *Ariel's* mini-guns at a few scattered Kimprak that had made it past the Wolfpack and *Tempest's* laser fire, destroying them instantly. But they were still close enough to see their fragments skimming over the gravity shield enveloping our ship, microscopic meteors blazing over it as they passed by like burning rain.

'Darn it, we have a denser region of Kimprak to get through dead ahead of us,' Erin said. 'This is going to be touch and go, whether we can make it through it.'

'Just do whatever it takes,' I said. Then I toggled the comm. 'John, is there any way you can throw some more firepower at that Kimprak cluster ahead of us?'

'We can't get a clear shot at them, but I know some people who might,' he replied.

Suddenly, zooming out of nowhere, came the Angelus Raptor, followed close on her heels by the *Sriracha*.

'Did someone just call for room service to clean up a mess?' Don's voice said over the comm.

Ruby laughed. 'We did, and don't worry, we tip well.'

'Then we'll make sure we do an extra special cleaning job just for you, ma'am,' Troy's voice said over the channel.

Both ships sped past *Ariel*, shredding the Kimprak cloud with their combined weapons fire.

But then my heart sank because just like in the Halls of

Dreams prediction, I spotted a huge meteoroid that the mother-ship had managed to throw out with one of its remaining mass launchers, heading straight towards us. Flanked on all sides, Erin had nowhere to go. With a sickening impact that shook every bone in my body, the meteoroid slammed into the side of *Ariel* sending her spinning.

Multiple warning alarms screamed out in the cockpit. Smoke began to billow into the cockpit and rapidly filled it, as respirators fell from the ceiling. I had an intense feeling of déjàvu we all quickly strapped them on.

'Hull breach. Eject now, structural integrity has been critically compromised,' Delphi announced.

As our ship began oscillating violently around us, I looked at the virtual cockpit and my mouth grew dry because I'd seen this exact moment in the vision of my future, but with one key difference. The *Sriracha* and *Falcon One* were here and they were doing everything they could to wipe out the stream of Kimprak now desperately being fired at us from the mothership. The Wolfpack drones hadn't been in the prediction either and they were diving through the swarm of Kimprak like sharks in a feeding frenzy through a shoal of fish. So it seemed Procession Planning really wasn't an exact science after all. But despite all of that, every other key detail was the one that I'd foreseen with Jack, and it was hard to see how this wasn't a one-way trip for me.

As the cockpit spun around us Erin fought for control. Jack looked at me and I could see in his expression that he recognised this moment too.

'Okay, Erin, let Delphi take over flying, we need to abandon ship,' I said.

'Delphi's going to have a hard time doing that because the stabilisers are shot to hell,' Erin replied. 'I need to manually fly her in if we have a chance of doing this.'

'We'll just have to take the chance,' I replied.

'But, Lauren—'

I cut her off with a sweep of my hand. 'That's a command, Erin, just do it.'

'Autopilot engaged,' Delphi said over the cacophony of alarms.

I shot a look at Ruby to cut off the protest that I could see she was already forming. 'Everyone to the escape capsule now, including you!' I shouted. 'Delphi, take over flight control to the navigation marker.'

'I have control,' Delphi replied.

Jack still hadn't said a word as we all unstrapped our harnesses, me playing along because I knew it was the only way for this to work.

We staggered across the tilting flight deck as the gimbals controlling the gyros had begun to fail.

Once again, just like in the prediction, Ruby and Erin entered the escape pod first. But then the script changed because it was Jack not me who paused behind them and then slapped his hand on door-close button.

'What the hell are you doing?' Ruby shouted as the door slammed shut behind her and Erin.

'Delphi, eject escape capsule now,' Jack said, turning to face me for the first time.

'Escape capsule ejected,' the AI replied.

The virtual cockpit was crawling with static, but I caught sight of the cylindrical capsule blasting away and turning as it began to head back towards *Tempest*.

Before I could say anything, Jack placed his finger on my lips. 'There's no point arguing about this because it's done now. We're both stubborn and neither of us is about to give in. Also, before you lecture me about what I just did, I've had time to give this a lot of thought. So here it is laid out for you, Lauren. I just can't live without you and that's the end of it.'

I stared at him and the sheer tenderness in his eyes. I knew in that moment that I would have done exactly the same if our roles had been reversed.

I slowly nodded. 'I love you, Jack Harper, from the top of my head to the tips of my toes.'

'And I love you, Lauren Stelleck, always have and always will.'

'Then like you said, that's all there is to it,' I replied as I leant in and kissed him. 'So let's go and finish this wild journey we've had together. I'll take the pilot's seat and you take over weapons to avoid us going down like Bonny and Clyde before we reach the target.'

Jack chuckled as he nodded. 'You do have a way with words, especially at times like these.'

'Hey, it's a gift,' I replied, grinning as we both took up the seats just vacated by Erin and Ruby.

The gaping fissure in the mothership was rushing up to meet us like a dark cave mouth. Threads of Kimprak crisscrossed the interior and I could almost feel their entire attention falling upon the single craft plummeting straight towards the heart of their mothership. I glanced at the view of our cargo bay, of the four warheads nestled in their cages.

Ariel was rattling and shaking, literally sounding like she was shaking herself apart. I could also see the REV drive indicator was rapidly overheating. She wouldn't last much longer, but then again, she didn't need to.

With a burst of mini-gun fire, Jack took out a group of Kimprak that had been speeding towards us. Already the script to the vision was severely deviating. Hope was starting to build inside me that we might actually have a chance to pull this manoeuvre off, just like that part of the vision had indicated we would.

I toggled the comm on. '*Sriracha*, you and *Falcon One* are to fall back.'

Don's face immediately popped up on a viewscreen. 'First, tell me why the hell you're still on board that ship?'

'Because Jack and I have to be here. The navigation system is shot to hell. We basically have no choice and there isn't time to discuss it.'

Don nodded. 'Damn it. There's so much I'd like to say. But the quick version is, I think I'm talking for every single person in the fleet when I say that we'll never forget the sacrifice you guys have made for us today.'

'Thank you and when you see Ruby and Erin, tell them how sorry I am that I had to deceive them, but this was for the best.'

Don nodded, and then just as we had done for Alvarez, he snapped me and Jack a salute.

I immediately choked up as I returned it and then Don's face was replaced by Troy's.

'You do know, that even now, I would trade places with you in a heartbeat if I could,' he said.

'That was never an option, but please promise me you won't turn your back on a command role. This fleet needs your talents, Troy.'

'Is that an order?'

'Technically not, as we are of equal ranks, so more like a friendly request.'

A smile flickered across his face. 'Then I will see what I can do. Good luck, my friends. It's been an honour knowing you both.'

'And you. Out,' I replied.

The video window went dark as I killed the comm button. Then on the virtual cockpit, we watched both ships peel away and begin to speed away from us back towards the rest of our fleet that was still fighting its way out of the Kimprak net.

'And then it was just two,' Jack said as he managed to take out another stream of Kimprak with the mini-guns.

'As dates go, I could think of a more relaxing venue,' I replied.

Jack laughed. 'You are so my woman.'

'And you will always be so much my man.' I glanced across at his chiselled features and those cobalt-blue eyes that were able to look into my very soul. 'I will see you in the next life, Jack Harper.'

He smiled at me and I glanced briefly ahead as we raced towards the hole that was almost filling the view. 'Delphi, set nuclear warheads to detonate in three seconds, conformation command code zeta-one.'

'Zeta-one code confirmed. Warheads are armed. Detonation in three...'

I reached out and took Jack's hand in mine.

'Two...'

I noticed a strange sensor trace on the tactical display but ignored it as my eyes clung onto Jack's, only barely aware of the ragged gouged asteroid walls rushing past as we headed into the enormous cavern beyond. I lost myself in the gaze of the man who I loved with my whole being.

'One...' Delphi seemed to say from a long way away as we squeezed each other's hands.

A bright light blazed through the cockpit and then our world went black.

CHAPTER TWENTY-NINE

As THE MULTIPLE nuclear explosions ripped through the hull of the mothership, *Ariel* blinked out of existence on the hologram. Lucy stared at the empty space as the AI equivalent of absolute anguish roared through her synthetic brain synaptic connections.

Lauren and Jack were gone, every particle in their physical bodies swept away by the raw power of atoms releasing their energy in a nuclear explosion that was now boiling outwards where they and *Ariel* had been just a moment ago. Even now, she could see the shock waves with *Tempest's* sensors, which were an extension of her own being, rippling out through space.

Many of the humans around her on the flight deck were staring in raw shock at the holographic display, some openly sobbing like Mike and Jodie who were hanging onto each other. The compulsion for Lucy was to do the same, but the person she would have thrown her arms round to find solace, wasn't here anymore.

It was at moments like this that she truly appreciated just how transient this species' lives really were.

Despite her own grief part of her artificial consciousness noted that the mothership was splitting apart into fragments, pieces blown apart from the brutal power of the nukes. Some segments were already tumbling into the atmosphere of Jupiter and were blazing with molten fire as they began to burn up. A chunk several kilometres wide had already sped straight down and had left a black ugly scar in the swirling gas clouds as it crashed through them. The rest of the fragments of what had been the mothership were of more immediate concern as they hurtled out of orbit, each fragment likely carrying the spores of poison that were the Kimprak. But Lucy made a silent promise to Lauren and Jack right then. Whatever it took, each and every one of them would be hunted down and destroyed. At least now, thanks to the bravery of her friends, there would be an afterwards for that to actually happen.

John, grim-faced, his legs planted slightly apart, hands clasped behind his back, raised his gaze from where he had been staring at the floor and turned at last towards Lucy. There were already standing orders in place that had been agreed upon with Lauren for this sort of eventuality and about how the command for the whole fleet would automatically pass to John if anything ever happened to her.

It was almost like she'd known.

Lucy looked across at John. He squeezed his eyes shut for a moment as he presumably gathered his thoughts before opening them again to gaze at her.

'Please tell me that it was all worth it and that damned thing is dead?' he said.

'Yes, I'm not reading any energy signatures in the main fragments other than individual Kimprak,' Lucy said. 'Also their net is losing integrity as they are no longer being controlled by the mothership.'

'Please show me,' John replied in a quiet voice.

With a quick order via the neural link and with a wave of her hand, Lucy zoomed the holographic display towards the net that was beginning to break apart as the human fleet had finally begun to escape its clutches.

'What are your orders, John?' Lucy said as he gazed at it.

'Orders, yes...' He breathed through his nose.

'Tell our fleet to fire at will and destroy every last one of those damned Kimprak. I can think of no better way to honour Lauren and Jack's sacrifices than that.'

Lucy nodded and connected immediately to their Battle Command system to relay the order. A short while later, both X-Craft and TR-3Bs were swooping through the strands of disintegrating nets and destroying the last of the Kimprak. Meanwhile, the Pangolins were already heading out to deal with the larger fragments of the mothership.

It was then that the *Tempest's* sensors lit up with a pulse of energy from one of the larger remaining chunks of the mothership, a single section of what had been its rear section. On closer inspection, Lucy could see that the transmission seemed to have originated from an array of antennas and dishes on the surface of what had been the mothership's hull. A quick analysis informed her that it was some sort of tight-beam communication burst packed with terabytes of data. Also, the signal was aimed at one specific area of sky in the constellation that the humans referred to as the Pleiades.

Was it a cry for help?

Lucy highlighted the fragment in the hologram. 'Commander, there appears to be some sort of communication facility on one of the larger fragments that has just begun broadcasting what could be some sort of distress signal.'

John frowned. 'Then we need to take it out as quickly as possible. Just how many of those Hammer torpedoes have we got left out there, Lucy?'

Lucy found her gaze had again locked onto the message on the hologram display that read, *Ariel, signal lost.*

'Lucy?' John repeated more gently as he saw what she was looking at.

The bulk of her AI consciousness still seemed to be locked onto trying to process what had happened to the two humans who had meant so much to her. With a considerable effort of will, she forced herself to respond.

'Yes, sorry, five hundred and thirty-six Hammers.'

'Then concentrate all of them on that fragment of the mothership that's still broadcasting,' John said.

Lucy nodded and at the speed of artificial thought, she transmitted the order to Battle Command to contact the torpedoes that remained. A moment later, every single one of them had powered up their rockets and were swooping down towards the fragment of the mothership.

Lucy quickly scanned the battlefield with *Tempest's* sensors and noted that *Sriracha* and *Falcon One* had already recovered Ruby and Erin's escape pod. Since then, they had almost single-handedly taken out many of the mothership fragments like they had a personal vendetta, which she then realised that they probably did, especially if Ruby got her hands on any of the *Sriracha's* weapon controls. For humans, something like this would always be personal, and much to her surprise it seemed the same held true for her. Even now, she felt the unfamiliar emotion of cold fury when she thought of the Kimprak.

The Hammer torpedoes were swooping straight towards the stern section of the mothership. The one piece of good news was that it was relatively low-tech and was simply broadcasting across the electromagnetic spectrum. That meant that if it was a distress signal, calling for backup would take countless light years to reach its intended destination. At least the humans would have plenty of time to prepare to deal with it.

With considerable satisfaction, Lucy watched the torpedoes reach their target and a ripple of explosions lit it up as the Hammers detonated across its surface. They might not have anything like the power of the nukes, but what they lacked in punch they more than made up for in sheer numbers. The rock fragment was sliced to pieces as the shrapnel hit it at extreme hyper-velocity.

Lucy confirmed the *Tempest's* sensor information before relaying it to the humans. 'The signal has been stopped.'

John gave her a relieved look as the remnant began to tip downwards towards the atmosphere of Jupiter.

It was then that Lucy noticed readings further out that had simply blinked into existence. If she'd been human, she might have panicked it was enemy reinforcements coming in. But her thoughts meshed into *Tempest's* sensor suite and informed her that these ships belonged to another alien race.

'John, we have hundreds of Tic Tac contacts and they appear to be heading for the fragments as well and have already begun engaging them.

John nodded. 'Better late than never, although we really could have done with their help thirty minutes ago. But at least now, they can help with the mopping-up.'

'I'm afraid that's the Greys all over,' Lucy said. 'Often late to the party, but at least they do eventually show up.'

Her heart clenched as she noticed just how broken Mike and Jodie looked, a mirror of exactly how she was feeling on the inside.

They, and the other humans on the flight deck, watched in silence, bearing witness as the remains of the Kimprak mothership started to burn up as it dropped into the atmosphere. It suddenly shattered, breaking up into hundreds of pieces and blazing trails streaking down into the clouds of ammonia ice. The pieces of rock started to wink out as the gas giant consumed them, helping to destroy the final fragments of the mechanised race that had travelled between the stars only to harvest and destroy.

Lucy felt the human's silence reaching into her as she handed over the final stages of overseeing this battle to the other avatars. It was then, at last, that she fully allowed herself to embrace the anguish that she'd fought to suppress and let it flood through her. It was then that Lucy began to weep for Jack, but for most of all for Lauren, a woman that, even though Lucy was an AI, she had truly loved.

CHAPTER THIRTY

ALICE SAT on the bridge of *Tempest* gazing out at Earth. It was a sight that would always take her breath away. But then her gaze fell upon the empty captain's seat where Lauren should have been sitting and as always she felt her heart breaking yet again. Not for the first time, Alice wished she'd just come out and told Lauren that she'd always seen her as a younger sister. In so many ways Lauren, with her passionate and often headstrong ways, had often reminded Alice of herself in her thirties. Now that vibrant shining light of a person had been extinguished, something that even now, Alice couldn't fully emotionally process.

Perhaps she never would.

Losing Jack had been hard too. He was someone she had always felt had been so good for Lauren, and her for him. Alice was far too used to losing people, Tom especially, but the loss of these two at the moment of a victory had cut her more deeply than anything ever had. Alice already knew that she would never get over it.

However, she also knew she wasn't alone in feeling like this and there was a large Lauren and Jack-shaped hole in everyone's lives who'd been close to them. To have fought so long to save Earth and then having been instrumental in helping to achieve victory was a testament to what extraordinary people they had both been. It certainly seemed like a cruel twist of fate that Lauren and Jack weren't here to witness the fruit of what had been achieved since that battle six months ago over the clouds of Jupiter. And today was the day when the next chapter would begin.

Through the windows of the Citadel, she could see the dozens of Angelus warships that had been constructed in *Tempest's* shipyard. There was everything from corvettes up to heavy cruisers and everything in between. Then, of course, there was also the new squadron of Raptor fighters that Troy had insisted they build and that were starting to fill up hangar bay three.

Lauren would have got such a kick out of all of this, Alice thought.

'You look lost in thought,' John said from behind her.

She turned to see him with a cup of coffee in one hand, mint tea in the other that he offered to her.

Alice smiled and took the tea. 'Thank you, and you're right. I was just thinking Lauren, in particular, should have been with us for this moment. She would have loved this as an astronomer.'

'Yes, I'm absolutely certain she would have loved the idea of journeying to the stars too,' John replied. 'My biggest regret is that I didn't have the time to get to know either her or Jack.'

'I can assure you that they were quite the team and both deeply special people. Whatever way you want to look at it, it's been a huge loss for our world, but their legacy is quite something to behold, isn't it?' She gestured around them at *Tempest* and the fleet of warships beyond the Citadel's windows.

'It is, and something tells me we're going to need all of it where we're headed. Lucy believes that the Pleiades cluster is almost certainly some sort of Kimprak stronghold. Of course, we will effectively be racing that distress signal that the mothership managed to send before it raises the alarm. But at least now *Tempest's* fusion drive is online and that can propel us near the speed of light.'

'The one small problem is, that the Pleiades is still roughly four hundred light-years away,' Alice replied.

'It would certainly help if Lucy and the other avatars ever find a way to reconstruct *Tempest's* missing jump drive,' John said.

'I know. However, don't forget the other little bombshell that Lucy dropped, that even if we do, we'll still need to find what the Angelus call a Navigator to be able to control it, a person with some sort of unique psychic ability.'

'She tried to explain that to me, but I'm afraid most of it went completely over my head, especially the bit about how they have a special genetic gift that allows them to directly connect to the ship's micro minds to be able to warp space between two points. Mike tried to explain it to me as well, but I gave up after the third holographic board of formula that he was trying to step me through,' John said. 'Anyway, all we can do is live in hope that they find a way around it so one day we can use *Tempest* to the full extent of her capabilities. At least we should be around to discover what's waiting for us at the Pleiades stellar nursery and to stop the Kimprak from threatening us again with what would almost certainly be a larger invasion force. At least being holed up in E8 within *Tempest* will make the voyage feel like no time at all.'

'To us maybe, but thanks to travelling close to the speed of light and Einstein's whole theory of time dilation, don't forget thousands and thousands of years will have passed here on Earth,' Alice said.

John took a sip of his coffee and nodded. 'Which makes this

departure all the more poignant. All of us will be saying goodbye to those we leave behind on Earth, knowing we'll never see them again. Grandchildren will grow old and die before us and countless generations after them. It's a sobering thought. I also find myself envying our settler teams who are bringing their entire families along on this voyage. Although, I'm also rather uncomfortable with the idea of civilians joining us for what is effectively a military voyage.'

'This is only a military voyage from your perspective, John,' Alice said correcting him. 'From where I stand, it is still at its heart very much a civilian voyage of exploration and will also give us the opportunity to establish colonies right across our galaxy. These are things I've dreamed of since I was a child. Of us becoming a multi-planet species, and now we finally have the tools to make it a reality. For a long time my goal was to establish a permanent base on Mars, but thanks to the Angelus, we can now raise our sights on seeding our race out there among the stars.'

'Well, I'm happy that the responsibility for all that will fall squarely on your shoulders rather than mine,' John said. 'The logistics alone of getting all those people on board and set up in the habitation zone would have given me a permanent migraine.'

'Oh, I'm more than happy to deal with all that, and the rest of it, as I know that we'll be safe with you and your forces protecting us. And if I haven't said it, I can't tell you how happy that your government chose you to command the military wing of our expedition.'

John smiled. 'Much better than being put out to pasture in the retirement that was rapidly looming for me. As long as I have a small section in one of the hydroponic zones for my own personal project, namely a vegetable garden, I'll be happy. I know Lucy insists that the molecular printed food is identical, but to my tastebuds, it's always tasted synthetic. And speaking of the devil, here is the lady herself.'

Alice turned to see Lucy heading towards them with a transparent tablet in her hand and a perplexed look on her face.

'The two people I wanted to see in the same place,' Lucy said as she approached them.

'Please tell me you're not about to tell us we have to abort our departure due to some problem with the fusion engines?' Alice said.

'Nope. Mike and Jodie are all over them and all the diagnostics are checking out beautifully. We should be able to depart on schedule in a few minutes for Psyche 16 to replenish our storage silos for our E8 molecular printers.'

John scratched the back of his neck. 'I can't believe how much faster the new engines are over the ion drive.'

'You better believe it, although it's always good to have the ion drive as a backup,' Lucy replied. 'Anyway, there is something I wanted you to see and which is why I was trying to track you down.' Lucy made a swiping gesture over the tablet towards the hologram, transferring the data that had been on her screen onto the larger 3D display.

Alice felt her heart clench as she and John turned to see a frozen image from the mothership battle. *Ariel* was clearly visible and had just entered through the fissure in the hull.

Lucy beckoned towards the two of them as she stepped into the hologram.

John narrowed his gaze first on the 3D model of *Ariel* and then on Lucy. 'Why exactly are you showing us this?'

'Because moments after the nukes that *Ariel* was carrying, exploded, I noticed a small gravitational anomaly in the blast wave as it expanded. I've been doing some frame-by-frame analysis and the conclusion is rather surprising. Here, let me show you. The next frame you're about to see is one-trillionth of a second after the first.'

With a flick of her finger, a white sphere had engulfed *Ariel* and its ID tag had winked off.

'That is the start of the nuclear shock wave that was about to rip the mothership apart, but what I wanted to draw your attention to is this.' Lucy waved her finger again and the view zoomed in on the edge of the explosion sphere where there appeared to be some sort of spherical shape at the heart of the nuclear explosion. The avatar gestured towards it. 'What you're seeing there is a distortion in space caused by a gravity field bubble.'

'Could it be anything to do with *Ariel's* REV field failing in those final moments?' Alice asked.

'That's what I thought at first, but it gets stranger. Here, let me show you. If we play the video on from this moment at a trillionth of a second per frame backwards, you'll see why it caught my interest.' She flicked her finger again and the recording started to play in reverse.

Frame by frame, *Ariel* was moving back out of the fissure but the gravity bubble was also moving at a right angle away towards the nose of the mothership where part of the remains of the *Vanguard* were still buried in it. As *Ariel* continued her reversed dive the gravity bubble distortion continued forwards until it cleared the mothership.

'Is that some sort of heavily cloaked spaceship?' John asked.

'No, none of gravity distortion analysis fits that. But what is very intriguing is that whatever it was, it seems it wasn't actually moving at all. It was literally stationary in space where all the movement we see in this playback is actually caused by the rotation of Jupiter and the mothership speeding round it.'

Alice stared at her. 'You're saying it was some sort of temporal anomaly sitting in space that *Ariel* just happened to fly into?'

'That's exactly what I'm saying, because after *Ariel* ran into it the anomaly simply vanished. Then it gets even stranger. Onboard *Tempest,* in a sealed-off lab that belonged to an Angelus research scientist called Tuul, there was a significant energy spike in what had been dormant systems, which then shut down again when *Ariel* was destroyed. A number of avatars have already begun an investigation of the equipment in there.'

'You're saying that this event could be linked?' John asked.

'It's certainly is an extraordinary coincidence if it isn't,' Lucy replied.

'So, what exactly was this Tuul researching, Lucy?' Alice asked.

'He was actively involved in researching time travel before it was banned by the Angelus authorities for being too dangerous.'

Alice stared at her. 'Time travel. Is that even possible?'

'We simply don't know. Tuul kept his work very secret before mysteriously disappearing,' Lucy replied. 'I can transfer all the data files we have on him for you to look at if you like?'

'Please do,' Alice said. Then her eyes widened as an astonishing thought hit her. 'And this,' —She made air quotes— '*temporal anomaly* just happened to arrive right next to *Ariel* just at the moment the nukes went off. So the question is whether it could—'

But Lucy was already holding up her hand to stop her. 'Your mind is heading exactly where mine first went, that this anomaly somehow plucked Lauren and Jack away before *Ariel* was wiped out. The problem with that idea is that our mystery ship arrived one-trillionth of a second too late and Ariel was already in the process of being blasted apart by then. I'm afraid even if whatever it was, was sent to rescue Lauren and Jack, it was too late to do it.'

'I see...' She took a long breath as she tried to gather her thoughts. 'Is there anything else you can tell us about this temporal anomaly then?'

'Nothing yet, but as I hate mysteries I'm going to keep working on it until I find out exactly what it was. Anyway, that's for another day because the other headline news is that the time for departure has come.'

Alice exchanged a look with John as her brief flicker of hope that her friends might still be alive died. 'In that case, let's get this journey to the stars underway.' She gestured towards the vacant captain's chair. 'John, I think the time has come for you to take your rightful place.'

He rubbed the back of his neck. 'It still feels too soon after losing Lauren.'

'Trust me, she would be the first to insist that you did,' Lucy said.

John held Alice's gaze for a moment and then nodded. 'Okay, if you insist.'

'I do,' Alice replied, smiling.

John moved towards the chair and sat down.

Alice cleared her throat. 'Delphi, please pass full control of *Tempest* to Commander John Hamilton.'

'*Tempest* recognises its new commander,' Delphi announced.

With that, the holographic displays in front of John's chair powered up and the seat adjusted subtly from the curves of Lauren's body to his own.

'Okay, then let's do this,' John said. 'Lucy, are we clear to depart?'

'We are, although there is something that's come to my attention just beneath our orbit that may be of interest. An Indian satellite called *Varuna* is currently making an uncontrolled entry into orbit. If you like, I could dispatch a Guardian to deal with it before we leave,' Lucy replied.

'Is it going to crash anywhere populated?' John asked.

'No, it's currently projected to crash into the sea.'

'In that case, probably better not to intervene and tip-off

India that something strange happened up here. So, when you're ready, please take us out, Lucy.'

'Roger that, Commander.'

Lucy turned towards the holographic display as Alice took her seat next to John, the one that had belonged to Jack, as a 3D model of *Tempest* appeared in the hologram.

With a look at the readouts being displayed around the model, Alice watched the power bars for the fusion engines begin to move upwards.

Alice raised her eyes to gaze out the window at the distant stars beyond Earth's moon. Then with the smoothest acceleration, the fusion engine powered up. *Tempest* began to accelerate away from humanity's homeworld to begin its journey that would one day hopefully lead it to the Pleiades constellation and whatever waited for them there.

And so it begins, Alice thought to herself with probably the same sense of excitement, anticipation, and fear that Lauren might have if she had still been sitting here as their voyage to the stars began.

AUTHOR NOTES

So here we are arriving together at the end of the **Earth Song** series. I hope it's taken you on as much a journey as it has me. I certainly hope you've become as invested in the characters despite Lauren and Jack's fiery heroic death!

I feel an enormous element of sadness leaving the **Earth Song** series behind so I set out to make sure that E**arth Roar** was a fitting finale. It has probably been the most complex book I have ever written layering in fiendishly complex large-scale battle sequences, the exploration of an extraordinary starship and the culmination of major character arcs for Lauren in particular.

These books have all been about taking someone relatively ordinary and dropping them into extraordinary situations and seeing how they would cope. Some might take issue with how Lauren rose to that challenge, but in many ways I would say they are missing the whole point of these books, because my personal belief is that people are extraordinary and can surprise themselves when they are thrust into situations far behind their comfort zones. It was that journey, that story thread, that has woven its way throughout the **Earth Song** series until, even though she didn't want the job, Lauren found herself thrust into the role of commander, which led to her making the ultimate sacrifice for everyone's sakes back on Earth. That is just how incredible and kickass Lauren had become.

The genesis of this book series was born out of the concept of Sentinel, an Angelus AI whose appearance in our world sparked the ideas that would eventually evolve into **Earth Song**.

But where did Sentinel come from?

Well, until now, I've kept quiet about it and there was a good reason for that. Some of you have followed my author's journey, which actually started back in 2006. This was when I left the computer games industry to pursue my passion for writing. Some of you may have already read my **Cloud Riders** trilogy. Now at long last, I have the rights back from my publisher and will be releasing the trilogy at the start of next year. They directly cover the origins of Sentinel and involve travel across parallel worlds in a somewhat unconventional manner. Think the movie Twister meets Jules Verne and even His Dark Materials, you would be getting pretty close to what **Cloud Riders** is all about. I wrote it suitable for everyone as a YA crossover, so as long as you don't mind teenage protagonists you may want to give these books a spin. For the very first time, it is available in hardback if that's your preference or just fancy upgrading your existing copy. There is a preorder link on the next page.

If you want to read the immediate sequel in the timeline to **Earth Roar,** then you might want to check out Sentinel's ongoing story in my **Fractured Light** trilogy the link for which will also follow. But of course, you are probably also dying to know about the new books I have planned. At this point in the story, we now have *Tempest* setting off on its journey to the Pleiades. Rest assured, eventually this will be picked up in a new series one day. But in the meantime, I have a new series to write which will help to weave together many aspects of the Multiverse Chronicles. I did tell you I love to write epic stories and I will forever blame reading Lord of the Rings as a teenager for sparking that particular obsession!

To hear the latest news about the new series, I would advise if you haven't already, to either sign up to my newsletter here: https://www.subscribepage.com/s6z3s9_copy or follow me on my Facebook author page here: https://www.facebook.com/GloudRidersNick

As always, I need to thank everyone for their support during the creation of **Earth Roar**. A huge shout out to my editor Hanna Elizabeth who was instrumental in helping to hone this book into the best state that it could be. I must particularly thank Catherine Coe who did the first read-through and whose insight has been invaluable as it has always been since the very beginning of my writing journey. I also have to single out my beta-reader, Joy Frances Saker, for doing an extraordinary job at picking up the few typo snafus that made it past the rest of us. Karen my wife has been my constant rock who has been with me every step of the way and is my moon, sun, and a whole lot more. But most of all I must thank you, dear reader, for continuing to turn the pages of what I write because I certainly wouldn't be where I am today without your belief and support. Thank you.

So, for now, I will bid you *au revoir* until we meet again in the next instalment in the Multiverse Chronicles series next year and that I'm already hard at work on. Meanwhile, whatever else you do in life, keep reading and keep dreaming.

Nick Cook, December 2021

LINKS

Do please leave that all important review for **Earth Roar** here:
https://geni.us/EarthRoar
Now you have finished the Earth Song series, are you ready for the prequel series, **Cloud Riders,** where something extraordinary is about to come crash landing into out world?

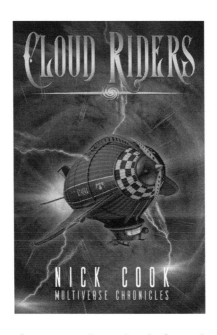

Twisters can rip lives apart, but what lurks within them is even more dangerous. Dom, comes from a family of storm chasers, but a year long drought has hit the US hard and even the tornadoes have vanished. With crops failing and the family diner about to go bust, Dom feels trapped, torn between supporting the family business and the urge to escape to a new life. When the first twister in months appears from nowhere and an airship emerges from the spout, Dom's world is turned upside down. Its pilots are explorers who make Dom an offer beyond his wildest dreams. But the visitors are also harbouring a terrible secret. Can Dom uncover the truth and make the right decision before everything he cares about is destroyed?

Cloud Riders is available here: https://geni.us/
CloudRidersTrilogy

The latest instalment of the Multiverse Chronicles is **Inflection Point** and will be launched in summer of 2022. **Inflec-**

tion point weaves together the story of new characters and old in an extraordinary journey across time.

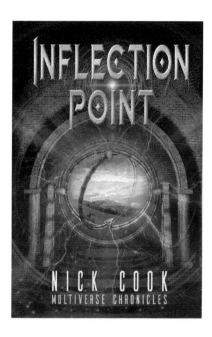

In Oxford on the eve of the outbreak of the First World War, Nathan Bishop is an electrician who is busy converting the colleges over from gas to electric light. However, his real passion is science and he idolises the famous Nikola Tesla who is working at the cutting edge of experimental science. To be involved in something like that seems an impossible dream for Nathan until the mysterious Professor Felix Schneider offers him the opportunity of a lifetime to work as an assistant in his home laboratory. It's an event that will change the course of his life forever. But as Nathan's world is torn apart by the coming war, he must embrace the opportunity to embark on an incredible journey that will determine not only the fate of those closest to him but one day far in the future even the survival of life across the whole galaxy as well.

The preorder link for **Inflection Point** is here: https://geni.us/
InflectionPoint

Now you have finished the Earth Song series you may also want to consider reading the ***Fractured Light*** trilogy. This continues the story of the AI *Sentinel* six years after the events covered in ***The Signal*** and also begins directly after the end of the ***Earth Song*** series. A secret hidden in human DNA is about to be unlocked, but can college students Jake and his underground hacker friend Chloe solve the mystery before reality itself starts to break down?

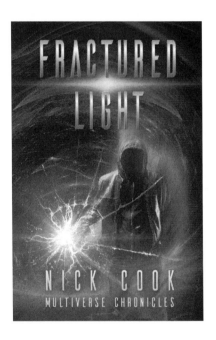

Is our reality all there is or could there be something lurking beneath it? Jake lost everything when his dad died during an experiment into dark energy. Ever since Jake has become an outsider in his home town, carrying the guilt for a catastrophic event that devastated their local community. Six years later on the way back from college, Jake witnesses a satellite crash-landing and starts receiving garbled messages hinting at a conspiracy. But when he then begins to see something lurking in the shadows he even begins to question his sanity. In desperation, Jake turns to his former best friend Chloe, an underground hacker who like many turned her back on him. But even if she believes Jake, do they still have enough time left to solve the mysteries that link all the events together and unlock an ancient secret hidden in human DNA? If they fail the coming darkness will devour all life across our world. Watch out for the shadows.

The **Fractured Light** trilogy is here: https://geni.us/ FracturedLightTrilogy

ALSO BY NICK COOK

The Cloud Riders Trilogy (Multiverse Chronicles)

The Earth Song Series (Multiverse Chronicles)

The Fractured Light Trilogy (Multiverse Chronicles)

Printed in Great Britain
by Amazon